ESCAPE!

Scott A. Ferguson, Sr.

ESCAPE!

HistriaYA

Las Vegas ♦ Chicago ♦ Palm Beach

Published in the United States of America by
Histria Books,
7181 N. Hualapai Way, Ste. 130-86
Las Vegas, NV 89166 USA
HistriaBooks.com

HistriaYA is an imprint of Histria Books dedicated to incredible books for Young Adult readers. Titles published under the various imprints of Histria Books are distributed worldwide.

All rights reserved. No part of this book may be reprinted or reproduced or utilized in any form or by any electronic, mechanical or other means, now known or hereafter invented, including photocopying and recording, or in any information storage or retrieval system, without the permission in writing from the Publisher.

Library of Congress Control Number: 2024944151

ISBN 978-1-59211-507-5 (paperback)
ISBN 978-1-59211-508-2 (eBook)

Copyright © 2024 by Scott A. Ferguson, Sr.

To my eldest son, Scott Jr., because of his love for history as well as his encouragement of me. Thank you.

PROLOGUE

"All right children, settle down," the teacher called out. Once everyone was in their seats, she began. "Today, as you know, we will have an assembly to commemorate the fiftieth anniversary of the end of the Great War. As a special treat, we will have a guest speaker today, Doctor Abigail de Groote. She is one of the few surviving war-time slave girls and she has agreed to share her story with us today. Now, I want everyone to line up, and we will quietly move to the auditorium."

He lined up behind his best friend, Freddie Watson, and they began walking to the auditorium. When they arrived, they went to their seats and began talking with friends and people from other classes. He looked around and saw his big sister looking at him. He smiled and she smiled back, both were excited and nervous.

After the rest of the classes took their seats, the lights dimmed, and the principal walked to the podium. He stood there for a moment or two as the auditorium became relatively quiet. "Good morning, boys and girls. Today, as you know, is the fiftieth anniversary of the end of the Great War. Now, I know that you all have been studying the war in your history classes and I know that some of you are bored by it. So, in an effort to humanize the war and show you the impact on the lives of those who lived through it, we have the honor and privilege of welcoming Dr. Abigail de Groote to our assembly. As some of you know, Dr. de Groote is one of the few surviving war-time slave girls from Agustis and she has graciously agreed to share her memories of her escape from the capital of the Empire of Truth and Light as well as the dangers she and her companions faced on that harrowing trek. And now, would you please join me in welcoming Dr. Abigail de Groote."

The assembled children all applauded as Abigail walked out on the stage. The children watched as a short, gray-haired woman who used a cane but stood very erect, walked across the stage and over to the podium. When she approached, the principal shook her hand warmly and thanked her once again. She smiled and told him that it was her pleasure. Then she turned and stood behind the podium.

As Dr. de Groote stood on stage, a large projection screen descended behind her. The room darkened and the screen blazed with an image of two hands, a forearm, and a small gold necklace attached to a gold chain. The back of the hands bore an elaborate branded 'S.' The forearm depicted a tattoo that read '35082.'

Then, in a slightly accented voice, she spoke. "You see, projected before you, photographs of the backs of my hands and my right forearm. These are the marks of a slave girl, and I will bear them until the day I die. Most people would consider them marks of shame, but I consider it an honor to bear them. I have borne them for fifty-six years.

"You also see my slave collar and leash. During the war, I was not allowed out in public without a collar and leash, just like any other animal.

"Today, I would like to tell you how I got those marks and how my friends and I escaped the fascists of the Empire of Truth and Light and came to your wonderful country. So, sit back and relax; it's a long story."

CHAPTER ONE

They had been in the shelter for over three days. Throughout that time, the sounds of explosions had gotten louder and louder. Finally, about two hours ago, the power died; the lights went out and the air circulation fans stopped. Throughout the shelter, she could hear some children screaming and others crying. She held on to her mother's arm with a death grip while her mother tried to soothe both her and her little brother.

Suddenly, there was a blinding light as the doors to the underground shelter were forced open and dozens of soldiers with flashlights and lanterns came pouring in. Other soldiers with machine guns and rifles began pushing and shoving them out of the shelters, toward the streets above. Still holding on to her mother, she got up and headed for the exit when she heard a soldier behind her begin shouting at someone. She looked around just in time to see the soldier try to pull a woman on a bench to her feet. When she refused to move, the soldier raised his machine gun and pointed it at her. The woman, obviously hysterical, curled into a ball crying so loudly that she probably didn't hear the soldier yell at her to move. He tried to prod the woman with the barrel of his gun, but she still didn't move. Suddenly, the soldier fired a burst and the woman fell to the floor, dead.

The other people screamed and began stampeding for the doors. She clung to her mother as hard as she could as they were shunted forward. Soon, they moved through the doors, up the stairway, and out into the bright sunshine. As she looked around, she couldn't believe her eyes; when she had gone into the shelter, the city was still filled with tall buildings and thousands of people. Now, almost every building had been reduced to piles of bricks and rubble. Instead of plain ordinary citizens, all she could see were hundreds of gray-clad soldiers and black-clad officers.

She looked across the street and her heart almost stopped. There, pointing directly at her, were at least twenty black army tanks—each with a machine gun and gunner on top of the turret. In her mind, every machine gun was pointed directly at her.

They had not taken more than ten steps when they approached a group of soldiers. Before she knew what was happening, a soldier had ripped her hands off her mother's arm and she was being corralled in with other girls while her mother and brother were being forced toward what was left of a building wall.

A group of soldiers surrounded the girls, their guns pointed into the group. Then, a black-clad officer began speaking through a loudspeaker. "The Army of Truth and Light has conquered your country, and your capital city has been destroyed. Since your government refused to bow to the inevitable and join the Empire, you, as citizens of the capital city, must pay the price."

The machine gunners on top of the tanks cocked their machine guns and pointed them at the people grouped against the building wall. The officer continued, "In accordance with the orders of our Supreme Commander, General Joshua, all males and any female old enough to have been with a man will be killed. All females too young to have been with a man, in other words, girls of thirteen and under, will become the property of the Empire of Truth and Light. They will be taken to Brighton where they will be processed and sold as slaves."

Without warning the machine gunners opened fire on the men and women, boys and older girls. She screamed out their names as her mother and brother were ruthlessly mowed down by the hail of bullets. The other girls were screaming, too, as they were forced to watch the carnage, but she couldn't hear them over her own screams.

Suddenly, it was silent except for the cries of the remaining prisoners. Through tears, she watched as a dozen soldiers and officers began walking through the dead, occasionally shooting survivors. Soon, that was over too, and only the group of younger girls was left alive.

The soldiers then began lining them up and herding them through the city to the train station. As they walked, she looked around at the destruction of the once beautiful city. Everywhere she looked, all she could see were dead bodies, destroyed buildings, and burning military vehicles. When they came near the capitol building, she could see flames shooting through its roof and out its windows. The president's mansion, which had been across the street from the capitol, had been leveled.

After about an hour of traipsing through the rubble-strewn streets, they finally arrived at the train station. When they moved around the heavily damaged building, she saw a long line of freight cars standing in front of the platforms. Everywhere she looked, there were soldiers forcing girls into the freight cars. Finally, it was her turn.

As she approached the open car door, she could see girls were being forced in from the other side too. When she hesitated, a soldier hit her in the back with the butt of his gun. She stumbled and would have fallen had there been enough room, but there wasn't. Instead, she knocked into another girl, and after apologizing, moved as far as she could toward the back of the car.

After a few minutes of maneuvering, she finally reached the wall of the car and leaned her back against it. It wasn't long after that that the doors closed with a boom, and they were left in semi-darkness. All around her, she could hear other girls sobbing and sniffling as they were forced to stand crammed together, their bodies pressing against one another.

The sun beat down on the roof of the boxcar, and before long, it became stiflingly hot. As they continued to stand in the sweltering heat and close quarters, they all began to sweat. It didn't take long before someone vomited. Of course, the smell of vomit made others vomit. Soon, it was all she could do to just breathe.

Eventually, the sun began going down and so did the temperature in the cramped boxcar. Once darkness had completely enveloped them, she began shivering from the cold. She guessed that it must have been near midnight when the car gave a sudden lurch and began moving. She hadn't realized that she had dozed off, but as soon as they began moving, she woke up again.

She looked around but couldn't see much in the dark and crowded boxcar. Even so, she could hear countless other girls sobbing and calling for their mothers. Tears fell down her cheeks as she realized that she, like everyone else, no longer had a family. She turned and finding a crack between the wooden planks that made up the wall, began watching the world pass by.

After a couple of hours, the train began slowing down and finally came to a stop. Then, without warning, it began going backward. She looked out the crack in the wall and discovered they were being moved onto a spur. As they came to a stop, she could see another train come barreling down the track they had just vacated. The moon was shining so she was able to see that the other train was a freight train carrying tanks and artillery towards the battlefront.

After about an hour, another train came flying down the track. This one, she noticed, was a passenger train; probably carrying soldiers to the battlefield. After another hour, their train began moving again and she stopped looking out the crack in the wall.

Sometime near daybreak, the train began to slow down again. When she looked out the crack, she could see they were in a railyard on the outskirts of what looked like a military base of some kind. She could see other trains standing on nearby tracks. Suddenly, they stopped, and after a few minutes, they could feel the engine disconnecting from the rest of the cars.

They sat again for hours. When the sun began beating on the roof again, she could feel the temperature begin to climb. Now, in addition to the smell of vomit, she could smell urine and feces. She realized she needed to relieve herself and was mortified when she could no longer hold it and felt the tears begin when the warm liquid began running down her leg. If she thought it couldn't get much worse, she was wrong.

She and the others spent most of that day trapped inside the sweltering stench of the freight car before they began moving again. As she felt the temperature beginning to fall, the car lurched again as another engine was attached. After a few minutes, the train was moving again, albeit very slowly.

About ten or fifteen minutes later, the train came to a stop again and there was relative quiet. She looked out the crack in the wall and discovered they were inside a huge concrete building. Before she could begin to figure out what that meant, the doors opened, and they were being herded out of the car.

Once outside, they were again instructed to form two lines and were soon marched away from the train toward a group of tables. Slowly, they were called forward and began being processed. She stood for what seemed like hours before it was her turn. She found herself standing in front of an older woman in a gray uniform.

"Name," the woman said in a bored voice.

"Abigail Henderson," she replied.

"Age?"

"Twelve."

The woman handed her a piece of paper and said, "You'll find your number on the top of that form. Memorize it because that is what you'll be known as while you are the property of the Empire. Follow the line on the floor to the next station. Next!"

Abigail moved off, following the dingy yellow line on the concrete floor. Eventually, she came to the next station and handed her paper to the woman sitting at a desk in front of a line of doors. The woman stamped the form, and two soldiers came over and took her by her arms. Before she could say or do anything, they took her into one of the rooms and strapped her to a chair. One of the soldiers grabbed her right arm and strapped it to the arm of the chair, the inside of her forearm facing up.

She was just about to ask what they were going to do to her when a man came in and began tattooing her number on her forearm. She opened her mouth to protest and one of the guards shoved a dirty rag into her mouth. Then, just as the man was finishing with the tattoo, her other arm was strapped to the chair. The man doing the tattoo loosened the straps and turned her right arm so that the back of her hand was facing up.

All this happened so fast that she didn't have time to react. Then, suddenly, another man came in with an iron rod with an elaborate 'S' on the end. Just as she realized what he was about to do, he pressed the letter onto the back of her right hand, and she screamed into her gag. He pulled it off her right hand and immediately pressed it against the back of her left hand, again causing her to scream. She struggled against the restraints the entire time, but it did no good. The pain was excruciating, and she almost blacked out from it; in fact, she wished she had.

Before they released the straps that were holding her down, another soldier came over and swabbed her brands and tattoo with iodine. As soon as they had released her arms, she reached up, pulled the rag from her mouth and began screaming at them. She hadn't said more than a couple of words when one of them backhanded her across the mouth and ordered her to be silent. The first time she ignored him, but after he hit her a second and a third time, she stopped talking.

She cried hysterically as she was pulled to her feet and dragged into the next room. Immediately upon entering this room, two women came over and roughly stripped her of her clothing. She was again manhandled into a chair and strapped down, this time including her head. As soon as the straps were pulled tight, a man came over and shoved another dirty rag into her mouth. Then she heard the barber's clippers, and as her eyes grew wide, the man began shaving off all her hair. Not stopping with her head, they took a straight razor and shaved off her eyebrows and even her eyelashes. Then, to her horror, they proceeded to shave all the rest of the hair off her body. When they had finished, Abigail had tears of frustration and humiliation streaming down the sides of her face.

They released her from the chair and pushed her through yet another door where two more women were waiting. They pushed her toward a wall and almost immediately began spraying her with a fire hose. She sputtered and gagged in the freezing water and then the women pounced on her. One of them held her arms behind her back while the other took a scrub brush and some harsh-smelling cleanser and began scrubbing her down. When she was done lathering her in the front, she grabbed Abigail's arms while the other woman scrubbed her back. Suddenly, they pushed her against the wall and sprayed her down with the fire hose again. She didn't even have time to catch her breath before they pushed her, still naked, out a door and into the next processing room.

As soon as she got her bearings, she saw a woman sitting in front of a wall of shelves. When she looked, she saw the shelves held garments that looked more like sacks than anything else. The woman never said anything, just looked her up and down, reached over and pulled a dress off a shelf, and handed it to her.

The dress looked like it had been fashioned out of a burlap sack, but she was grateful for something, anything, to cover herself. She pulled it over her head and saw that it came down to the middle of her thighs. Then, she moved through the door to which the woman behind the counter had pointed. Here, she saw nurses and doctors all tending to other girls. One of the nurses motioned to her and she walked over.

The nurse beckoned toward the examination table, and she jumped onto it. As soon as she was seated, a doctor came over and listened to her heart and breathing and took her blood pressure and temperature. Then, without saying anything, the nurse handed the doctor a syringe. As he was injecting the contents into Abigail's arm, the nurse was preparing a second syringe. After the third injection, the doctor left and the nurse said, "You're finished. Leave."

She stood up, a little dizzy, and staggered through the door into a large dining hall. As she looked around, a guard standing next to the door muttered, "Better grab some food while you can."

She looked at him and he nodded toward a door on the far wall that had a pile of cafeteria trays standing on a counter next to it. She suddenly realized she hadn't eaten since the day before her capture. As quickly as she could, she staggered over, grabbed a tray, and went through the door. The smell made her stomach growl and her mouth water as she looked at the mounds and mounds of food. A woman behind the counter began piling food on a plate and handed it to her. As she moved along, another woman handed her a tall glass of watery milk and, finally, she helped herself to two glasses of murky water.

She quickly found a seat and began devouring the food. It tasted horrible, but she was so hungry it didn't matter. When she was about halfway through, an old man came over, grabbed her right arm, turned it over, and read her number. He never said a word as he walked away.

She was just finishing her meal when a soldier came over and grabbed her right arm. After reading her number, he said, "Follow me."

She got up, picked up her tray, and followed the man towards the door. She deposited her dirty dishes in the basins and followed him out of the cafeteria. He led her down a corridor and around three or four corners until she was totally lost. At last, he opened a door and motioned for her to enter.

She walked in and was met by a wizened old woman. The woman looked at her number and said, "Go to the back of the room and get a mattress and pillow. Your bunk is 82, near the back on the right. Once you've done that, someone will bring you a blanket. Move quickly, lights out in fifteen minutes, and once the lights are out, you are not allowed to leave your bunk for any reason, so if you need to use the bathroom, you'll have to move quickly."

She nearly ran to the back of the room and grabbed the first mattress and pillow she found. She sprinted to her bunk, which was near the bathroom, and threw the mattress and pillow into place. A matron walked over and gave her a thin piece of material that was supposed to be a blanket. After throwing it on her bunk, she ran to the bathroom. She was just climbing up to her bunk when the lights were turned off.

CHAPTER TWO

Still breathing heavily, she lay back on her mattress. Her poor body was exhausted and the pain in her hands was nearly unbearable. Her mind was still trying to process what had happened over the last few days. Whenever she closed her eyes, she could see the tank gunners firing their machine guns, and even though she hadn't actually seen it, she watched the bullets rip through her mother's body. Tears flowed gently as the sense of loss overpowered her. The cinema in her mind continued the horror by forcing her to watch one of the black-clad army officers walk over and shoot her brother in the head. She watched, horrified, as the blood flowed from both her brother's and her mother's bodies.

Eventually, the film must have come to an end because it wasn't long before Abigail awoke to the sound of whistles and matrons bellowing at them. As she got out of bed, she couldn't understand how she had ever fallen asleep, considering the pain in her hands and arms. She could hardly move her arms as she half-climbed half-fell out of her bunk. Finally, she made it to the bathroom and then the cafeteria. She sat by herself and ate the slop they euphemistically called gruel. When she had finished and pondered what was going to happen next, a man in a black army officer's uniform arrived. At least a dozen armed soldiers followed suit.

All the girls stopped what they were doing and looked at the man. He walked to the front of the cafeteria, near the doors to the food line, and cleared his throat. "I am sure that most of you are wondering what is going to happen to you next." He smiled as he continued, "You will remain in quarantine for the next three days. At the end of the quarantine, provided you aren't sick or dead, you will be transported to the auction. There, you will be sold to the highest bidder and become his or her property for the rest of your miserable lives."

He looked around at the disconsolate faces and smiled. "Don't look so sad, most of you will be sold to pimps or perverts and will probably be dead within five years, so odds are the rest of your miserable lives won't be too long anyway." He exchanged knowing looks with a couple of the guards and said, "Does anyone have any questions?"

A girl of about eight, who was sitting near the front of the room, raised her hand. He nodded at her and told her to stand up. She did so and was just about to ask her question when a guard hit her in the mouth with the butt of his gun. She screamed in pain and fell to the floor, her mouth spraying teeth and blood everywhere.

The man in the black uniform glowered as he looked around the room. "Understand this: you are slaves. Property. You have no opinion, and no one cares what you think. You will speak only when spoken to and will follow all commands, no matter what they are. Do I make myself clear or do you need another demonstration?" When there was no response he smiled and said, "Good. You may now go back to your dormitories where you will receive further instructions."

They all stood at the same time and began shuffling to their barracks and their bunks. Once back in their beds, the head matron came in and gave them instructions. She told them that for the next three days or so, they would be allowed out of bed only to go to meals twice a day and the bathroom three times a day. If they needed to leave their beds at any other time, they must request permission from one of the matrons before getting up. Ominously, she told them there would be no exceptions and anyone caught out of bed without permission would receive ten stripes with the leather strap.

Lying on her bunk, the only thing Abigail could do was think. At that moment, her world consisted of nothing but pain. The physical pain from the inoculations, tattooing, and branding; the emotional pain from watching her family being murdered; and the physiological pain from the humiliation she had endured from the moment the soldiers burst into the bomb shelter three days ago. Was it really only three days ago? She wasn't sure, but it seemed like a lifetime.

Without thinking, she crawled out of her bunk and walked to the bathroom. When she walked back to her bunk, the head matron was waiting for her with a smile on her face and a leather strap in her hand. She was gently slapping her free hand with the strap and Abigail felt her heart sink. "Some people must think the rules don't apply to them," she hissed. "Well, one of those special people is about to learn a lesson in obedience."

Before she could even breathe, two of the other matrons grabbed her arms and turned her around so she was facing the bunks. The head matron called out in a loud voice, "The rest of you listen up! This is what happens when you do not follow the rules!" Then, to Abigail, she said, "Don't worry, dearie, this won't leave a mark and ruin you for your auction. You'll still bring a pretty penny from the pimps and perverts."

She swung the strap, and it landed on the back of Abigail's thighs with a resounding crack. The pain buckled her knees, but the two matrons held her up. Again and again, the strap struck her thighs, and again and again, Abigail screamed in agony. Finally, after the tenth stripe, the matrons holding her threw her onto her bunk, and laughing at her, walked away to continue patrolling the barracks.

She lay face down on her mattress, her face buried in her pillow, screaming until the pain became bearable. As the tears ebbed, she gently began to probe the damage with her still aching hands. There didn't seem to be much damage, just some bumps and heated skin. That was good, she thought. She tried rolling over, but the pain in her legs made her quickly change her mind.

While she was feeling her injured legs, the old man she had seen in the cafeteria came over and told her to lie flat on her stomach. He examined the back of her legs and said, "They're red and there are a few welts, but they'll be fine by tomorrow." Then, he looked around, and once he was sure there was no one around, he handed her a pill and whispered, "Take that at dinner, it will help with the pain, and you should be able to sleep tonight."

She was just about to thank him when he placed his finger on her lips, and without saying anything else, walked away. She lay there thinking about the old man when the whistles blew for dinner. She gingerly hopped down and made her way to the dining hall with the others.

After dinner, she quickly washed up and used the bathroom. She returned to her bunk well before the 'lights out' whistles sounded. At first, the pain from her hands, arms, and legs felt like it would keep her from sleeping, but then the pill took effect, and she slept through the night without waking once. When she woke in the morning, she was pleased to find the pain was now down to an almost bearable dull ache.

This routine continued until the following Monday, the day before the big auction. They were once again shaved, sprayed down, given a clean dress, and even a pair of cloth slippers. Finally, just before dinner, each girl was inspected and those needing medical attention were taken care of before they ate.

The next morning, they were woken before the sun had come up. Quickly, they were fed and then led to the loading docks where at least a dozen trucks were waiting to take them to the auction. The guards pushed and shoved them, forcing them into the back of the trucks. It wasn't long before the trucks lined up in a convoy and they were on their way to the auction house.

It didn't take long to get there, and it took a surprisingly short time to unload the girls. They were then sorted by age and forced into cages. After the last of the heavy, iron-barred doors were closed, hundreds of men and women came in and began walking between the cages, looking at all the girls. Abigail looked at them with a vague disinterested look on her face when, suddenly, she saw the old man who had given her the pill the other day. When he saw her, she could see the recognition in his eyes. As their eyes met, he didn't say anything. He just winked and kept on walking.

After about an hour, the gawkers, as Abigail thought of them, left and the auction began. They started with the babies. Abigail listened as the auctioneer sold every infant and toddler. It was afternoon when they finally got to the twelve-year-olds.

One by one, the girls were taken out of the cage and paraded up on a stage where the potential buyers could see them clearly. Each girl was called out by her number, not her name, and it took Abigail a second to realize they were calling her when they called out her number.

"And here comes number 35082, another twelve-year-old from Agustis." The auctioneer looked down at a sheet of paper and said, "As you can see, she is slightly smaller than normal, only four and a half feet tall, and weighing only sixty-five pounds. She has green eyes, and when she had hair, it was dirty blonde." There was a small chuckle at the mention of her missing hair and Abigail blushed as she stepped on to the podium.

She tried to look at the people in the audience, but the bright lights glaring in her face prevented her from seeing anything or anyone clearly. Then the auctioneer began, "We'll start the bidding at fifty muntens. Do I hear fifty muntens?"

A hand went up and the auctioneer nodded, "Thank you, sir. I have fifty. Can I get sixty?" Another hand went up and he said, "I have sixty. Can I get seventy?"

Abigail heard a voice call out, "I'll give one hundred!"

"One hundred! Thank you, sir," the auctioneer said.

Then, another voice called out, "One hundred fifty!"

Before the auctioneer could acknowledge the bid, the other voice called out, "Two hundred!"

This continued, each person raising the bid by fifty until they reached five hundred muntens. The auctioneer called out, "We have five hundred. Do I hear any more? You sir?"

The man must have shaken his head because the auctioneer called out, "Anyone else? The bid stands at five hundred muntens. Can I get five-twenty?"

Now, a new voice called out, "I'll give you five-twenty."

"Five-twenty, thank you, sir. I now have a bid of five hundred and twenty muntens. Can I get five-fifty?"

There was silence for a few seconds. Then the auctioneer called out, "The bid is five hundred twenty muntens. Are there any other bidders? Five hundred twenty going once…five hundred twenty going twice…five hundred twenty going three times." He brought his gavel down with a bang and called out, "Lot 35082 has been sold to bidder 612 for five hundred twenty muntens!"

Abigail was in complete shock when the auctioneer announced she had been sold. How could that be? There was no slavery anymore. Slavery ended almost a hundred years ago in a country thousands of miles away. How could she, a modern girl, be sold to another person just like a car or even a dog? Suddenly, a soldier grabbed her, pulled her off the stage, and pushed her toward what she assumed must be the cashier's cage. The auctioneer was calling out the next girl's number as they approached the cashier. When she saw her new owner, she gasped.

CHAPTER THREE

She stood dumbfounded as the soldier removed her shackles and bound her hands in front of her. She was still looking at the old man as the soldier placed a heavy leather collar around her neck and attached what appeared to be a dog leash to it. The man turned around and smiled at her as the soldier handed him the other end of the leash. Without pulling on it he said, "Shall we go?" and she followed him out of the building.

He led her to an old luxury car and opened the passenger's door for her to get in. Once she was inside, he went around and got behind the wheel. She was still goggling at him as he started the car. He looked at her and said, "Well 35082, what's your real name?"

She came to her senses and replied, "Abigail, Abigail Henderson."

He smiled at her and said, "A pleasure to meet you, Abigail Henderson, my name is Dr. Kurt van Heflin. Do you go by Abby, Gail, or Abigail?"

"Abigail," she replied.

As he nodded, he reached over and removed the heavy collar from her neck and the bindings from her wrists. When he was done, he said, "I don't believe you will be needing these restraints. I believe you'll be perfectly happy with us. Besides, where would you go?"

As they pulled out of the parking lot, Abigail screwed up her courage and asked, "Why did you buy me?"

He sighed and said, "A few months ago, there was a fever going around and my daughter and granddaughter came down with it. Despite my best efforts, my daughter died, and my granddaughter lost her vision. I bought you to be a companion and a friend to her. She is very shy and doesn't have any friends. Anyway, it will be your job to help her adjust to her blindness and to help her to resume a normal life, or as normal as possible. You will escort her everywhere she goes. In short, you will be her eyes from now on."

After digesting this information Abigail asked, "Yes but, why me? Why didn't you pick one of the other twelve-year-olds that were auctioned before me?"

The doctor was silent for a moment or two. Finally, he said, "You remind me of my daughter when she was your age. Your face is like hers, even the freckles across the bridge of your nose. Knowing the fates most of the girls face, I couldn't let that happen to…"

She didn't say anything as they continued to drive away from the auction house. After a few minutes, the doctor pulled over and parked near some shops. He got out and walked around the car, opening her door. She gave him a quizzical look and he said, "I'm guessing you don't have any other clothes and you can't go around wearing just a gunny sack. You'll need some dresses and the like, won't you?"

She nodded and got out of the car. When they opened the door to the shop, a little bell tinkled, and by the time the door closed, a woman came over and said, "Dr. van Heflin, how good to see you! How's that beautiful granddaughter of yours doing?" Then, before he could respond she noticed Abigail and said, "And who do we have here?"

The doctor smiled and said, "Mrs. Braun, allow me to introduce Abigail Henderson. Abigail, this is Mrs. Braun, a friend of the family. Gretchen, Abigail will be Inga's new companion. But, before I introduce them to each other, I thought we should get Abigail some clothes. As you can see, the Empire isn't very generous with the clothing they give their captives."

Mrs. Braun looked Abigail up and down and said, "No, I can see they aren't very generous at all." She smiled and said, "Come with me dear, and we'll find something nicer than that sack you're wearing."

An hour later, Abigail and the doctor left the shop with every article of clothing she could want, except shoes. The doctor explained they would stop for those next. At the shoe store, the doctor bought her two new pairs of shoes, a pair of slippers, and a pair of winter boots. It was late afternoon when they finally parked in front of her new home.

The house was in the center of a row of townhouses. It was three stories tall and built of brick. They walked up the stoop and a middle-aged woman opened the door for them. She stood aside to allow them in and as Abigail entered, she smiled and nodded to her. Blushing, Abigail returned the gesture and followed the doctor into the entrance hall.

Once the door was closed, the doctor introduced Abigail to the housekeeper, "Abigail, this is Mrs. Lotte van der Walle, she's our housekeeper. Mrs. van der Walle, this is Abigail Henderson, Inga's new companion."

Mrs. van der Walle took Abigail's hand, causing Abigail to wince from the pain and pressure in her brands. She shook it vigorously, saying, "Thank goodness you're here, my dear! Miss Inga is sorely in need of a companion now that…" She let the sentence remain unfinished.

Abigail blushed as the doctor, clearly irritated, said, "Now that Inga is blind and all alone in the world? Was that what you meant to say? Yes, so tragic, but I'm sure Abigail will be able to help her, and we'll be one big happy family again in no time. However, in the meantime, can you take Abigail up to her room and help her get settled? I think I'll talk to Inga before we introduce them."

The doctor didn't wait for an answer; he just turned his back on them and began climbing the stairs. Mrs. van der Walle lowered her head and mumbled something Abigail didn't quite understand. Then, as the doctor reached the landing, Mrs. van der Walle looked up and said to Abigail, "Would you like to see your room?"

Abigail nodded as Mrs. van der Walle asked, "But where's your luggage, dear?"

Again, Abigail blushed as she replied, "I don't have any, ma'am, just a couple of dresses and stuff and they're still out in the car."

Suddenly, Mrs. van der Walle saw the brands on Abigail's hands, and she gasped. They were still red and swollen so they were hard to miss. "Oh my," Mrs. van der Walle said, "I can see why you don't have any luggage. Are you allowed to go outside without your collar and leash? Aren't they required by law?"

Abigail replied, "I don't know. Dr. van Heflin removed the collar when we got in the car, and I didn't wear it when we went in the dress shop or the shoe store."

Mrs. van der Walle sighed and said, "No matter. I'll show you to your room and then I'll go collect your things. That way you won't be seen outside without your collar. Come on."

She led Abigail up to the second floor and into a small room next to Inga's. She knew her room was next to Inga's because she could hear the doctor's voice through the closed door. When she walked into the room, she saw a twin bed, a dresser with a mirror, and a small closet. There was no window. Mrs. van der Walle said, "When this house was built, this room was the linen press, but now it's your room. The bathroom is next to Inga's room and the doctor's room is on the other side of that. My room, by the way, is upstairs on the third floor. Now, you stay here and get comfortable while I get your things from the car." Mrs. van der Walle smiled at her as she left.

Abigail sat down on the edge of the bed and bounced once or twice. Then she saw herself in the mirror. She couldn't believe it was really her staring back. The girl in the mirror was bald, hairless, skinny, and scared. The pale green eyes that were looking back at her showed terror and panic lurking just below the surface. She looked down at her hands and saw the swollen, red 'S' on the backs of both of them. A tear trickled from one eye and then the other. How could anyone have done this to another person? To her?

Mrs. van der Walle tapped lightly on the door. Abigail wiped her eyes and said, "Come in," and she walked in carrying all of Abigail's new clothes. She smiled and handed Abigail the bags while she went to the closet to hang up the dresses, skirts, and blouses. Abigail placed her underwear and things in the drawers and looked up in time to see Mrs. van der Walle watching her.

She came over and wiped the remaining tears from her eyes and said, softly, "I know you've been through a terrible ordeal, but that's all over now. You'll be safe and cared for here. You'll see."

She gave Abigail a quick hug and hurried from the room. Abigail moved back to the bed and sat down. She was just wiping the final tear from her eyes when the doctor tapped on her door. She quickly got up and opened it. The old man smiled at her and said, "Ready to meet Inga?"

Abigail nodded and tried to smile. He took her hand and led her to Inga's bedroom door. After knocking, they entered and the doctor said, "Inga, honey, this is the girl I was telling you about."

Abigail saw Inga turn toward her grandfather's voice. Inga, she saw, was a pretty ten-year-old with short, curly, dark brown hair that framed her big, brown eyes. She was slightly taller than the average ten-year-old, and a little on the heavy side, but otherwise, a typical little girl. "Hello," Abigail said softly.

Inga said, "My grandfather told me he bought you today. How much did he pay for you?"

Before the doctor could object, Abigail said, "He paid five hundred twenty muntens for me, and then probably spent another one hundred muntens or so buying me clothes and other things I didn't have but needed."

"Well," Inga said, turning back to the wall, "he wasted his money. I don't need anyone, and I certainly don't need a slave girl leading me around like a guide dog."

"Inga, we talked about this," the doctor chastised. "Abigail is a part of our family now and she only wants to be your friend and to help you. I'm sure you two will become fast friends once you've gotten to know one another."

"I don't want any friends, and I don't need her pity."

Abigail interjected, "I don't pity you; I kinda envy you."

That brought Inga up short. "Envy me? Why?"

Abigail moved over to the bed and sat down. "Well, you have your grandfather, and he loves you very much, and I don't have any family left. Your family is rich, and even when my family was alive, we never had very much. There were four of us and we lived in a little apartment, you see. And then, you have your freedom, and I am supposed to wear a collar and leash whenever I go outside, just like any other dog."

As she was speaking, the doctor smiled at her and quietly left. Now, Inga moved over and sat beside Abigail on the edge of the bed. In a soft voice, she asked, "What happened to your family?"

Abigail replied, "When the war started, my father left and joined the army and we never heard from him again. When your army forced us to leave the bomb shelter, they shot my mother, little brother, and a bunch of other people right in front of me and some other girls."

"Oh, how horrible!" Inga gasped. "Then what happened?"

Abigail went on to describe her life since that fateful day and Inga sat spellbound. When she was finished, Inga asked her to describe herself and Abigail took her hand and placed it on her face, allowing her to feel the features. As she was feeling her face, Abigail said, "I'm twelve, but I'm small for my age. I'm only four and a half feet tall, and I weigh sixty-five pounds. I'm supposed to have blonde hair, but as you can feel, I don't have any. Oh, and my eyes are kinda pale green. My mother always told me that my eyes are my best feature." Suddenly, she remembered Inga's blindness and gasped, "Oh I'm so sorry, that was... I didn't mean to..."

Inga smiled and said, "That's all right, my mother told me my eyes were pretty too. Do you think they're pretty?"

Abigail looked into the light brown eyes of the little girl sitting next to her and said, "Yes, I think they're beautiful. I think you are too."

CHAPTER FOUR

The two girls sat for a few moments in silence until Mrs. van der Walle called them for dinner. Abigail led Inga down to the dining room and sat her in her usual place and stood behind her. When the doctor sat down, he looked at Abigail and said, "What are you waiting for? Aren't you going to sit down and eat? Yours is the seat next to Inga's."

Abigail took the seat, and they began dinner. When they were finished, they all moved into the living room that had a large console radio. She and Inga sat on the sofa while the doctor turned on the radio and tuned in to "Sherlock Holmes," which they liked to listen to. After it was over, they listened to "The Big Band Dance Party" and then it was time for the evening news.

The announcer began by extolling the successes of the Army of Truth and Light and then they listened to General Joshua giving a speech to the national assembly on the inevitability and certainty of their ruling the continent and returning it to the paradise of freedom and purity it was intended to be. Then, after a quick check of the weather, the news was over, and it was time for the girls to go to bed.

Abigail helped Inga back to her room and turned down her bed while she changed and washed up. After tucking the younger girl in for the night, Abigail crawled into her own bed. Although her body was ready for sleep, her mind was still trying to process the changes the day had brought. She tossed and turned for some time before sleep overtook her and that horrible dream began yet again.

This time, there was a change. Instead of waking up and trying to comfort herself, there was someone there to hold her until the terror subsided. When she started screaming, the doctor rushed in, and seeing the terror in her eyes, took her in his arms and comforted her until she overcame the panic and the tears stopped. Through her sniffles, she said, "I'm sorry. I didn't mean to scream and wake everyone up. It was just that dream again."

She described the dream to the doctor. He assured her that he understood. She didn't need to apologize for anything. He told her that he thought that the horrors she had lived through were enough to give anyone nightmares. Once she had herself back under control, he got her a glass of water. She gratefully took it and drank it down. She thanked him as he tucked her in. Then, the doctor turned out the light and left the room.

The next morning, after breakfast, Abigail talked Inga into going out for a walk. It was the first time she had been out since recovering from the fever and she seemed to enjoy it. They stopped at the neighborhood playground, and they played on the swings. Abigail even talked her into going down the slide a few times.

They were both having fun until, suddenly, a constable stood in front of them. He looked at Abigail's hands and then at her lack of collar and leash and said, "Come here, girl."

Abigail stopped pushing Inga on the swing and went over and stood in front of the constable. He looked down at her and said, "Who owns you?"

Abigail blushed and looked at her shoes. Before she could answer, however, Inga spoke up and said, "My grandfather bought her yesterday." Then she added, "Why, who wants to know?"

The constable looked at her and said, "I do, missy."

Abigail could see the constable was getting angry, so she interjected, "Sir, Inga is blind, so she doesn't know you're a constable. She wasn't trying to be rude."

Once he heard that, his angry look disappeared and was replaced with one of concern. "I'm sorry," he said, "I didn't know." Then, he addressed Inga and said, "Young lady, I'm Constable Bart de Vos and I see that your slave isn't wearing a collar and leash. I don't know if you're aware, but all slaves must be on a leash whenever they are in public. Being caught without one could result in a heavy fine for the owner and the slave being confiscated. But, since you just got her, I'll be lenient and just escort you home. Then, I can explain the law to your grandfather, and he can make sure this never happens again."

As the constable explained, Abigail's face became redder and redder. Finally, when he had finished, she turned back to Inga, thereby hiding her tears of humiliation from him. She wiped the tears away as she took Inga's arm and the three of them walked back to the doctor's house.

Once there, Constable de Vos explained the law to the doctor and left with a cheery wave. When he was gone, the doctor turned to Abigail and said, "I'm sorry my dear, I didn't think anyone would enforce that stupid law. I know it will be humiliating for you, but we must follow the law. I'll tell you what, once I'm through seeing patients this afternoon, I'll see if I can find something that will fulfill the requirements of the law but be as unobtrusive as possible. In the meantime, maybe you two should stay home for the rest of the day."

Abigail, still blushing, nodded her agreement and led Inga up to her room. They read and listened to big band music on the radio until it was time for dinner.

When dinner was over and the family was listening to "The Shadow," the doctor said, "Abigail, I went downtown today, and I got you something."

He pulled a small bag out and handed it to her, saying, "I know it's humiliating to have to be on a leash, but perhaps this one won't be so bad."

When she opened the bag, she saw a small gold necklace with a tiny ring on it. Attached to the ring was a gold chain that was about three feet long. She looked up at him and he said, "The woman in the shop said that was the smallest, most unobtrusive one they had. I figure that Inga can hold the leash when you lead her wherever you're going. Considering how small it is, I bet nobody will ever see it."

Abigail thanked him and returned to her seat beside Inga. During the radio program, she showed it to Inga and they both agreed it was probably the best they could hope for.

Life fell into a routine for the rest of the summer until the first week of August. It was a Sunday night when the doctor told the girls that they were all going to the secondary school the next morning to enroll them in classes. So, that night, both girls took baths and laid out their clothes for the next day.

Abigail woke up before the alarm and it wasn't long before she and Inga were dressed and sitting at the table finishing their breakfast. After the doctor finished his breakfast, they all climbed into the old car and drove six blocks to the Elsa Van Damme Academy for Young Ladies.

It took them a little while to find the headmaster's office, but once they did, it wasn't long before they were sitting in the anteroom, filling out the proper forms for both girls to be enrolled in fall classes. The doctor turned in the paperwork and they waited about fifteen minutes before they were escorted into the headmaster's office for an interview.

The headmaster's name was Professor Bruno von Hapsburg and he was about the doctor's age. He looked over Inga's application and finally said, "I see that your granddaughter is blind, is that correct Doctor?"

"Yes, she is. She has been for about six months now."

The headmaster put the application paperwork down and said, "I'm sorry Doctor, but the Elsa Van Damme Academy cannot admit your granddaughter. Unfortunately, we do not have enough staff members to properly assist her with her daily assignments. I'm sure you can appreciate that it would be extremely difficult, if not impossible, for her to complete the reading and writing required of our students. Perhaps you should consider St. Ann's across town. I understand they have an excellent program for blind students."

He put Inga's application aside and picked up Abigail's. He looked at it for a moment and said, "Doctor, I'm afraid we cannot accept Miss Henderson's application either. The law states that slaves cannot be enrolled in school for any reason."

The doctor thought for a moment or two and then said, "We were really hoping Inga could be enrolled here because your school is the closest to our home and St. Ann's does not have any openings. We were also hoping Abigail could continue her education because she is a very bright young lady. However, since, as you say, slaves are not allowed to attend classes, perhaps we can combine both desires. How would it be if Inga was enrolled as a first-year student and Abigail accompanied her to her classes? Abigail could aid her with reading and writing and that way both girls would receive an education, and since she isn't actually a student, you won't be breaking the law. I would even be willing to pay tuition for Abigail, just as if she were enrolled."

The headmaster thought about it for a few moments and said, "Abigail would not be allowed to participate in classes, other than to read and write for Inga, correct?"

The doctor nodded.

"Well, since she won't be an actual student, I don't see how that would violate the law. However, I think it would be best if I check with the school's board of directors before I agree to the arrangement."

The doctor replied, "Can that be done before the beginning of the school year? I wouldn't want Inga to miss any school at all if possible."

The headmaster stood, signaling the interview was over and said, "I have a meeting with the board tomorrow, I'll bring it up then and I should be able to call you tomorrow evening and let you know our decision."

The doctor and the girls stood. The doctor shook the headmaster's hand and said, "That will be most satisfactory, Headmaster. I look forward to hearing from you tomorrow evening."

***

Just before dinner, Mrs. van der Walle answered the telephone and called the doctor. He picked up the phone and said, "Hello? ... Yes, this is Doctor van Heflin." He listened for a moment or two and said, "Yes, I understand. Yes, that will be more than satisfactory. I will inform them both and they will see you on the first of September. Thank you, Headmaster, and please express our gratitude to the board the next time you see them. Yes, goodbye."

When he hung up the phone, he called Inga and Abigail into his study and told them the good news. "The headmaster said that the board of directors has agreed to allow you to attend classes beginning in September. But, they said that Abigail will have to follow a few rules."

Both girls looked at him with interest as he continued. "The first rule is that you are not to answer any questions unless they are directed to you specifically. You are not allowed to interact with any of the students or staff unless they initiate the contact. When you and Inga talk in class, you must keep your voice down to a murmur or a whisper. Lastly, because you are older than Inga, they assume you are more advanced and, for that reason, as well as others, you will not be allowed to help Inga with any answers."

Both girls agreed and left the room. As soon as they were out of the study, they burst out laughing with excitement. When they got to Inga's room they plopped down on the bed and Inga said, "I knew they'd let us in! This is going to be so much fun; I can't wait!"

Suddenly she stopped and said, "Oh Abigail, I forgot, you've already passed the first year. You're not going to be bored, are you?"

"No, I'll be all right," she replied.

The following week, Inga received a letter from the school telling her that she had been accepted. The letter went on to explain what books and school supplies she would need and what her uniform was going to be. At the bottom of the letter, there was a handwritten note explaining that, even though Abigail was not 'officially' a student, she would be expected to be dressed in the same uniform and would be required to follow the same rules and guidelines as a 'real student.'

The next day, the doctor and the girls went to the uniform shop suggested in the letter and bought their uniforms. Next, they went to the bookstore and purchased Inga's schoolbooks and a bag to carry them. Lastly, they went to the stationary store and purchased their pens, pencils, and paper for the year.

After lunch, the doctor took both girls to the beauty shop for their pre-school haircuts. Since Abigail's hair was just beginning to grow out, she didn't need a haircut, so she got her nails done instead. When the girl saw her brands, she was hesitant to do her nails until the owner told her that even slave girls liked to look nice.

At last, it was the night before their first day at school and they were both excited and a little apprehensive, too. Inga was nervous because she desperately wanted to fit in, and Abigail was apprehensive because of her status as a slave. How would the other kids treat her, she wondered? She would soon find out.

CHAPTER FIVE

The two girls were up and dressed at least an hour before they had to leave for the first day of classes. The doctor and Mrs. van der Walle both smiled when they came down so early. They bolted down their breakfast and urged the doctor to do the same. He, on the other hand, decided to take his time, more for his and Mrs. van der Walle's amusement than for any other reason.

At last, he was ready to go, and they all piled into the old car for the six-block trip to school. When he pulled up in front, the doctor got out and walked to the passenger's side of the car. As the two girls got out, he gave them both a hug and wished them a good day. Abigail was slightly surprised but quite pleased by the gesture.

She took Inga by the arm and led her into the vestibule and, eventually, to their locker. After depositing Inga's books, they headed to their first class. When they entered the classroom, Abigail looked around and saw the teacher sitting at his desk. When he looked up, he motioned for them to come over.

Abigail whispered to Inga that the teacher wanted to see them as they walked over and stood in front of his desk. Both girls were nervous when the teacher said, "You must be Inga van de Clerk and Abigail Henderson." They both nodded and he continued, "I'm Professor Lindert Kelder, your history professor, and homeroom teacher. Headmaster von Hapsburg told us about your special circumstances and considering those circumstances, I would suggest you take the two seats directly in front of my desk. That way, Miss Henderson will be able to see everything on the board and relay it to you without any difficulty and I can give you any additional assistance you may need."

Inga thanked him and they took their seats just as the rest of the class began coming in. Soon, the class was called to order and the professor began by introducing Inga and her 'companion,' Abigail. He went on to explain that Abigail was a slave and was there only to assist Inga with reading, writing, and guiding her wherever she needed to go. He told them that Abigail had been instructed to only interact with the others when directly addressed.

Throughout the teacher's speech, Abigail's face got redder and redder and, by the time he had finished, she had tears of humiliation running down her cheeks. Some of the other students noticed but didn't say anything. Inga noticed Abigail shaking and knew she must have been mortified by the speech. She gave Abigail's arm a slight squeeze and that little gesture helped her to persevere.

The rest of the class went without a hitch. When the bell rang, Abigail grabbed their books and they left the classroom, along with the other girls. Abigail gripped Inga's arm tighter than she normally would so they wouldn't get separated as they made their way to the next class. When they walked in, the teacher called them up to her desk and the scene from the first-period class was repeated. Once the other students were seated, the professor began by explaining about Abigail and Inga.

When the bell rang, Inga told Abigail she needed to use the restroom, so they stopped in the nearest one. When they walked in, they saw a group of girls standing near the window, smoking cigarettes. One of the girls noticed them and said, "Hey, there's that blind girl and her pet slave! Hey slave girl!"

Abigail blushed but didn't say anything. As she guided Inga to the door of the nearest stall, the girl called out, "We don't allow animals to use the bathrooms in this school, why don't you go outside and pee in the bushes like the other pets?"

The bully's gang of friends all laughed as Abigail's blush deepened but she still didn't say anything. The bully kept at her. She called out, "It's bad enough we have to put up with a freak but to have to put up with the stench of a puny slave is just too much! How's it feel to be a blind girl's seeing-eye dog? I'll bet your mommy would be so proud!"

Abigail was shaking with rage when she suddenly heard an adult's voice say, "What are you girls doing? You're not smoking, are you? Put those cigarettes out and get to class."

As they were filing out of the restroom, the teacher reached out and took the bully by the arm and said, "Bertha, I believe you owe these girls an apology, you were being very rude when I came in."

Bertha mumbled a half-hearted semi-apology to Abigail and Inga and tried to continue out into the corridor, but the teacher continued to hold her back. She looked the bully in the eye and softly said, "If I ever catch you bullying anyone else, I will ensure you're expelled; I don't care who your grandfather is. Do I make myself clear?"

Bertha stared daggers at the teacher but nodded and looked down. Once the teacher released her arm, she hurried out of the restroom. The teacher looked over at Abigail and Inga and smiled. She said, "You must be Inga van de Clerk and Abigail Henderson, I'm Professor Betina Svensson, your Dutch teacher and you're in my next class." She smiled at them and continued, "If you're ready, why don't we walk to class together?"

Their language class began just as the other two did with the exception that Professor Svensson made it sound as if it was a pleasure to have them in her class.

All too soon the class ended, and it was lunchtime. They were both famished, so they grabbed their lunches from the locker and hurried to the cafeteria. They had just found a place to sit and were about to start on their lunch when another first-year girl came over and said, "May I sit here with you?"

Inga smiled and said that was fine. As the girl sat down, she introduced herself. "My name is Frida Weisz. I know who you two are, the whole school is talking about you. Are you really blind?"

Inga nodded and Frida asked, "Have you always been blind or did something happen?"

Inga explained about her illness and the loss of her mother and when she was finished Frida said, "Oh, you poor thing! Oh, how terrible. So, you really can't see anything at all? No shadows, no light, nothing?"

Inga replied, "Nope, not a thing. Not for almost seven months now, I think."

"So, who do you live with since your mother is gone? Do you live with your father?"

Inga shook her head and said, "My father left to be an officer in the army when the Supreme Commander took over, so my mother and I went to live with her father. My father was a tank commander, and he was killed in the Battle of Rotherham about a year before we got sick. Now there's only my grandfather and me left." Before anyone said anything, she added, "And now, Abigail is part of our family too."

There was silence for a few seconds. Then Inga, more to break the silence than anything else, asked, "What about you? Is your family still together? Any relatives in the army?"

Frida said, "No, my father is too old to be in the army, he's over fifty. Instead, he's in charge of the civil defense wardens in the city. Momma left us when I was a little girl, and I really don't remember her so there's just Papa and me. Oh, and my dog Mittsy. I do have a cousin that's in the "De Jeugdleider Korps" (Youth Leaders Corps) at his school but that's the closest to anyone being in the army in my family."

When lunch was over, they went to their afternoon classes, and all went without incident. At last, the final bell rang, and they headed for the door and home. They were passing the last doorway when an oversized foot came out of nowhere, tripping Abigail, who went sprawling on her face to gales of laughter from some of the other students. As she was getting up, that same oversized foot came down on her back and an all too familiar voice said, "I told you, slave girl, animals belong outside."

Bertha laughed and walked out the door just as Frida rushed over to help Abigail get up and collect their books. At first, Inga hadn't known what had happened. She just knew that one moment Abigail was guiding her down the hall, and the next, she was standing alone. It frightened her.

Soon they had collected their books and things and, after thanking Frida for her help, walked out to the old car and the doctor. Abigail was still angry and somewhat embarrassed when they climbed into the back seat. The doctor smiled at them and asked about their first day.

Inga described their day in great detail while her grandfather drove them home. She continued her description all the way into the house and even followed him into his study. When she finally ended her monologue, the doctor looked at Abigail and said, "And how was your day?"

Abigail thought about it for a moment or two before she answered. Should she tell him the truth or just say it was fine? She decided on the truth; after all, he was as close to family as she had now. When she had finished her description with the retelling of Bertha's attack, the doctor sighed. "Abigail, I'm sorry about that girl Bertha but there will always be some people who need to bully others so they can feel good about themselves. It sounds like this Bertha is one of those. I would suggest that you try to avoid her as much as you can in the future."

Abigail agreed and they left the study, heading for Inga's room and homework. It didn't take too long and, once they were done, they headed for the backyard and the warm afternoon sunshine. About an hour later, it was time for dinner and then the evening radio shows. Before they knew it, it was bedtime. Although both girls wanted to stay up later, it wasn't very long after their heads hit the pillow that they were both sound asleep. For the first time in weeks, Abigail didn't have her usual nightmare.

The next day began better than the first and it wasn't long before they fell into a routine. Abigail kept a constant lookout for Bertha or any of the girls from the bathroom, but, since they were seventh-year students and Abigail and Inga were in their first year, they didn't see much of each other, only occasionally passing in the hall. Abigail made it a point not to use the bathroom where they had first encountered Bertha if she could help it.

As the week progressed, Abigail noticed another thing. Day after day, more and more of the first-year girls came over and sat at their table during lunch. The first day it was Frida but the next day there was Gertie and Helga. By the end of the week, there must have been almost a dozen girls sitting with them. And they weren't just talking to Inga; they were talking to Abigail too. It made her feel accepted.

Finally, Friday came and the end of the first week was at hand. When the final bell rang, Abigail and Inga got their stuff from their locker and headed outside for the ride home but, for whatever reason, the doctor wasn't there. They stood at the top of the stairs, near the front door of the school, and waited patiently. As she was looking down the street for the familiar old sedan Abigail suddenly felt something hit her on the back of her head. Without warning, she was falling down the stone steps, landing in a heap at their foot.

At first, she didn't feel any pain, but then she looked at her left arm and saw it sticking out at a funny angle. Then the pain came. Tears were falling down her cheeks as she sat up and cradled her arm. She looked up and saw Inga standing at the top of the stairs, looking lost and confused. Abigail called her and directed her down the steps.

Just then, the doctor pulled up in front of the school. Immediately, he jumped out of the car and came to Abigail's side. One look at her arm and he knew it was broken. He quickly placed Inga in the back seat and went to care for Abigail's arm. Carefully, he used a newspaper and a belt to splint her arm and gently placed her in the back seat too.

It was only a few minutes before they were home, and Abigail was being ushered into the doctor's basement clinic. Mrs. van der Walle had taken Inga to her room and quickly returned to the clinic to help the doctor set the arm. She helped Abigail onto the examining table and held her hand as the doctor used ether to put her to sleep before he set her arm. As she fell asleep, she thought she heard a man's voice moan. *I wonder who that was*, she asked herself. The last thought she had was that she must remember to ask the doctor about it when she woke up.

She woke up two hours later in her bed, her arm in a cast, with no memory of the moaning man.

CHAPTER SIX

The following Monday brought the second week of school. When their friends saw Abigail's arm in a sling, naturally everyone asked what had happened. It wasn't a very good story, since Abigail had no knowledge of how she ended up at the foot of the steps with a broken arm. She did mention feeling someone or something hit her on the back of the head though.

"I bet I know what happened," said Frida. "I bet it was Bertha who hit you in the back of the head. Mark my words, she'll be bragging about it to the whole school by lunchtime, you wait and see."

It was true. By lunchtime everyone in the school knew that Bertha van de Poole had hit that slave girl, Abigail Henderson, in the back of the head, causing her to fall and break her arm. Funny, nobody was impressed. Almost everyone felt sorry for the slave girl and that only made Bertha angrier.

It came to a head on Thursday when Bertha cornered Abigail and Inga in the cafeteria. They had arrived before their friends and were consequently sitting alone when Bertha came up behind Abigail. She grabbed her lunch and threw it on the floor. Then she grabbed Abigail by the collar of her blouse, forced her to her hands and knees, and pushed her face into what was left of her lunch. As she did this, she cried, "Animals don't eat at tables, slave girl, they eat off the floor. Now eat it!"

Inga heard the older girl and Abigail's sputtering and called out for help. Almost instantly, there was a voice that said, "Bertha van de Poole, what did I tell you the last time?"

Professor Svensson pulled Bertha off Abigail and said, "The headmaster's office Bertha, now!"

Inga felt around and found Abigail still on her hands and knees, sobbing hysterically. She pulled her up and held her while she cried out her humiliation. As they sat there, their friends and other girls who had witnessed the attack surrounded them and offered their sympathies. After a few minutes, Abigail had calmed down enough to sit beside Inga, who offered to share her lunch. They were just finishing when Professor Svensson came back in and approached them.

Abigail looked up apprehensively as she approached. She looked down at them and said, "I took Bertha to the headmaster's office and now he wants to see you too."

Abigail and Inga rose together but the professor said, "Frida, I know you have a study period after lunch, so would you please take Inga to her next class and stay with her? We shouldn't be too long."

Before she could answer, Professor Svensson took Abigail by the arm and walked out of the cafeteria. As they were walking to the headmaster's office, Professor Svensson said, "I want you to know that the rest of us don't feel like Bertha does. It's not your fault that your home country was invaded and conquered. I'm sure the headmaster will not hold your status against you."

They walked up to the headmaster's door and the professor knocked lightly. They heard a voice say, "Come in," and they entered the office.

Abigail saw Bertha sitting in a chair in front of the headmaster's desk and the headmaster sitting behind it. They stopped in front of the desk and Professor Svensson said, "Here she is, Headmaster. As you can see, her left arm is in a cast, thanks to Miss van de Poole and, as I told you, I found her trying to force Abigail to eat her lunch off the cafeteria floor. And this isn't the first time she's bullied Miss Henderson. I've been told that on the first day of school, as Abigail and Inga were leaving, she tripped Abigail and stepped on her back as she tried to get up. Headmaster, these are the actions of a bully and someone who I believe should not be enrolled in our academy. In any case, these are not the actions we, as an institution of learning, should condone or allow to go unpunished."

"Miss Henderson," the headmaster said, "how did you break your arm?"

Abigail told him and then he asked about the tripping incident and Abigail confirmed that story too. Lastly, she explained the verbal abuse she received the first time she met Bertha. The headmaster sighed then he looked at Bertha and said, "Are these accusations true, Miss van de Poole?"

"No sir," Bertha replied. "I would never treat another human being that way, not even a slave."

"Headmaster, I have witnesses who would gladly tell you about these instances," Professor Svensson said. "I can have them brought to the office if you'd like."

"No, that won't be necessary Professor, thank you," he said. Then he turned to Abigail and said, "Miss Henderson, as a non-student you have very few rights and privileges in this school. Additionally, as a slave, you have even less standing in society as well as in school. However, one of the few rights you do have is the right to be free from injury while on school property. Therefore, I would like to offer you an apology for Miss van de Poole's actions." As he was speaking, Bertha began to protest but he cut her off.

"Miss van de Poole, this is not the first time you've been accused of bullying fellow students. I believe I told you the last time that any more accusations of bullying would result in suspension, did I not?" Bertha nodded and the headmaster continued. "Therefore, effective immediately, you will be suspended from this school until your guardian comes in for a conference with me and your homeroom professor. Please wait in the outer office while I dictate a letter to your grandfather, explaining the situation and what he needs to do to resolve it."

Once Bertha had left the office, he looked at Abigail and said, "Miss Henderson, even if you are a slave and not a student, you are not required to tolerate mistreatment by anyone in this school. Please express our sincere apology to your owner and tell him that I personally assure you this will not happen again."

Abigail blushed at the mention of her owner but said, "Yes, Headmaster. I'll tell the doctor what you've said, sir."

The headmaster nodded and said, "Very well, you may go," and Abigail hurried from the office. She avoided Bertha's glower as she hurried out the door.

As she was walking down the hall, Professor Svensson called, "Abigail, please wait a moment."

She hurried down the hall and, when she caught up with her said, "Abigail, even though Bertha will be out of school for a few days, I don't want you to think she's gone for good. Her grandfather is a very important man, as I'm sure you know, and is a large contributor to the school. You can breathe easy for a while, but she'll be back. Just keep looking over your shoulder when she does get back." She smiled and patted Abigail's shoulder, then turned and headed for her classroom.

The next day, Bertha was not at school but on the following Monday morning, Abigail was again called to the office. When she knocked and was allowed entry, she saw Bertha and an older man, who could only be her grandfather, standing next to the headmaster's desk. When she glanced around the office, she was surprised to see Dr. van Heflin standing on the other side of the headmaster. He smiled and approached her, giving her a quick hug as the headmaster said, "Miss Henderson, this is Mayor van de Poole." The man nodded to her, and the headmaster continued, "He is here to express his and his family's remorse for the actions of his granddaughter."

The mayor came toward her and offered his hand. He smiled as she took it and said, "My dear young lady, please forgive my granddaughter for her... disrespectful actions toward you. I can assure you she was not brought up that way."

Abigail blushed but didn't say anything. Instead, the doctor said, "I'm sure Abigail will be able to forgive Bertha and will be more than happy to let bygones be bygones."

The mayor looked at Bertha and said, "Bertha, honey, don't you have something to say?"

Bertha looked at Abigail's feet and said, "Sorry. It won't happen again." Then, she walked over and forcibly took Abigail's hand and shook it. She dropped it as soon as she thought she could with a look of revulsion and disgust on her face.

Abigail saw the look on Bertha's face and knew this wasn't over, but she didn't say anything. Instead, the headmaster smiled and said, "I sincerely hope this will be the end of this conflict and you two can learn to coexist." Then, he looked directly at Bertha and said, "Miss van de Poole, if anything like these reported incidents happens again, or if you're involved in any other reported bullying incidents, you will be expelled. Do I make myself clear?"

Bertha looked down and mumbled, "Yes sir."

"Very well, you may both go back to class."

As Abigail turned to go, the doctor bent down and gave her a kiss on the forehead and a smile. She hurried to class and whispered what happened to Inga. When they were in the cafeteria, Abigail told their friends about the meeting and Bertha's promise to behave. None of them believed she'd keep that promise.

The rest of the week remained routine, and Abigail didn't see anything of Bertha or her gang of friends. Meanwhile, the group of first years at their lunch table continued to grow until there simply wasn't any more room. Inga, whom the doctor described as shy, really wasn't and was quite enjoying the attention.

Near the end of the week, Frida invited them to come over to her house after school on Friday. When Inga asked for permission, the doctor agreed, provided they called him when they were ready to come home. They agreed and when Friday came, they walked with Frida to her house, which was about eight blocks away.

Abigail had never seen that part of the city and really enjoyed looking at all the different houses as they walked. Whenever Inga asked, she would describe the neighborhood and all the different houses. When they arrived at Frida's house, Abigail described it to Inga and Frida blushed. She hadn't realized how grand it would seem to the other girls.

Once inside, Frida showed them her room and the rest of the house. They had just finished the tour when Frida's father came in the front door. Frida was surprised when she saw her cousin come in behind him. Frida said, "Papa, this is Inga van de Clerk and her companion, Abigail Henderson."

He smiled and shook both girls' hands while Frida went on, "Inga, Abigail, this is my father Heindrik Weisz, and my cousin, Jurren van der Meij."

When Abigail looked at Jurren, she could feel the hairs on the back of her neck stand on end. He was wearing a black uniform similar to the one army officers wore. The only difference was the "De Jeugdleider Korps (Youth Leader's Corps)" emblem on his epaulets instead of rank designations—those were on the collar of his uniform shirt.

Jurren nodded to both girls and Frida giggled. "Jurren," she said between giggles, "Inga is blind and can't see you nodding."

Jurren blushed and took Inga's hand, saying how pleased he was to meet her. Then he took Abigail's hand and she involuntarily shuddered as he smiled and told her how pleased he was to meet her too. Then he saw the "S" on the back of her hand and his smile disappeared instantly. He looked at her and said, "So, you're a slave? Where are you from?"

Abigail turned red but looked him in the eye and said, "I'm from Agustis."

He sneered and said, "Oh yes, Agustis. They fell in, what, three days?" He chuckled and said, "You must be glad to be here in the Empire. So, are your masters treating you well?"

Before she could answer, Inga said, "Abigail is my friend and like a sister to me. She's no more a slave in my family than you are. We all love her very much. In fact, I don't know what I'd do without her."

Just then, Frida's father said, "Why don't we see what's for dinner tonight, shall we?" Then he called out, "Mrs. Rothsburger, what's for dinner?"

The rest of the evening went well enough. After dinner, Frida, Inga, and Abigail went into the living room and listened to big band music until it was time for them to go home. Frida's cousin came in too, but he just sat in a chair and watched the girls. Whenever Abigail looked toward him, she had the feeling he was watching her. It made her feel creepy.

The doctor came and picked them up at ten and they told him about their visit on the way home. It wasn't long after arriving home that both girls went to bed.

CHAPTER SEVEN

It was the middle of the night when Abigail woke from a fitful sleep. At first, she thought it was the thunderstorm that had woken her, but soon she realized her left arm was aching. She lay still on her back for a few minutes, feeling her heartbeat pounding a painful beat in her arm. She tried ignoring it, but she just couldn't. After tossing and turning for almost an hour, she decided to go to the kitchen for a snack. She pulled her dressing gown on over her arm and stepped into her slippers as she headed for the door. She quietly made her way down the stairs and was almost to the kitchen when she passed the door to the basement. Suddenly she froze, fear rising in her heart as she could have sworn she heard voices drifting up the stairs from the doctor's clinic.

She took a steadying breath and opened the door. She listened for a few moments until she heard the voices again. This time, she heard the doctor's voice, but who were the others? Slowly, quietly she began going down the stairs when the stairway light suddenly came on. She jumped when she looked down to the landing and saw a man with blood all over the right arm and shoulder of his coat. Almost at once the doctor came around the corner and seeing the man looking up the stairs, followed his gaze. When he saw Abigail, he swore under his breath then called up to her, "Abigail, go back to sleep. I'll explain in the morning."

Before she could stop herself, she replied, "My arm was aching. It woke me up and I couldn't get back to sleep so I thought I'd get a snack and that's when I heard you. I'm sorry."

She was just turning to go when the doctor called, "Come down here and I'll give you something for the pain but then it's back to bed for you."

Tentatively, she walked down the steps. When she reached the bottom, she saw the man with the bloody arm was really a boy in his late teens. She looked at his face and saw the panic in his eyes and the sheen of perspiration on his face. As she approached, he swayed, and Abigail reached out her good arm to steady him. When she took hold of one of his arms the doctor rushed forward and took hold of the other. He said, "Bring him in here," and they led him into one of the examining rooms. Once the doctor had helped him onto the table, he smiled at Abigail.

Before he could say anything she said, "Doctor, do you need any help treating him? I'm not really tired; I could try to help if you need me."

The doctor nodded and said, "Help me get his coat off so we can see what we're dealing with."

It took them a while to get the coat off without causing the man too much pain. Finally, they succeeded, and Abigail saw several bullet wounds in the man's shoulder and arm. The doctor sighed and said, "Can you go to the supply cabinet and get me the ether? We'll need to put him to sleep before we can remove those bullets."

Abigail rushed out of the examining room and hurried to the supply closet in the next room. Having never seen an ether container, it took her a few minutes to find the right one. Once she did, she grabbed it and ran back to the room. After she had given it to the doctor, he said, "Now go into exam room one and you'll see some gauze masks. Bring me one, please."

Again, she rushed out of the room and sprinted to the supply cabinet. This time it only took her seconds to locate the masks and in less than a minute she was back with the doctor, carrying two of the masks. She panted, "I brought you two, just in case."

He nodded and took them from her, saying, "Good thinking."

Then he turned to the man and explained what he was about to do. As Abigail listened, she realized he was going to expect her to help him treat the bullet wounds. She took a deep breath and swallowed her fears. The doctor looked over to her and said, "Ready?"

She nodded and he said, "All right, hold this over his nose and mouth while I administer the ether. You won't be much help to me passed out on the floor so try not to breathe in too much of the fumes."

She nodded and after placing the mask over the man's mouth and nose leaned back as far as she could while the doctor poured the ether onto the mask. Try as she might, she couldn't help but breathe in some of the anesthesia and was slightly woozy when the doctor stopped pouring and capped the bottle. He checked the man's eyes and pulse, making sure he was truly asleep before he told her to remove the mask and put it in the trash container that had a lid.

She did as she was told and returned in time to watch the doctor begin probing the wounds for the bullets. After he removed the sixth bullet, he took a deep breath and said, "I think that was the last one. Help me turn him over, just to make sure."

They turned him over and found one more. After the doctor removed that one, they bandaged the wounds and the doctor moved to the sink and washed his hands. While he was doing that, Abigail took a blanket and covered the man while he continued to sleep on. The doctor turned and smiled at her as he said, "Thank you for helping me with that man. Normally, Mrs. van der Walle assists me, but as you know, she's at her son's for the weekend." He wrapped his arm around her shoulder and began guiding her towards the door. As they walked, he said, "Let's tell his friends that he'll be all right and then I'll give you something for your arm."

They walked out into the waiting area and Abigail saw about a half dozen men, all carrying machine guns and covered with black commando makeup. The doctor approached the leader and said, "He'll be fine now. He just needs rest while he heals. He'll probably be asleep for a few hours, but then you can take him with you. When you leave, make sure you're not seen."

The leader thanked him and then the doctor led Abigail into the other examining room. As she sat on the table, the doctor prepared a shot for her. After giving her the injection, they went up to the kitchen and had a quick snack. Fifteen minutes later, Abigail was back in her bed and five minutes after that she was sound asleep.

The next morning, Inga was surprised Abigail was still asleep. When she shook her and asked why she was still sleeping at ten in the morning, Abigail had the good sense to tell her that her arm had kept her up most of the night and that the doctor had to give her something to help her sleep. She didn't mention the man in the clinic.

When they came down for breakfast, she saw the doctor sitting at the table drinking his coffee and reading the newspaper. After greeting them, he asked Abigail to help him prepare breakfast and they left Inga sitting in the dining room. Once they were alone in the kitchen, the doctor said softly, "Abigail, please don't mention last night to Inga. If anyone found out about me helping those men, I could be executed, and I don't want to worry her unnecessarily."

Shock appeared on Abigail's face. "Why?" she asked.

The doctor explained, "Those men are from the underground. That's a group of men and women who are opposed to the rule of the Supreme Commander and are fighting as best they can. The young man we helped last night was shot during a sabotage mission at the munitions factory not far from the city. Unfortunately, they were discovered before they could carry out their mission. Anyway, Mrs. van der Walle and I have been helping the resistance by treating their injured whenever we can. We've gone to great lengths to ensure Inga doesn't know and I'd appreciate it if you would not tell her."

Abigail, still shocked by the information the doctor had just shared, assured him that their secret was safe with her. She even went so far as to offer to assist him if he ever needed her and he thought there was something she could do to help. He thanked her and they returned to the dining room as soon as the oatmeal was ready.

Nothing more was said for the rest of the day and Mrs. van der Walle returned home in time to make dinner. After dinner, Abigail and Inga went into the living room and turned on the radio. As they were getting settled in for the evening's programs, Abigail could just hear the doctor speaking to Mrs. van der Walle. She assumed he was telling her about the night before. She was sure of it a few minutes later when the doctor and Mrs. van der Walle came in and she winked at Abigail.

***

The following Monday at lunch, Frida told them how impressed her father had been with them and Abigail blushed. "What about your cousin, Jurren," she asked.

Frida looked down and said, "He didn't say."

Abigail didn't respond but Inga did, "Frida, I know I'm blind, but I could hear the scorn in his voice when he spoke to Abigail. Are you telling me he didn't say anything after we left?"

Frida blushed and said, "He said he thought Abigail was pretty–for a slave."

Abigail laughed. "That was it? I'm surprised."

Frida blushed even more and added, "Well, he did mention he wished he could buy his own slave girl."

The other girls all giggled and one of them said, "Yeah, I wonder what he'd do with a slave girl."

They all giggled even more, but Abigail didn't. Instead, she thought back to what the army officer in the cafeteria said about pimps and perverts. She shivered involuntarily.

It wasn't long before the topic changed to the upcoming interschool dance and what everyone was going to wear. She was surprised when Rosalie asked her what she was going to wear. "I'm not sure we're going." She looked at Inga and said, "Inga, are we going to the dance?"

"I hadn't thought about it," she replied. "What do you think? Do you want to go?"

Before she could answer, they heard a loud explosion and the floor shook. Suddenly, all the bells were ringing, and teachers began shepherding them to the basement. Abigail, being the only one to have lived in a war zone, knew immediately what had happened. She leaned over and whispered to Inga, "That explosion wasn't very close, so I don't think we have anything to worry about. The teachers are making us go into the basement just as a precaution. We shouldn't be there too long."

Inga nodded as they began going down the stairs. When they reached the basement, the teachers began organizing them by class. As they lined up, Abigail could hear some of the girls sobbing and even a few praying. She could feel Inga's grip tighten as more and more of the girls began to panic. Abigail put her arm around the younger girl and began assuring her that there was nothing to worry about. While she was assuring Inga, she could see the teachers moving through the crowded hallway doing the same for the other girls.

Finally, after about thirty minutes, they received the all-clear and began shuffling back up the stairs and on to their next classes. Once everyone was seated, the professor informed them that the explosion that had prompted their evacuation to the basement was over ten miles away at a military base and was caused by an artillery accident. Having heard artillery before, Abigail knew this was a lie.

The rest of the day continued without any more incidents. Even so, everyone was glad to hear the last bell of the day. Abigail had a difficult time holding on to Inga as it seemed everyone was in a hurry to get out of the building. Finally, they made their way out and began looking for the doctor. He wasn't there.

They waited for almost half an hour before Abigail suggested they just walk home. It was only six blocks away after all. Inga agreed and they decided to follow the route the doctor always took when he drove them to or from school. The weather was still warm, so the walk was actually quite pleasant, and it wasn't long before they were knocking on the front door. Neither of them had a key as they had never needed one.

They knocked for a while before Abigail suggested they go around back and see if they could get in that way. Inga agreed and they walked around the block and up the alley, finally arriving at their back gate. They reached the back door and began knocking. After a few minutes, Abigail stopped knocking. "Where do you think they are," she asked.

Inga shook her head as she said, "I don't know. What do you think we should do now?"

Suddenly, Abigail saw the stairway and door to the doctor's clinic and had a thought. What if the doctor and Mrs. van der Walle were in the clinic helping someone from the underground? She knew she couldn't bring Inga through there because of her promise to the doctor. Then, she got an idea. "Inga," she said, "You wait here, and I'll see if I can find a way in, and then I'll come and open the back door."

Inga agreed and sat on the steps while Abigail snuck down and tried the clinic door. Abigail quietly turned the knob, then grinned as she felt the latch pop open. Sneaking in, she gently closed the door behind her, being careful to make as little noise as possible. When she turned around, she was shocked to see ten or twelve men all pointing guns at her. She raised her hands and said, "Please don't shoot; I live here!"

Just then, Mrs. van der Walle hustled into the waiting area and, seeing the guns exclaimed, "Stop! She lives here!"

As the men lowered their weapons, she looked at Abigail and asked, "What are you doing here? Why aren't you in school? Where's Inga?"

Abigail replied, "School's out and we walked home. Inga is sitting on the back door steps waiting for me to open the door. Why didn't you answer the door when we knocked?"

Mrs. van der Walle suddenly looked panicked and rushed up the stairs to the kitchen. Abigail followed in her wake. She had just reached the top of the stairs when the doctor called out for Mrs. van der Walle to come and help him, but she didn't hear him. Abigail quickly called out to Mrs. van der Walle, but she was already opening the door and bringing Inga inside. While Mrs. van der Walle was occupied, Abigail quietly went back downstairs and into the examining room. The doctor looked up from the patient and was surprised to see her. As he looked back down, he said, "Where's Inga?"

"She's upstairs with Mrs. van der Walle. Can I help?"

He nodded and she came around to his side of the table. As she did before, she helped the doctor for the rest of the night.

CHAPTER EIGHT

It was nearly midnight before Abigail and the doctor came up from the clinic. Mrs. van der Walle met them with bowls of soup and sandwiches. They sat at the kitchen table, both exhausted, and ate in silence. After a few minutes, Mrs. van der Walle asked, "Doctor, what are we going to tell Inga about you two being gone for so long? She asked me numerous times, but I just kept changing the subject."

They all jumped as a voice said, "Yes, what are you going to tell Inga?"

They looked up as Inga came into the room and sat down at the table. "Grandpapa, did you really think I didn't know about you sneaking off to the clinic at all hours of the day and night? I know I'm blind, but I'm not stupid."

He looked down at his soup bowl and said, "Inga, honey, I didn't want you to worry."

"Well, it's too late. Didn't you think I'd worry when you disappeared for hours with no explanation?"

He sighed and said, "Inga, I've been treating people who get hurt, sometimes at night. I didn't think you'd be interested. I'm sorry if you've been worried. It's really nothing."

"Grandpapa, I've heard some of the voices coming from the clinic and I know you've been helping the people fighting against the Empire. As I've said, I'm blind, not stupid."

"Well, if you've known, why haven't you said anything about it," he asked.

"Because it's your business and I didn't want you to think I was spying on you."

"Inga, honey," Mrs. van der Walle began, "we didn't tell you because we felt you had enough to deal with, having to learn to live with your blindness. We felt you were too young to know about the underground members we were helping."

"Well, that didn't work out either, did it? In case you haven't noticed I'm not a baby anymore. I will be eleven next week." After a moment she added, "Why? Why do you take the chance? What would happen if you got caught?"

Doctor van Heflin took her hand and said, "I expect that if we were to be caught helping the resistance, we would be considered traitors and executed. That's why it's so important that we never talk about it anywhere but here in our own house.

"As for the why, well it's because of Abigail and other girls like her. Whenever I have to go to the processing center, I see these young girls who are frightened and some of them injured or maimed, and I know what's in store for them and it turns my stomach. Most of them end up being sexually and physically abused and eventually killed by cruel, wicked men and women. They're used for horrific things, and some are beaten to death. It continues with each country the empire conquers. Countless girls are sold like cattle and the guards just laugh and count the money. I swear, if I had the money, I'd buy every one of them, but I just can't, and it kills me a little inside every time I have to watch. This is the only way I can help stop these animals, by helping the resistance end this reign of perversion and terror."

Abigail had tears in her eyes when he finished. She reached across the table and taking his hand whispered, "Thank you, Doctor."

Inga took a few minutes to digest what he told her. Finally, she said, "Grandpapa, I have about a hundred muntens saved up if that would help you save another girl."

He reached over and gave her a hug. She leaned her head against his shoulder and sighed. He gave her a squeeze and said, "Thank you, honey, we'll see. But, in the meantime, I think it's time we all got some sleep."

Mrs. van der Walle cleaned up while the doctor took the two girls up to their rooms. Once they were washed up and in bed, he gave them both a kiss and they all went to sleep.

***

The next day everybody was talking about the attack on the munitions factory just outside of town. "It was on the news last night," Frida said as they sat around the lunch table. "The reporter said that a group of terrorists attacked the factory and the explosion killed twenty workers and closed the plant for at least a month. He said there was a ten-thousand-munten reward for any information on the terrorists."

After the other girls thoroughly discussed the topic, the talk turned to the dance. There were two weeks before the dance and almost everyone was going. "The political science teacher told all the sixth years that it is every girl's civic responsibility to do what they can to aid and comfort present and future soldiers and that dancing and socializing with them is the best way we can help keep their morale high," Helga told them. "My sister told me that he also told them that they have to look as pretty as they can so that the boys…how'd he put it? Oh, yeah, we're supposed to look pretty so that the boys will remember what they are fighting for."

Everybody giggled at that. Then Gertie leaned over and asked Inga, "So, are you and Abigail going to go? It's in two weeks, you know."

Abigail looked over at Inga and saw she was at a loss. "We'll see," she interjected. "We'll have to ask Inga's grandfather first, in case he may have other plans."

As it turned out, he thought it was a great idea and that weekend they went to the dress shop so they could get new party dresses for the dance. Mrs. Braun was glad to help them both find just the right dress. Doctor van Heflin sat for hours as they tried on dress after dress. Finally, they both had the perfect dress, and they were off to the shoe store for their first pair of 'grown-up' shoes. Lastly, they went to the jewelry store, and each got new earrings and a small necklace.

The following week passed without incident but felt like an eternity. Even Inga's birthday celebration didn't make the time move any faster. Eventually, the night of the dance arrived, and the doctor drove them to the school.

The girls walked into the cafeteria and Abigail gasped at the sight. Instead of the plain, off-white walls and long tables, the walls were covered with posters and student "art" from both schools, promoting the war effort. The long lunch tables had been replaced with dozens of round tables. A small band on the stage played the latest big band songs.

Abigail spotted their friends and guided Inga over to their table. They all greeted them and made room for them to sit. No sooner had they sat down than Frida leaned over and told them that her cousin Jurren had just been there asking about them. She told them that his friends were dying to meet Abigail as they had never met a girl from Agustis before. Abigail laughed, but inside she cringed—she knew what they really meant.

Suddenly, Jurren was standing next to her and Inga. Abigail felt her flesh crawl when she saw that he was wearing his uniform. She leaned over and told Inga he was there, and she blushed. He leaned down and asked Inga to dance and she blushed even more, but got up and headed to the dance floor.

Abigail was sitting alone watching Inga and Jurren when she felt a tap on the shoulder. She looked up and saw a blond boy wearing a Youth Leaders uniform and smiling down at her. She shyly smiled at him as he asked her to dance. Being a slave, she wasn't sure if she should, or even if she would be allowed to, but she decided to say yes. As they walked onto the dance floor, the boy whispered into Abigail's ear. "My name is Otto de Koster," he said.

Since the song was a slow one, Otto placed one arm around Abigail's waist and took her hand with his other hand and they began slowly moving across the dance floor. He asked a few questions about her, and the conversation remained light. As they were dancing, Abigail felt his hand move slightly south of proper and she gently but firmly pulled it back above her waist. When this happened for the third time, she said, "Otto, I don't know what you think you're doing, but I'm not that kind of a girl. Please keep your hands off my backside. It's creepy."

He didn't say anything, but leaned down and kissed her. While he was kissing her, she struggled to get free. When she finally did, she stepped back from him and slapped his face as hard as she could. He staggered back a step or two and then backhanded her back. She fell to the floor and almost instantly Professor Svensson and a man in a major's uniform were there. Professor Svensson helped Abigail up and looked at her swollen, red cheek. The major quickly ordered Otto to attention and began questioning him about what happened.

"I tried to kiss that slave and she had the audacity to slap me! Me, a lieutenant in the Youth Leaders Corps slapped by a little slave girl! She should be grateful I didn't kill her for her insolence!"

Before the major could respond, Professor Svensson said, "Abigail is a member of the Elsa Van Damme Academy family. We do not see her as a slave but a wonderful young woman and companion to Miss van de Clerk." Then, addressing the major, she continued, "Major Smoot, I don't know what you teach your cadets, but assaulting a young girl at a school dance is not acceptable behavior."

The major looked at Otto and said, "Lieutenant, you will apologize to the slave for your actions. We do not condone treating other people's property with such cavalier indifference. You will then apologize to her owner and the rest of the academy. Do I make myself clear?"

Otto clicked his heels and said, "Yes Major." Then he turned to Abigail and said, rather stiffly, "Please forgive me, my actions were... regrettable."

He walked over to Inga, who was still standing with Jurren, and said, "Miss van de Clerk, please forgive me for trying to take liberties with your property without asking your permission."

Without waiting for her response, he walked in front of the stage and said, in a loud voice, "Students and faculty of the Elsa Van Damme Academy please accept my apology for my actions toward your... mascot."

There was stunned silence in the room as he walked over to his table and sat down. Professor Svensson led Abigail, who was still crying, back to her seat and directed one of the other girls to go get a cloth with some ice in it for her face. While they were waiting, Inga and Jurren came back to the table. Inga sat next to Abigail and was trying to calm her when Frida turned on Jurren and said, "This is all your fault—you and your fascist friends! Thinking you're better than everybody else just because of that stupid uniform you wear! You make me sick!"

"Frida, I didn't do anything to that slave girl, and I sure didn't tell Otto to do anything either. I wouldn't touch her even if she wanted me to!"

He stormed away, back to his friends and schoolmates as the band began playing again. Soon, the dance floor was filled with couples swinging to the latest big band sounds. One by one, boys came to their table and began asking the other girls to dance and they accepted. At last, there were only Inga and Abigail left when two boys came over and stood, waiting to be acknowledged. Abigail leaned over and told Inga of their presence and she asked them what they wanted. When they approached, the tallest one said, "My name is Lars, and this is my brother Daan." They both bowed and he continued, "Please understand that we do not feel as the lieutenant does, and we're embarrassed to be from the same school as he is."

Inga said, "Thank you, Lars," and was about to turn away from him when he continued. "We were wondering if it would be all right if we asked you ladies to dance." Before they could answer he added, "We promise not to grope you or try to kiss you...without your permission, that is."

Inga leaned over to Abigail and whispered, "What do you think? Should we take the chance?"

Abigail thought about it for a moment or two. At first, she wanted to say no, but then she thought that sitting at this table for the rest of the dance would not be fair to Inga, so with many reservations and misgivings, she said, "Why not?"

They both got up and the two boys smiled as they took the girls' hands and led them to the dance floor. Abigail took the boy's hand and tensed as he placed his other hand on her waist. They had been dancing for a few minutes when he began asking her about herself.

As they swayed around the dance floor, Abigail relaxed and told him her story. Then, she asked him about himself, and he told her that he was also twelve, and lived on a farm outside of the city with his parents, brother, and little sister. When she asked, he told her that his father was employed at the munitions factory and had been slightly hurt in the explosions the week before.

Before she realized it, they had danced through several songs. She looked around for Inga and found her sitting with Daan and some of his friends, sipping punch and having a good time. Lars asked Abigail if she wanted any punch, and they joined Inga and Daan. The rest of the dance was spent with the brothers and their friends.

When the bandleader announced the last dance, Abigail and Lars and Inga and Daan returned to the floor. Both couples danced closer than was strictly allowed and when the song ended the brothers escorted them out to wait for the doctor. When the doctor pulled up, Abigail turned to Lars and thanked him and Daan for making what started as a disaster of an evening into a good time. Then, giving Lars a quick kiss, she took Inga's arm and hurried to the waiting car.

CHAPTER NINE

The doctor smiled as the girls climbed into the back seat. He began to drive home. Inga told him all about the dance, including the unpleasantness with Otto, and the fun they had had with Lars and Daan. The doctor only meant to tease her when he asked if she had kissed Daan. When Inga didn't answer, Abigail looked over at her just in time to see her blush and lower her head. She giggled and Inga's blush deepened. The doctor chuckled and said, "Abigail, our little girl is growing up."

The next week at school, the dance was all the other girls wanted to talk about, especially the incident between Otto and Abigail. On her part, Abigail would have liked to forget about the whole thing, but the bruise on her cheek made that hard to do. Frida told them that the two boys with whom they were dancing drove Jurren crazy by asking about them all the time. Abigail blushed and was about to respond when they felt the ground shake and, shortly thereafter, heard the explosion. Almost immediately, the bells began ringing and the teachers herded them back into the basement hallway that served as their bomb shelter.

This time, while they were in the shelter, they heard and felt a series of explosions, each coming closer and closer. With each explosion, Abigail felt Inga's grip on her arm tighten. Finally, after almost two hours in that dingy, musty hallway, they were allowed to return to their classes. Most of the other girls were shaken and kept asking the professors about the explosions, but they didn't know any more than the girls.

While listening to the radio after dinner, they finally found out what had happened. When the news came on, the reporter told them that there had been a series of terrorist attacks around the city. The terrorists damaged three railroad bridges and attacked an army truck convoy. According to the reporter, no serious injuries occurred. However, the attacks caused serious property damage. In order to protect citizens from further attacks, the army and State Security Service planned to increase patrols and arrest identified suspects immediately. Speechless, the doctor, Abigail, and Inga looked at each other with fear in their eyes.

Abigail remained on edge for weeks afterward. Every day on the way home from school, she felt sure police would be waiting to arrest them. But, with each day that passed with no one carted off to jail, Abigail relaxed. Then, one day in school, Greta told Abigail and Inga that her neighbor's house was raided. The police suspected the father of sabotage and took him into custody. Abigail's heart raced as Greta described the raid in gruesome detail.

That evening, Abigail told the doctor about the raid. "I am aware," he said. "But there is no need to worry, my dear. That man had nothing to do with the resistance cell that we assist, so do not fret."

After the discussion with the doctor, Abigail spoke with Inga. "Do you feel any better after hearing what the doctor said?"

"No," replied Inga.

"Me neither," Abigail mumbled.

For almost a month, everything was quiet. Then, a huge explosion rocked the whole school on the day before Christmas break. Once again, they shuffled into the basement hallway and were forced to stand around for hours. When they were finally allowed out, it was dark. Everyone was sent to their homerooms and allowed to leave only when their parents came and picked them up. It was a long process, and Abigail and Inga had to wait until almost six o'clock before they were allowed to leave. When they went to get into the car, they were surprised to see Mrs. van der Walle instead of the doctor.

Mrs. van der Walle noticed the shocked look on the girls' faces. She explained to them that enemy airplanes dropped bombs on a munitions factory, which caused the explosion they had heard earlier. The doctor had been called to the site to aid the injured workers. She told the girls that the doctor would tell them more news when he got home.

But the doctor didn't come home that evening. They ate dinner and listened to the radio reports and even stayed up late, but he still wasn't home when they went to bed just after one o'clock in the morning. The next morning, he still wasn't home, and the girls began to worry. Finally, after just over 24 hours, the doctor came in. He was exhausted, and it showed in his face and in his eyes.

Still, he smiled when the two girls rushed up and hugged him. Then they all went to the kitchen, and he told them about the factory while Mrs. van der Walle made him something to eat. "The factory building itself isn't in too bad shape. After all, it was designed to withstand explosions, but the storage yards and the railhead were completely destroyed. I don't know how many explosives were destroyed, but the windows of every building for miles around have been blown out. The buildings nearest to the yard were completely disintegrated; there was nothing left but piles of rubble."

He took a bite of food and then continued, "I must have treated hundreds of injuries; everything from cuts from flying glass to workers with missing limbs to those who were disemboweled. It was horrible."

After eating, he excused himself and shuffled off to a quick bath and much-needed sleep. Mrs. van der Walle and the girls talked for a while and then went into the living room for that evening's radio shows. When the news came on, the announcer told them that the air corps would soon begin patrolling the skies above the city.

The first days of January brought a new sight and sound to their lives—fighter planes flying over the city. Most of the population had never seen an airplane, let alone fighters, but there they were circling over the city. It was only a few days before the first enemy air attack and almost the entire city stopped what they were doing when they heard the air raid sirens blaring. But, instead of heading for shelters, as they had been instructed to do, almost everyone looked up to watch the battle.

Abigail and Inga were back at school when the attack began so they didn't get to see the battle taking place above. Instead, they, along with their schoolmates were stuck in the basement corridor for hour after hour. Then, suddenly they all heard a huge explosion, which rocked the entire building. Several girls screamed in fear. After waiting for what seemed like forever, the 'all clear' was sounded and they went back upstairs. As they exited the staircase leading up from the basement, they were all shocked to see that almost all the windows in the school had been blown out. They all asked the teachers, but they couldn't tell them what had happened. Finally, the headmaster came across the public address system and told them that an enemy plane crashed about three blocks away and caused damage to their school.

This time, the girls had to wait for their guardian to actually come in and get them. It was the doctor who came to get them, and as they were going to the car, Abigail could see pillars of thick black smoke rising from various places around the city. The doctor told them that there was indeed a crashed aircraft not far from the school, but that it was one of the empire's fighters that had gone down.

From then on Abigail became very popular at school. Students and professors alike would come up to her and ask her about the various explosions. Once or twice, they asked about her opinion of how the war was going. She smiled to herself because she would almost always tell them that it depended on their perspective. When they looked shocked, she would laugh and tell them that a few air raids didn't mean that the empire was losing the war and that they needn't worry too much.

The Monday after the air raids began, there was an assembly in the cafeteria. When Abigail and Inga came through the doors, Abigail's heart almost stopped. There standing in front of the assembly with the headmaster was the same army officer that had addressed her and the other slaves in the processing center. Her pulse was still racing when they took their seats.

The headmaster began the assembly by leading the girls in singing the national anthem. Once everyone had sat down, he introduced the army officer as Lieutenant Colonel Maximillian Vonn Friedenberg and told them that he was the school's new military liaison and information officer. He explained that, since the air raids and the sabotage attacks had begun, the empire felt it was important to keep the citizens of the capital informed, and that included the students, too. He went on to say that the empire expected the children to inform their families of what they were told.

Finally, the colonel began speaking. "Thank you, Headmaster, for your kind introduction. And thank you, girls, for your warm welcome."

Inga leaned over to Abigail and whispered, "What warm welcome? Nobody has made a sound."

He continued, "Our most gracious leadership has asked me to address your concerns about some of the more distressing events of the last few weeks. First, let me assure you that there is nothing to be concerned about. There have been a few instances of sabotage around some military installations and involving some valuable infrastructure around the city. Although the sound of the explosions can be frightening, there was only minor damage, and no one was seriously injured. Most importantly, the war effort was not disrupted in the least. These attacks only produced minor inconveniences and should not concern you or your families." He smiled and Abigail, remembering the last time she saw him smile, shivered.

After a moment, he continued. "As I know you are aware, the enemy began a campaign of harassing air raids on military targets in and around the city. I admit that this move by the enemy was not expected and we in the armed forces were caught off guard. However, you may rest easy from now on because the air corps has shifted some of its assets to provide protection for the capital and its citizens. So, in the near future, you will be hearing and seeing more fighter aircraft in the sky above you. This should not be a cause of concern. Instead, it should reassure you that our Supreme Commander has taken steps to protect you and your families."

Abigail looked around and saw that this information didn't get the reaction the colonel was looking for. Quite the contrary, most of the girls around her and Inga looked close to panic. As she was thinking this, the colonel asked if there were any questions and one of the older girls in the back row raised her hand. The colonel nodded at her. She stood and said, "Thank you for the information but wasn't that one of our airplanes that crashed three blocks from the school? Are they fighting right over the city? Isn't that dangerous?"

The colonel leaned over to one of his aides and whispered something and then said, "Thank you for asking such an intelligent question. Yes, one of our fighter planes did crash near the school, but it wasn't from any battle that may or may not have been going on in the sky. That specific plane crashed because of mechanical failure. You'll be happy to know that the pilot was able to bail out before the plane crashed and parachuted to safety. He is currently receiving medical treatment, but he should be back up in the skies keeping you and your families safe in just a few days."

The girl smiled and sat back down. The colonel looked around and asked, "Any more questions?"

No one raised their hands, so he thanked them for their attention and left the room. Before they were dismissed, the headmaster told them that the basement "bomb shelter" would be undergoing major renovations over the next summer so that all the students and faculty would be able to shelter there comfortably for hours, and even days, if necessary. Finally, they were allowed to return to their class schedules, and they all got up to leave.

As they were queuing up at the door, Abigail saw a man in a suit move over and 'guide' the girl who had asked the question out another door. She felt the hairs on the back of her neck tingle as she watched the girl go.

That night they told the doctor and he said he wasn't surprised. "I figured they would assign people to the schools sooner or later. It stands to reason that they'd want to keep an eye and an ear open to what was being said in people's homes and the best way to do that is to listen to what children and young people tell each other. You two will have to be extremely guarded in what you say and to whom you say it while you're at school. Remember, all our lives may depend on it."

The Friday after the assembly, Abigail and Inga were walking through the halls, heading for their next class when two armed soldiers stepped in front of them. Abigail's heart was in her throat when one of them said, "The colonel wants to see you two in the headmaster's office. Follow us."

When the soldiers opened the headmaster's office door, Abigail saw that everything had changed. First, the headmaster was working at a small desk in the corner and Colonel Vonn Friedenberg was sitting at his old desk. Also, instead of the diplomas and paintings that used to hang on the walls, now there was a huge picture of the Supreme Commander behind the desk and maps and pictures of tanks and fighter airplanes all around the rest of the room. The flag of the empire and a military ensign were displayed behind the desk, one on each side of the Supreme Commander's picture.

The soldiers saluted the colonel and left the two girls standing in front of the desk. The colonel smiled at them and said, "Please be seated."

Abigail directed Inga to a chair and they both sat. The colonel stood and walked to the front of the desk. He leaned against it in what he obviously thought was a casual manner, but really only served to put Abigail's nerves on edge. He reached over and took Abigail's right hand and looked at her brand. He then turned her arm over and saw her registration number tattooed there. He looked at her and said, "Why are you in my school, slave? Doesn't your master know it's illegal to educate a slave?"

Before she could answer the colonel looked at the headmaster and demanded, "Headmaster, why is there a slave in my school? Don't you know you could be arrested for educating an enemy of the state?"

Inga spoke up and said, "Abigail is acting as my eyes, sir. I'm blind and my grandfather bought her so she could help me with my schooling. She isn't here as a student, only as my helper."

The colonel looked from the two girls to the headmaster and back again. "Is this true," he asked Professor von Hapsburg. "Is it legal?"

The headmaster said, "It is true, Colonel. Abigail is here as Miss van de Clerk's aide only. As far as it being legal, the school's board of directors is satisfied that the arrangement does not violate the law. Since she's been here, Abigail has followed all the conditions set forth for her by the board."

The colonel stared at him for a moment or two and then turned to the girls. "I see. Tell me slave, who is your master?"

"Doctor Kurt van Heflin bought me during the summer last year, sir," Abigail answered.

"I see. What were the conditions you were given for being here?"

"I am to help Inga by reading to her and writing whatever needs to be written. I'm not allowed to interact with the other students, faculty, or staff members unless they initiate the contact. I'm not allowed to participate in a class unless directly addressed, and I'm not allowed to help Inga by giving her any answers to any schoolwork or homework. I'm also required to wear the school uniform so that I don't stand out or draw attention to myself in any way."

He scrutinized Abigail for a few moments before he leaned over her and said, "Very well, girl, you may stay. But if you put even one toe out of line you and the blind girl will be out of here so fast it will make your head swim. What's more, your master will find things will become very uncomfortable. You see, we've been watching him for some time now. We know about his radical views and subversive leanings. It's only a matter of time before we have him arrested for one thing or another. Now, get to class."

As they hustled out of the office, both girls were shaking with fright.

When they got home, they told the doctor and he laughed. "He was only trying to frighten you. No one knows what I do for the resistance and there's no one watching me. All the same, you need to be very careful around Colonel Vonn Friedenberg. I've seen how he operates at the processing center. Abigail, I believe you were there when he had a girl's teeth knocked out for simply asking a question. Please, girls, don't give him any reason to question you again."

CHAPTER TEN

Abigail couldn't believe she had been living with the doctor and Inga for four years now. In that time, both she and Inga had changed dramatically. While she had only grown to be five feet tall and now weighed a whopping one hundred pounds, Inga had shot past her to be almost five and a half feet tall and outweighed her by at least twenty pounds.

Other things had changed, too. Abigail's dirty blonde hair grew back and reached the center of her back. She liked to wear it in a braid, which Mrs. van der Walle braided for her. On the other hand, Inga had continued to keep her curly hair cut just above her collar. Both girls had grown in beauty and grace, too, and it wouldn't be long, the doctor thought, before boys were camping out on their front doorstep, begging for dates.

Along with all the physical changes, there had been other changes too. Their relationship had become closer than ever. Now, instead of being friends, they were more like sisters. They were so close that they could sometimes predict what the other was going to do or say. When that happened, both would break out into fits of laughter.

Their school life had changed quite a bit in the last four years, too. The headmaster was gone. Colonel Vonn Friedenberg was now in charge, and he had brought about many changes. For example, during their second year, the army installed an anti-aircraft battery on the roof of the school. One or two parents complained, and their daughters were gone from school the next day, never to be heard from again.

Many of the professors had left as well. Now, almost all their classes were taught by army officers or military veterans. In fact, Abigail's favorite teacher was an army veteran who was missing his right arm. He was still young and most of the girls had crushes on him. Abigail told Inga that his piercing blue eyes were what dreams were made of. It didn't hurt that he had a quick sense of humor, too.

Frida was still their best friend, but they had lots of other friends. Almost every other weekend, they were at Frida's, and more often than not, Jurren and some of his friends were there, too. Abigail still didn't like him, but Inga was still taken with him.

The doctor continued to help the resistance by treating their injured fighters. As the war dragged on, supplies became scarce, so it became more and more difficult. What started as only the occasional resistance fighter soon began to include enemy airmen. As more injured pilots came to them, the cases were more difficult and took more time to treat. Soon, it was all Dr. van Heflin and Mrs. van der Walle could do to keep up. Abigail aided them whenever she could and was actually becoming quite good at it.

One night, there was a knock on the door. The doctor answered it and found one of his contacts from the underground with an injured man leaning on him. The doctor led them to one of the examining rooms and called Abigail to come down and help him. When she walked into the room, she felt her heart skip a beat as she saw the injured man. He was a year or two older than she was and had the most beautiful face she had ever seen.

She came back to herself and hurried into the room to help treat the man. The doctor and the comrade of the injured man placed him on the table while she ran and got the ether and a mask. It wasn't long before he was anesthetized and being treated. While she helped the doctor treat his numerous injuries, she couldn't keep her eyes off his face. She blushed as they removed his clothing and she saw his broad shoulders and strong chest; the holes and the blood were something of a distraction, though. She shook her head and once again brought herself back to the task at hand.

The doctor removed three bullets from his shoulder, repaired his severely broken leg, set his arm, and patched up his other injuries. After almost five hours, they were finished. They walked into the waiting room to let the resistance member know that he was going to live, but he could not be moved for at least a month. The man nodded and said he would let the others know and that someone would come back in a week to check on him.

Abigail didn't know how she made it through school the next day, considering she had been helping the doctor all night with the injured airman. But somehow, she made it home that afternoon and was just about to go up to her room for a nap when the doctor called her into the kitchen. "Abigail," he said, "can you bring our patient something to eat? Mrs. van der Walle had to go out for a while, and I've got patients waiting."

Abigail agreed and went downstairs to see what the patient might want to eat. When she knocked on the door, the man called, "Come in," in a heavily accented voice. She smiled as she opened the door and saw the man sitting up. She blushed as she said, "Dr. van Heflin asked me to make you something to eat. What would you like?"

She looked into his eyes and almost forgot to breathe; she couldn't remember ever seeing such deep blue eyes. He smiled and said, in broken Dutch, "I not no wordy four dine."

She giggled and he turned red. She said, very slowly, "What language do you speak?"

He said, "Anglosian, Agustian, and Franco."

Her eyes lit up when she heard he spoke her native language. "You speak Agustian? I'm from Agustis! It's my native language!"

His face lit up too. "My father is from Agustis! What a small world!"

"Whereabouts in Agustis is your father from," she asked.

"He's from a small town just outside the capital called Dunwich. Do you know where it is?"

"Yes, of course. My grandparents had a small farm just north of Dunwich; I've been there lots of times!"

They had been talking for about an hour when Abigail suddenly said, "You know, we've been talking all this time, and I don't know your name."

He smiled and said, "Corporal Benjamin Albert Nicholson at your service, ma'am! And you are?"

She too smiled and said, "Abigail Rachel Henderson."

He held out his left hand and said, "Pleased to meet you Abigail Rachel Henderson."

When she took his hand to shake it, he looked down and saw her brand. He looked at her and said, "Oh my God! What is that on your hand?"

She blushed and said, "When Agustis fell, I was taken as a slave." She showed him her other hand and said, "These are my brands and this," she turned her tattoo up so he could see it, "is my registration number."

He looked confused when he said, "And I thought the doctor was all right…"

"Oh, but he is," she interjected. "He and his granddaughter have been like family to me ever since I came to live with them. And they treat me like family too. Oh, please don't think ill of the doctor, he's a gem!"

"But he bought you?"

"Yes, he got me about four years ago, right after Inga, that's his granddaughter, was struck blind from an illness. I was supposed to help her with her schoolwork and getting around but now, we're more like sisters than anything else. In fact, it's because of her that I have been able to continue my schooling. It's against the law for slaves to be educated you see, so the only way I could continue going to school was as Inga's eyes. I read everything to her and write her answers and that way we both learn."

"Still, being a slave. It must be embarrassing sometimes."

"Well, at first it bothered me because some people treated me like dirt but now, I'm treated just like any other girl. It's not too bad…except for having to wear a collar and a leash when we go out."

Benjamin looked closer at her necklace and realized, with a shock, that it was really a slave's collar with a little hook for a leash. He sat dumbfounded for a few seconds, finally coming to himself when she said, "Oh, I almost forgot, I was supposed to be getting you something to eat. What would you like?"

He told her and she ran off to the kitchen, promising to return shortly with his dinner. True to her word, she was back in less than half an hour with a large bowl of soup and fresh bread and, to his surprise, another visitor. She put the soup and bread on a table and said, "Benjamin, I'd like you to meet Inga van de Clerk. Inga, this is my new friend, Benjamin Nicholson."

Inga nodded in his general direction and said, "I'm pleased to meet you," in Dutch, which he didn't really understand, but Abigail interpreted for him.

As Benjamin ate, the two girls kept him company. They talked about the war and their home lives. Benjamin told them about living in the United Colonies and about his family. During the conversation, Abigail learned that Benjamin was only eighteen. They also learned that this was his first mission and that his airplane was shot down three nights ago. He told them that only he and one other gunner had survived the crash. "We thought we were goners when the guys from the underground found us. I really couldn't fight, and Sergeant Smithers only had his .45 and two magazines. We were never happier than when the men coming through the underbrush used the code word."

It was almost ten o'clock when the doctor came in and ushered the girls out, saying Benjamin needed his rest and they needed their sleep too considering they had school in the morning. They all agreed, said goodnight, and went back upstairs and to bed. When they got to Inga's room, they spent the next hour talking about everything they learned from Benjamin. When she finally crawled into her own bed, Abigail was smiling to herself, but she wasn't quite sure why.

The next day seemed to drag on forever. Abigail couldn't wait to get home and visit with Benjamin some more. She found herself daydreaming about him and more than once Inga had to nudge her to bring her back to reality. When it happened for the fourth time, Inga said, "Will you stop thinking about Benjamin? We have schoolwork to do, and it won't do itself you know."

Frida leaned over and whispered, "Who is Benjamin?"

They both blushed, but Inga replied, "A boy my grandfather treated in his clinic the other day. I think Abigail has a crush on him because he speaks Agustian."

Abigail blushed and nudged Inga and all three girls began giggling. The teacher came over and said, "Ladies, I fail to see how the defeat of the Franconian Empire is a laughing matter. Is there something you'd like to share with the class?"

They were all blushing when Inga muttered an apology for the three of them. When lunch came, Frida began questioning them about Benjamin and Inga was more than willing to tell her anything she wanted to know. When Frida asked her where Benjamin was from, Abigail broke into the conversation and said, "A little town not too far from where I lived in Agustis, but his family moved here before the war, and they've been here ever since. In fact, he told me he wants to join the army as soon as he's well enough."

While she was telling Frida this, she stepped on Inga's foot, so she knew not to correct her. Still, some of the other girls were now paying attention. Abigail had a bad feeling about that but there was nothing she could do about it now. Frida seemed to get the message and stopped asking about him. Instead, she asked them if they were coming over on Friday. They said they were.

The day was finally over and, after finishing their homework, Abigail headed for the clinic. He was sitting in a chair when she came in. She blushed as he smiled and greeted her. "I thought you might have forgotten me," he said as she came in.

They talked until dinnertime and she went upstairs to eat, promising to come back with his dinner and to sit with him while he ate. Half an hour later, she came in with Inga and a tray of food. They talked until Mrs. van der Walle came and got the girls for bed.

When Friday came, the three girls walked to Frida's house. They spent most of the walk talking about people they knew. When they reached Frida's, they went directly to her room and closed the door. Frida turned from the closed door and said, "Okay, spill the real story about this Benjamin boy. Who is he really and what's the truth about him?"

Abigail felt trapped. She replied, "We told you, he's a boy that Doctor van Heflin was treating for an injury, and we sort of hit it off when he found out I was from Agustis. There really isn't much else to tell you."

Frida looked from Abigail to Inga and back again. "Bull," she said, "There's more to this story and I know it. Why just looking at you two I can tell you're lying. Now out with it."

Before either girl could respond, Frida plopped on the bed and said, "Oh my God, he's really an enemy airman, isn't he?"

Abigail felt herself turning red, but still, she said, "No, of course not. How could an enemy airman wind up at Doctor van Heflin's clinic? No, he really is just a boy who happened to be from a little town in Agustis that we met in the clinic. In fact, he said he lives just outside of Brighton on a farm with his mother and father and two younger brothers."

"What's his last name," Frida asked.

Before she could stop her, Inga said, "His last name is van Nicholsen."

"Liar," said an unexpected voice.

CHAPTER ELEVEN

Abigail felt the hairs on the back of her neck rise as Jurren strolled into the room. "There are no former Agustians living in the empire. They are all either enemies of the state or slaves, so your story doesn't ring true. More likely, your grandfather has been helping the underground by providing medical treatment to traitors and foreigners. And that makes you two traitors, too."

Abigail felt her mouth go dry as she looked into those cold brown eyes. She said, "Of course he isn't aiding the enemy! Don't be foolish. Doctor van Heflin is as loyal to the empire as anyone I know. Why he even volunteers at the slave processing center whenever there are new slaves to be processed. Inga's father gave his life for the empire, and you have the audacity to accuse her grandfather of treason? How dare you!"

All three girls glared at him, but Jurren just smiled and said, "Suit yourself, but if I were you, I'd come up with a better story to explain the enemy fighter in your basement if anyone else should ask, and I can assure you, they will."

Before any of them could stop him, he turned and walked out. Abigail sprang from the bed and followed him, begging him to stay and hear her explanation. When he slammed the front door in her face, she bolted for the telephone. The doctor answered on the second ring. He listened as she explained what had happened and told her that he would pick them up in fifteen minutes. After she hung up the phone, she ran up the stairs to Inga and Frida. She said, "Frida, we're sorry but we've got to go home right away. Inga, Grandpapa is coming to pick us up. He'll be here in a few minutes."

Frida burst into tears and cried, "Jurren was right! You are helping the enemy! How could you!?"

Abigail said, "Frida, don't be ridiculous, of course we aren't helping the enemy. It's just that Inga's grandfather wants us home when the police show up so we can explain how Jurren misunderstood the facts. Everything will be fine, and we'll see you on Monday."

Before Frida could say anything, Abigail took Inga by the arm, and they headed out the front door to wait for the doctor. They didn't have to wait very long as the old sedan came around the corner after only a few minutes. They hustled into the back seat and the doctor took off for home. As they drove, Abigail answered his questions while Inga began sobbing. In between her sobs, she kept saying how sorry she was about the whole thing and how it was all her fault for mentioning it where someone else could hear them.

"No, it was my fault for daydreaming about him. You couldn't have known Frida was close enough to overhear us."

The doctor interjected, "No matter who is to blame, the damage is done. Now we have to figure out what to do about it." As they pulled up in front of the townhouse, he added, "Don't mention this to anyone. Don't say anything while I get hold of my contact and we figure out what to do. In fact, I think it would be best if you wait up in Inga's room for me. I shouldn't be too long."

As they climbed the steps he added, "Inga, dry your eyes now, no more tears. Abigail, straight up to Inga's room. Let me deal with Mrs. van der Walle." He opened the door and whispered, "Go."

As the girls rushed up the stairs, Abigail heard Mrs. van der Walle talking to the doctor. She closed the door to Inga's room just as the telephone rang. Abigail led Inga to the bed and walked over to the radio, tuned it to a music station, and quickly moved to the window. She pulled the curtains slightly apart and looked down on the street in front of the house. She sighed with relief when she didn't see anyone out there. She had just walked back to the bed when there was a knock on the door. The doctor came in. He closed the door and walked over to look at both girls and said, "I've alerted my contact, and he assures me that they'll know if and when the police decide to come calling. In the meantime, we're to act as if nothing has happened."

Before he could continue, Abigail interrupted, "What about Benjamin? What's going to happen to him?"

The doctor said, "We have a way to hide him that should be safe. I'll need you and Mrs. van der Walle to help me move him, but once he's safely tucked away, we should be okay.

"Now listen very carefully. My contact tells me that it's not unusual for the secret police to show up in the middle of the night and roust people. Their usual method is to separate family members for questioning, often telling them that one of the others has confessed. Whatever you do, don't believe them, and don't tell them anything other than our cover story. I can't stress enough that all of our lives depend on everyone sticking to the same story."

Inga burst into tears and the doctor took her in his embrace and tried to soothe her fears. After a few minutes, she regained control over herself, and he continued. "The cover story is that a young man came to my clinic with a broken arm and while Abigail was helping me set it, he started flirting with her and told her he was from Agustis and she believed him. Turns out he really was just trying to get her to go out on a date. I've talked it over with my contact and he's agreed to provide a boy who can speak Agustian and will be briefed on the cover story." He got up, walked over to the window, and peeked out at the street. Then he turned back to them and said, "Mrs. van der Walle has some food ready if you're hungry."

They all walked downstairs to the kitchen and had a bite to eat. Then the doctor, Mrs. van der Walle, and Abigail went down to the clinic to tell Benjamin what had happened and to move him into the secret room behind the doctor's office. Abigail watched his eyes as the doctor gave him the news. When he was finished, she found she couldn't look him in the eye. All she could do was keep saying how sorry she was. He took her hand and smiled at her. "Don't worry about it. What's done is done and we'll just have to deal with whatever comes our way. That's all."

He chuckled and continued, "Really, I'm kinda flattered that you were talking about me. I didn't think I made that much of an impression."

Abigail blushed as she looked at him and he laughed. A few minutes later, as they were moving him into the hidden room, he wasn't laughing anymore. Instead, he was gritting his teeth and sweating from the effort. Finally, he was situated in the room and the doctor gave him something for the pain while Abigail and Mrs. van der Walle went upstairs to get his dinner. Abigail stayed and talked with him while he ate. When she had gathered the dirty dishes and was leaving, he called out, "Hey, don't forget I'm down here. I like a little company once in a while."

She smiled and blushed as she closed the hidden panel and went upstairs.

The weekend seemed to take a month to pass by, but suddenly it was Monday and they were off to school. Both girls' hearts were pounding like steam engines as they walked through the front doors and headed for their locker and classes. The day slowly dragged on until it was finally lunchtime. They quickly grabbed their lunches and headed for their usual table, hoping to see Frida there.

They had just sat down when Frida came in the door. She looked directly at them and proceeded to sit at another table. Abigail murmured this to Inga as the rest of their friends came and sat down. Gertie plopped down next to Inga and immediately asked, "Is it true that your grandfather has been helping the resistance fighters?"

Inga immediately went into the cover story and the tension at the table seemed to melt away. Abigail even told them the name of the boy in question and told them that he lived about three blocks away from them. It wasn't long before the other girls began teasing Abigail about having a boyfriend. Both girls began to breathe easier.

The afternoon classes were uneventful. The best thing of all happened as they were walking out the door toward the doctor's old car. They had just reached the top of the steps when Frida called out, asking them to wait. When she caught up, she said, "Helga and Rosalie told me about what you said at lunch today. Is it really true? Was he really just flirting with you?"

Abigail blushed and said, "Yeah, he turned out to be a tease. I'm so embarrassed that I was taken in by his lies."

Once they were in the car, Abigail told the doctor about their day and the story they had spread. He told them that they had done well, but to keep it up as they were not out of the woods yet. No sooner had he told them that than Abigail felt her heart jump into her throat at the sight of a man in an overcoat and a fedora standing across the street from their house.

Once they were inside, the doctor told them that the man had shown up around lunchtime and that he wasn't the only one. There were two men watching the alley and a dark sedan was constantly driving around the block. "They're not even trying to hide the fact that they're watching us," he told them.

The surveillance continued for about a week until late on Thursday night. Just as they were getting ready for bed, there was a knock on the door. Mrs. van der Walle answered it and a man in a dark overcoat walked in as if he owned the place. He was followed by about a dozen other men, all wearing dark overcoats and matching fedoras. The doctor came out of the study and asked, "What's the meaning of this? Who are you?"

The first man motioned to the other men, and they moved to secure every door in the house. He walked over to stand in front of the doctor and produced his identification. "My name is Inspector Eric Hoffmann, I'm with the State Security

Service. We have information that you may be hiding an enemy combatant in your clinic."

After looking at the man's identification, the doctor said, "Well Inspector, why don't I just take you down to the clinic and you can see for yourself that we're not hiding anyone." As he began leading the way, he added, "As you will see, we're not really set up for long-term care of patients. We're just set up for minor injuries and illnesses."

When they reached the bottom of the steps, the inspector and two other men began searching every nook and cranny of the clinic. Meanwhile, Mrs. van der Walle guided three other security agents into every room on the main floor. Abigail and Inga had just put on their dressing gowns when four agents came up the stairs to search the bedrooms.

Abigail went into Inga's room and the two girls sat on the bed while two of the agents searched Inga's room. The other two men were searching Abigail's and the doctor's rooms. After leaving one agent at the front door and one at the back, the last three went up to the third floor to search. After about two hours of searching, they found nothing.

When the search was finished, Inspector Hoffmann gathered everyone in the living room and began the questioning. "Doctor van Heflin, as I told you when we arrived, we have information that you have been giving aid to the enemies of the empire. We have it from a reliable source that an individual named Benjamin van Nicholsen was seen and treated by you in your clinic sometime within the last two weeks. Now, we've checked and there are no families living on any farms near Brighton with that last name. Our source also tells us that Benjamin van Nicholsen is allegedly from Agustis and he moved here with his family before the war. Does any of this sound familiar?"

Abigail raised her hand and said, "Excuse me, sir, but I think I know where this is coming from."

The inspector looked at her and said, "And you are?"

Abigail replied, "My name is Abigail Henderson, sir. I'm Inga's slave."

The inspector said, "I'm not used to being addressed by slaves, but just this once, I'll let you speak. Where do you think this came from, girl?"

Abigail could feel her face glowing with irritation, but tried to keep the anger out of her voice as she explained about Frida and her cousin Jurren and the overheard conversation. Then she told him their cover story and finished by telling him how embarrassed she was about the whole misunderstanding. Once she was done, there was silence as the inspector finished writing his notes. He looked at Inga and said, "Is this true?"

Inga nodded and said, "Yes, sir. It's true."

Then he said, "What did you say were the full names of this Frida and her cousin? And where did you say they lived?"

Inga told him their last names and Frida's address but added that they didn't know Jurren's address.

The inspector continued questioning them for another hour or so. Then, out of the blue, he looked at Abigail and said, "So, slave girl, is the doctor a tender lover, or is he rough?"

Abigail was taken aback, but the doctor quickly came to her aid. "Abigail is not a sex slave, Inspector. She is Inga's companion and helper, nothing more."

The inspector turned to Inga and said, "Oh, so she's your sex toy. Very interesting."

Inga blushed as the doctor interjected, "I told you, Inspector, Abigail is not a sex slave. She never has been and never will be. She is my granddaughter's best friend and companion. She helps Inga with her schoolwork and guides her wherever she needs to go. We consider her a member of our family."

The inspector looked at the doctor and said, "You know what I think, Doctor? I think you and your whole family are liars and traitors and if I had one little bit of evidence, I'd have all of you in front of a firing squad in a heartbeat." He stood up and the other agents did, too. "I suggest you and your little girls be very careful what you do and say from now on. I'll be watching all of you."

The doctor stood and the inspector said, "Don't bother seeing us out, we know the way."

They all began breathing again once they heard the door slam.

CHAPTER TWELVE

Abigail burst into tears as soon as the front door closed. Inga moved over next to her on the couch and held her as she sobbed. The doctor quickly went to the vestibule to make sure the security agents were gone. Hurrying back into the living room he said, "Abigail, get a hold of yourself. I need you to go check on our friend downstairs. Quickly!" Then he turned to Mrs. van der Walle and said, "Lotte, no doubt our friends have made a mess of everything, but there's also the chance they placed listening devices somewhere in the house. Can you check each room and see if you can find them? I'll check the clinic." Turning to Inga he said, "Inga, honey, can you check yours and Abigail's rooms for any hidden microphones? Check under tables and the beds, between the mattresses, anywhere you can think of. And if either of you finds one, don't do anything, just let me know."

They all went about their assigned duties. Abigail dried her eyes as she hustled down the steps and into the storage room. She reached under the third shelf and tripped the latch so the whole shelving unit swung forward. When the hidden door opened, Benjamin looked up and was about to say something when Abigail motioned for him to remain silent. She closed the door and said, "We were just visited by the State Security." He paled at the mention of the secret police but she quickly added, "They're gone now, so you needn't worry. It's just that you'll have to stay hidden for a while longer."

He looked in her eyes and saw she'd been crying. He raised himself up onto one elbow and said, "They didn't hurt you, did they?"

She blushed slightly as she wiped her eyes again and said, "No they didn't hurt any of us. They just said some really cruel things and I was so frightened. But I'm better now. Anyway, we need to keep you hidden for a while until they get tired of watching us and the house."

He pulled the blankets off himself and began to get up, saying, "I've put you all in danger. I've got to leave."

She saw him break out in a cold sweat as he tried to swing his legs out of the bed. She rushed over and pushed him back down, saying, "Benjamin, don't! You're not ready to get up yet. You'll tear your stitches! Besides, they're watching both the front and the back of the house. You wouldn't get ten feet before they arrested you–or worse. You need to just stay here until they get bored and go someplace else."

He lay back down, and she tucked his blankets in again. As she worked, he looked at her. When she noticed him looking at her, she blushed. He asked, "Why are you doing this?"

"Doing what?"

"Helping me. Putting yourselves in danger for someone you don't know and never met before in your life."

She finished with the blankets and looked at him. Then she turned the back of her hands towards him and said, "I watched my mother and little brother be shot to death by these animals. When I was being processed as a slave, I heard the guards all laughing as they told us that most of us would be sold to pimps and perverts and probably wouldn't live five years. I suffered through the processing and know what it's like to be treated like an animal—worse than an animal. Doctor van Heflin feels that we should do everything within our power to stop these animals before they destroy any more lives. I agree with him."

"Well, I guess that if you feel that strongly, the least I can do is express my appreciation the best way I can."

Before she realized what he meant, he reached up and pulled her face towards his and kissed her on the lips. Her eyes bulged out as their lips met and her heart pounded. After a few seconds, or perhaps a year or two, he let her go and she stood back up, still dazed. Without saying anything, she turned and walked out of the room, closing the door behind her. She thought she heard him calling her as she closed the door, but she wasn't sure. It didn't matter, she wasn't in control of herself anyway.

Benjamin was sure he'd blown any chance he'd had with the girl when she walked out the door. He was also sure that at any moment the door would burst open and the doctor would come in bellowing at him like a wounded lion and ordering him out of his house. Then, he had visions of the secret police barging through the door and carrying him off to some POW camp somewhere where he'd die a slow and painful death.

Abigail's lips were still tingling where they had come into contact with his. She walked, as if in a dream, back up to the kitchen and almost ran into Mrs. van der

Walle. "Abigail, honey, is there something wrong," she asked as reached out and stopped her before they collided.

Abigail seemed to come out of her stupor and said, "He kissed me."

"Who kissed you, dear?"

"Benjamin. We were talking and he reached up and kissed me."

"Are you all right? Should I go down and have a talk with him?"

Abigail shook herself and suddenly smiled. "No," she said, "It's all right, I liked it." She smiled and added, "I've got to tell Inga. She'll flip!"

Mrs. van der Walle smiled and shook her head as the girl tore out of the kitchen calling Inga as she bolted up the stairs. Moments later, she heard both girls scream with happiness as she was sure Abigail had shared her secret with Inga. Just then, the doctor came in with raised eyebrows and she laughed as she told him about the kiss.

After two very long hours, they had finished searching the house for listening devices, finding only three. They didn't remove them, just marked their location so they didn't say anything incriminating near them. The doctor went up to Abigail's room and told the girls where the devices were. "There's one in exam room #1, one in the kitchen, and one in Inga's room. Now, so we don't forget they're there, I've put a large red sign on the wall next to their location. Inga, I know you can't see the signs, so you'll have to remember where they are. The one in the kitchen is under the chair nearest the window. The one in your room is under the foot of your bed. The one in the exam room is under the table. They shouldn't pose too much trouble, except for the one in your room, so if you two want to talk about anything sensitive in nature, please do it in Abigail's room."

He looked at his watch and said, "It's late, so I think you'd best be getting to bed. You still have school tomorrow and I don't think it'd be wise for you to miss it."

Abigail and Inga got up off the bed and began walking out the door when the doctor said, "Abigail, may I have a word with you?" When both girls stopped, he added, "In private, please."

Inga felt a little left out but continued into her room and got ready for bed. Meanwhile, the doctor said, "I hear Benjamin kissed you this evening, is that correct?"

He smiled as she began blushing and he continued, "I see that it is. Well, I have to ask, how did you react?"

At first, she didn't understand, but then she did. A look of shock came over her face as she tore out of the room and ran down the stairs. She seemed to fly as she dashed through the basement door and slid to a stop in front of the secret door.

Benjamin jumped as the door was suddenly thrown open. It was his turn to be taken aback as he expected to see the doctor come rampaging in, but instead saw Abigail's flushed face. He was just about to apologize for kissing her when she rushed in, leaned down, and kissed him full on the mouth. When they broke apart, she smiled at him and said, "Good night."

Before he could respond, or even react, she ran back out the door and up the stairs. He smiled as he lay back down. *Girls are strange*, he thought as he drifted off to sleep.

The next morning, they all acted as if nothing had happened. They left for school at the regular time and went about their day as usual. The doctor saw patients all day and Mrs. van der Walle went shopping and ran errands all morning. The entire time, a man across the street and one at each end of the alley watched their comings and goings. The dark sedan continued to cruise the neighborhood.

When they arrived at school, it was obvious to everyone that they hadn't gotten any sleep the night before. Frida asked them at lunch what happened, and Inga told her about the secret police's visit but didn't mention the listening devices. Frida and the others listened with rapt attention and were impressed at the end of the story. When they were done, Frida said, "I can't wait to tell Jurren about the boy and the secret police. I bet he'll feel bad when he finds out how much trouble he's caused."

Abigail said, "You mean you haven't seen him since he ran out of your house last Friday?"

"Oh, he hasn't been around. When Papa heard what he'd done, he banned him from our house. He said he really likes you girls, and he hates snitches. Since Jurren snitched on you girls, he didn't want him around our house. But after I tell him, I'm sure he'll be sorry, and Papa will forgive him."

Abigail didn't think Jurren would be sorry at all, but she didn't say anything. Inga did, however. "Well, when you tell him about what he's done, tell him that I never want to see him again! He almost destroyed my whole family!"

The weekend was long but quiet. The men were still watching the house and they were all on pins and needles. They expected the police to come barging in and arrest them all, but that didn't happen. Abigail spent as much time with Benjamin as she could. Sometimes, she brought Inga with her, but she always seemed to come down near bedtime by herself. She began to relish their goodnight kisses.

The following week was also quiet. Frida gave them a letter from Jurren at lunch on Monday. The letter said he was really sorry that he accused them of being traitors and that he was glad they weren't in too much trouble. After Abigail read the letter out loud, Inga commented that it didn't get much worse than having the secret police watch everything they do. Frida did note that at least they weren't under arrest. Inga's only reply was, "Yet."

***

It was close to three o'clock in the morning on Sunday morning when Inspector Hoffmann and his goons beat on the front door until the doctor opened it for them. Once again, they came in uninvited and gathered the family in the living room. Both Inga and Abigail were rousted out of bed. They barely had time to grab their dressing gowns as they were hustled to the living room. As the police did the last time, they searched the house. Again, they found nothing incriminating.

When they were finished, the inspector turned to the doctor and said, "Well, I see you found our microphones. I bet you feel very proud of yourselves. Well, I've got news for you: you didn't find all of them. What's more, we now know the name of your Agustian-speaking boyfriend and he said he has no idea who you are or what we were talking about."

Before anyone could respond, he nodded at one of his men and he moved over to Abigail and took her by the arm. She felt her stomach drop and she tried to get away, but the man just tightened his grip. The inspector continued, "I think I know how this misunderstanding happened. You see, little Miss Abigail here doesn't look like a slave anymore."

The man forced Abigail into the kitchen chair that another security agent had brought into the living room and forced her arms behind the chair back, causing her to gasp with pain. Another agent took a length of cord and roughly tied her to the chair. When the doctor and Mrs. van der Walle moved to come to Abigail's defense, three agents raised machine pistols and aimed them at their chests.

The inspector continued, "You recall when you first bought her, she didn't have any hair? Everyone could tell just by looking at her that she was a slave, but you've let her hair grow out. Well, I think we should shave her again, just so no one will be confused about what she really is."

Abigail began to cry when an agent pulled out a set of barber's clippers and plugged them into the outlet. She began to beg as he turned them on, but the inspector only laughed. She struggled, twisting her head this way and that, but another man came over and grabbed her by the jaw, forcing her to stop moving her head. She began to scream, but he just laughed and stuffed a rag into her mouth. Over and over again, the clippers moved along her head until all her beautifully braided blonde hair lay in a heap on the floor. Then, to add insult to injury, the man took the clippers and shaved off her eyebrows. When he was done, the inspector said, "There, now everyone will know what you are."

They released her and shoved her over to the doctor and Mrs. van der Walle. They grabbed her so she didn't fall, and while they were helping Abigail steady herself, one of the agents grabbed Inga and forced her into the chair. "You know," the inspector said, "since you and the slave are like sisters, I think it's only fitting that you should look like sisters, don't you?"

Before anyone could respond, Inga found herself receiving the same treatment as Abigail. After a few minutes, she too had been shaved and shoved towards the rest of the family. While both girls were sobbing, the inspector walked over, leaned close to the doctor's ear, and softly said, "You have one week to produce the enemy soldier, or we'll be back. Personally, I hope you don't. Then I'll get to have more fun at your expense."

With that, the inspector and his henchmen left the house, slamming the door behind them.

CHAPTER THIRTEEN

Abigail and Inga were inconsolable as they watched Mrs. van der Walle sweep up the hair and clean up the living room. The doctor tried to comfort them, but without any success. He assured them that he'd take them to get wigs if they wanted, but then Inga pointed out that they didn't make wigs for missing eyebrows. Finally, between sobs, Abigail said that she would proudly go out with only a headscarf. She was, after all, just a slave.

Before the doctor could respond, Inga straightened up and said, "If Abigail can stand being seen without hair, then so can I. No, Grandpapa, I'll just wear a headscarf, too. We'll show the world how sadistic the secret police really are."

Before going to bed, four microphones were found while cleaning up the mess. The next morning being Sunday, they all went to church. When they walked into the church, they could hear the people murmuring when they saw Abigail and Inga. Both girls held their heads high and ignored the comments they overheard.

They received the same reaction on Monday morning when they walked into school. In the middle of their first class they were called to the colonel's office. They knocked and entered, standing in front of the desk until they were acknowledged. Colonel Vonn Friedenberg didn't ask them to sit down. He just said, "Miss van de Clerk, is this some kind of political statement, or have you become a slave too?"

Inga explained and the colonel sat dumbfounded for a few seconds. Finally, he said, "Very well, you may go back to class."

The rest of the day was spent with the other students all staring and talking about them and not even lowering their voices. It wasn't long before everyone in school knew that the secret police had visited Inga van de Clerk and her family in the middle of the night and shaved both girls' heads. The reason the secret police did this was a matter of conjecture and rumor, most of which weren't even close to the real reason, but that didn't matter. By the end of the day, most of the other students were actively avoiding both Inga and Abigail. Sadly, this included some of their friends.

When they arrived at school on Tuesday, they were immediately called to the colonel's office. After they were seated in front of his desk, he called his aide and told him to send someone in. Both girls turned to see a young man in a Youth Leaders Corps uniform come in and approach the desk. Abigail felt her stomach drop as she recognized the boy. He saluted the colonel, and once he was acknowledged, he took a seat next to Inga. Abigail had a bad feeling when the colonel smiled.

"Miss van de Clerk, this is Youth Leader Major Otto de Koster. From now on, he'll be your personal aide in all your classes." Then, he looked at Abigail and said, "Your presence in this school has become a distraction that we can no longer tolerate. Therefore, since Major de Koster will now be assisting Miss van de Clerk, you will no longer be allowed to attend classes after today." He handed an envelope to Abigail and said, "Please give this to your owner. It explains everything. You may all go to class now."

As they stood to leave, Abigail reached for Inga's arm, but Otto took hold of Inga and said, "Since I will be her escort from now on, I'll take her from here."

Abigail felt tears brimming in her eyes as she fell in behind Inga and Otto and followed them to class. The rest of the day was a haze to both girls. The doctor was shocked when he pulled up in front of the school and saw a boy leading Inga to the car instead of Abigail. Otto smiled at him as he guided Inga into the back seat of the car. Once he was out of the way, Abigail climbed in and handed the doctor the letter. They sat there while he read it and then he pulled away without saying anything.

That night, Abigail was virtually silent as she went about her usual routine. After helping Inga with her homework, she went down to see Benjamin. He smiled as she came in, but the smile immediately faded when he saw the look on her face. He sat up and asked her what happened. She told him, and when she finished, he held out his arms and she fell into them and cried into his chest. He held her, gently stroking her back as she allowed her feelings to escape.

When she finally had no more tears, she felt much better and gave him a little smile. He smiled back, leaned down, and gave her a gentle kiss. She gave him a squeeze, thanked him, and left to get his dinner.

The next morning, Abigail rode to school with Inga and felt her heart sink when she saw Otto waiting for her when they pulled up. He smiled at her as he helped Inga out and escorted her into school. Her heart nearly broke as they drove away.

While they were driving back home, the doctor told her that from now on she could help him in the clinic, and when Inga got home, she could help her with her homework. "Hopefully, by helping her, you can keep up your education too." She nodded but didn't respond.

The new routine was just settling in when the end of the week came and Abigail and Inga were invited to Frida's. Since Abigail wasn't there to walk Inga to Frida's, she and the doctor picked them both up at school and drove all three of them. When they arrived, Frida and Inga sympathized with Abigail and she began to feel slightly better. Soon, the other two girls were telling Abigail about the happenings of the week. They all giggled when Frida told them what the other girls were saying about Inga being escorted around the school by such a handsome boy. When the air-raid alarm sounded Frida said that all the other girls were jockeying for position so they could stand beside Otto in the shelter. They all giggled when Frida said that some of them even tried to rub against him while they waited for the all clear.

By the time they went home that evening, Abigail was feeling better about the new routine—until about two o'clock that morning.

The week was up, and Inspector Hoffmann and his friends were back. As with the last time, they tossed every room, and after about two hours, gathered the family in the living room. The inspector looked at the doctor and said, "Well doctor, the week is up. Have you decided to turn the enemy soldier over or shall we find another way to persuade you?"

The doctor sighed and said, "Inspector, as I have told you every time you and your men have been here, we are not now harboring, nor have we ever harbored an enemy of the state. As your countless searches of the house have proven, there is no one here but my granddaughter, her companion, our housekeeper, and of course, me. I truly don't know what else I can say or do to convince you of the truth."

The inspector smiled and said, "Well, if that's your answer, I guess we shall proceed with the persuasion."

As soon as he said this, four agents grabbed the doctor and Mrs. van der Walle and held them by their arms. At the same time, four more agents grabbed Abigail and Inga by their arms and moved away from the others. The inspector said, "Slave, do you remember what happened in the dormitories when someone left their bunk without permission?"

The memories came flooding back of the stripes she received in the dorm and she felt her knees almost buckle. Apprehensively, she nodded, and the inspector said, "Sergeant, since the little slave seems to have vivid recollections of those consequences, perhaps we should start with Miss Inga. I don't think she should be the only girl here not to have had the experience."

The doctor struggled against the two men holding him and bellowed, "Inspector, no! Don't do that to a defenseless blind girl! Why not do it to me instead?"

The inspector nodded at one of the other agents and he pushed a gag into the doctor's mouth. "Because, dear Doctor, I believe this will leave a more lasting impression on you and it may just convince you that we're serious about the enemy you've been hiding these last few weeks. Maybe when you watch your granddaughter writhing in pain, you'll finally come to your senses and cooperate with us."

He nodded and the two men holding Inga forced her up against the wall as a third man pulled a wide leather strap out from under his overcoat. Abigail began struggling and screaming, but the men holding her just gripped her arms tighter and she soon found her mouth gagged too.

"If memory serves me, slaves received ten stripes for leaving their bunks without permission, so I think we'll start with those and then we'll see what comes next. Sergeant, you may proceed when ready."

Inga screamed as the leather strap whistled through the air and struck the back of her thighs. When Mrs. van der Walle began to scream she, too, had a gag shoved into her mouth. Tears were flowing down everyone's cheeks as the strap struck flesh again and again. Finally, the tenth stripe was administered, and the inspector turned to the doctor and said, "Well, now the slave's little sister knows what it feels like to be caught breaking the rules. And now, just so they can still look like sisters, why don't we refresh the slave's memory a little too?"

Abigail struggled as the two men holding her shoved her against the wall. She tried to beg and plead with the inspector, but the gag in her mouth prevented anyone from understanding what she was trying to say. The first stripe stung and burned and the next was worse. Again and again, the leather strap struck the back of her legs until the tenth stripe.

"Now Doctor, are you going to tell me what I want to know, or shall we continue?"

The doctor was red in the face and was perspiring when he shook his head. The inspector nodded and one of the agents removed the gag. The doctor screamed, "I'll kill you, you son of a…" One of the men slapped him across the face and he sputtered. As he began to curse the inspector again, he was backhanded. After the third time, he bellowed, "I told you, you bastard, there's no one here! There never have been any enemy soldiers, no saboteurs, or members of the underground or any terrorist groups! There has been nobody but plain, honest citizens! What are you, deaf? I've been telling you that since the first time you came here, and I'll be telling you that no matter what you do to any of us. You can kill me if you wish, but that won't change the truth!"

The man with the leather strap swung and struck the doctor in the face. With blood flowing freely from his nose, the doctor was gagged again. The inspector motioned and the man turned towards Inga. "Five more stripes, I think, or are you going to tell me where he is?"

Inga screamed as the strap made contact with her already injured legs. After the fifth stripe, the inspector pointed to Abigail and said, "Even 'em up."

Abigail felt the sting of the strap on her already throbbing legs as she received the next five. She took a shuddering breath after the fifth blow landed, but quickly lost it when the next one hit. After the last five, she couldn't feel the back of her legs anymore. All she could feel was excruciating pain and searing heat. Somewhere during this ordeal, she realized that her legs had buckled and the two agents were actually holding her up.

"Oscar, you gave the slave five more than the mistress!! Now you'll have to give the other one five more, just to even things up."

Again they all heard the crack of leather striking skin until, at last, the fifth stripe had been laid on. Abigail wanted to scream when she saw Inga hanging limply in the arms of her tormentors. She felt sick when she saw the blood trickling down the back of her legs. Part of her mind wondered if she was bleeding too. She was afraid she was.

The inspector motioned and the agents released the doctor and Mrs. van der Walle. At the same time, the others released Inga and Abigail and they both collapsed to the floor, nearly hysterical from the pain shooting through the back of their legs. The doctor gently turned both girls over and began to treat their injuries as the inspector said, "This time, I'll give you two weeks to come to your senses. If you don't comply after that, I won't guarantee these two will survive our next visit."

The agents all shuffled out the door as the family began the process of recovery. The doctor crawled over to Inga and examined the back of her legs while Mrs. van der Walle attended to Abigail. It wasn't long before each girl was taken down to the clinic where their legs were cleaned and dressed. The pain medication was taking effect while the doctor was bandaging Abigail's legs. As the pain lessened, she said, "I don't understand, Doctor. The last time my legs only had a few welts. Why did they bleed this time?"

"Last time an experienced matron was wielding the strap. This time an inexperienced man, who was probably using his full strength, was using it. Add to that that you received twice as many stripes as last time. Don't worry, though. I don't think there'll be any scarring."

"How's Inga?"

The doctor grimaced as he replied, "She's not doing as well as you are. You see, you knew what to expect, but she didn't. Physically, she has no more injuries than you do, but emotionally she's much worse than you." Before she could say anything the doctor added, "If you feel up to it, can you try to comfort her? You know what she's going through and can comfort her much better than Mrs. van der Walle or I can."

Abigail nodded, and when he was finished bandaging her legs, he helped her gingerly to her feet. At first, she felt a bit wobbly, but after the first few steps, she felt better. The doctor led her to the stairs, and she slowly made her way up to her bedroom where Inga was lying on the bed. She carefully sat on the edge of the bed and placed her hand on Inga's back. She began rubbing it as she asked, "Are you all right?"

"My legs are killing me, but I guess I'm okay. Did you really go through that when you were being processed?"

Abigail told her the story but added, "I only received ten stripes and those from a woman, not a man using all his strength. This time was much worse, believe me."

They talked for about an hour as Mrs. van der Walle straightened up the house and made everyone a midnight snack. When it was ready, the girls slowly made their way down to the kitchen. They all remembered the hidden microphone, and while they ate, the doctor passed each a note. After reading it, Abigail whispered its contents to Inga and the conversation began. For the next half hour, they all followed their scripted story. Finally, the doctor suggested they all go to bed, and they stood to leave. Abigail whispered into the doctor's ear and quietly snuck down to say good night to Benjamin.

When she opened the door, he was sitting up in his bed. At first, he smiled, but almost immediately saw the bandages on her legs. He jumped up and hobbled over to her. She motioned for him to remain silent until the door was closed. Then he took her in his arms and said, "Oh my God, Abigail, what happened?"

She explained and calmed his anger as best she could. All the time they were talking, he continued to hold her. When she was finished, she leaned her head against his chest and allowed herself to rest, just for a moment. He gently led her over to his bed and made her sit down. Suddenly she felt herself deflate like a balloon until, without realizing it, she laid her head on his pillow and fell asleep.

He gently placed her injured legs on the bed, took off her slippers, and covered her with the bedsheet. He shuffled over and sat in the chair watching her sleep. Suddenly, he felt the doctor gently shaking him awake. The doctor smiled down at him and said, "Thank you for being such a good friend to Abigail. She really needs a friend during this. Did she tell you that she's been banned from school?"

He nodded and thought, *Why is he telling me this?* The doctor continued, "I know this has been difficult for you, too, but it should be coming to an end soon, one way or another."

He stared at Abigail for a few moments and took a deep breath, letting it out slowly. Finally, he looked at Benjamin and said, "I think I should wake her up and bring her up to her room. You need your sleep and so does she." He smiled and added, "I'll send her back down with your breakfast later this morning."

He moved over and began shaking Abigail. When she opened her eyes the doctor smiled and said, "I think it's time you went to sleep in your own bed and let Benjamin sleep in his. Come on, I'll help you up the stairs."

She blushed and began stammering some sort of excuse, but he just waved it away, saying, "It's been a very long, very difficult day. It's no wonder you fell asleep. Don't give it another thought."

As the doctor led her out the door, she turned and smiled at Benjamin and he winked at her. They slowly made their way up to her room and she gratefully fell into her nice soft bed. Within minutes, she was asleep.

CHAPTER FOURTEEN

Abigail awoke stiff and sore. It took her a few minutes to finally force her legs out of bed and to actually carry her weight. At last, she made her way to the bathroom and then to check on Inga. When she hobbled into her room, she saw Inga trying to sit on the edge of the bed without actually sitting. If she wasn't in so much pain it would have been comical. Eventually, she made her way over to the bed and said, "You look about the way I feel. Need some help standing up?"

Inga looked in her direction and half smiled, half grimaced. She nodded and Abigail helped steady her on her feet. She helped her to the bathroom and then down to the kitchen for a little breakfast. When they arrived in the dining room, the doctor looked up from his paper and grimaced. After they gingerly sat down, he said, "I take it, by the looks on your faces, that you're not going to want to go to church this morning."

He laughed at the look Inga gave him and said, "Well, I can understand that. I, on the other hand, can't wait to get to church this morning. I want to speak to the minister." He winked at Abigail, and she winked back. She knew he wasn't going to speak to the minister; he was going to talk to his underground contact. She nudged Inga and said, "Well, pray for us when you get there, won't you? I don't think we're in any condition to do much today and Inga still has homework to finish. Maybe, when you get home, we can go for a walk if it's nice and our legs are up to it."

He left a few minutes later and Mrs. van der Walle brought them their breakfast. Abigail quickly ate hers, and pointing downstairs, asked if she could have seconds. Mrs. van der Walle went into the kitchen and soon came back with a tray for Benjamin. While Abigail hobbled down to the secret room, Mrs. van der Walle helped Inga back to her room to get dressed for the day.

When Abigail knocked and entered his room, she found Benjamin sitting in his easy chair reading yesterday's newspaper. She smiled shyly at him and placed his tray on the bedside table. He put the paper down and moved over to examine the wonderful meal she had brought him. They talked while he ate, and she thanked him for his consolation and understanding the night before. Then she apologized for falling asleep in his bed. "Don't be silly," he said with a chuckle, "I've always wanted to get a pretty girl like you into bed, but somehow I just assumed she'd be awake when I did it."

She blushed as he laughed and that made him laugh even more. They continued to talk for a while as she made his bed and straightened up. They were laughing and generally enjoying each other's company until there was a knock on the door and the doctor came in. Their smiles disappeared as soon as they saw the look on the doctor's face. He sat on the edge of the bed and said, "I spoke to my contact this morning and he and I feel that it's getting too dangerous for us to remain in Brighton very much longer. Between Abigail no longer being allowed at school and Inspector Hoffmann terrorizing us every few days, things are quickly getting out of hand. He feels that we should leave and soon."

Abigail was shocked. Where were they going to go? How would they ever escape with the secret police watching their every move? And what about Benjamin? The doctor saw the look on her face and said, "Abigail, you look worried."

She explained her concerns and he told her that they were working on a plan, but they hadn't fleshed out the details yet. "In the meantime, I need you to talk to Inga and explain to her what's happening. Try to reassure her so she doesn't worry too much. I don't want her to act all nervous while she's alone at school. We both know that it was the secret police behind your replacement with that boy. By the way, wasn't he the one who got in trouble for slapping you at the dance in your first year?"

Abigail nodded and he continued, "Well that's all the more reason for her to be on her guard. I'm sure he was assigned to spy on her and to try to get information out of her during the school day."

Abigail agreed and the doctor asked her to go now as he needed to speak to Benjamin alone. Abigail got up slowly, and after giving Benjamin a peck on the cheek, made her way up to Inga's room. They moved into Abigail's room and began working on homework. While they worked, Abigail told her about the doctor and his contact deciding they needed to escape. After she told her of their suspicions about Otto de Koster, and their concern about her safety and security while she was at school, Inga was visibly shaken. She reassured her as much as she could, considering her own misgivings about the plan.

The next day being Monday, the doctor and Abigail took Inga to school. Abigail helped her out of the car and handed her over to Otto de Koster. He smiled at her, but Abigail couldn't quite return the gesture. As she handed Inga over she said, "Take it slowly today; her legs are a little sore."

They watched him escort Inga into the school and then they drove back home in silence. Once they got there, they were walking down the stairs to the clinic when the doctor reminded her about the microphone in exam room #1. He needn't have bothered as they didn't have any patients. All morning the waiting room remained empty. Finally, near closing time, a mother brought her son in with a deep gash on the back of his head. Abigail brought them into exam room #2 and was assisting the doctor as he stitched up the boy's head when the mother said, "Do you know about the men outside in the alley? They're actually sending your patients away. The only reason they let me in was that he was bleeding so badly. Who are they?"

The doctor explained they were from the government, and they mistakenly thought he was trying to charge his patients too much for his services and not paying enough taxes. "They've been here for a while, but this is the first I've heard of them actually sending my patients away. I guess I must really make too much money."

They all laughed, but Abigail could tell his was forced, as was hers. Finally, they finished and the mother offered to pay for the stitches. The doctor told her that they were on the house and that she should tell the men that he didn't charge her. She agreed and left. On the way to pick up Inga, they agreed that they were going to have to escape soon if the government was actively trying to keep him from making a living.

Once Inga was in the car, they asked her about her day. She told them that Otto was a terrible assistant and she felt as if she were falling behind. "He doesn't tell me anything. He only asks about what you do in your clinic and what Abigail and I talk about when we're alone." She reached into her school bag and pulled out a piece of paper and handed it to Abigail. She saw it was a test and Inga had done very poorly. After a moment or two, Inga said, "He wouldn't tell me what the grade was, just that we passed, but I think it must not be very good. The professor said he was disappointed when he handed it to me." Abigail didn't say anything as she put it back into Inga's bag.

The next few days were the same. Otto continued to try to pump Inga for information and the secret police kept scaring away the doctor's patients. Meanwhile, Mrs. van der Walle told them that she was now being followed whenever she ran any errands. She told them that the dark sedan that had been driving around the neighborhood now followed her wherever she went.

When the weekend came, they were all nervous that Inspector Hoffmann would pay them another visit, but he didn't. On Sunday morning, they all went to church, and afterward, the doctor disappeared for a while. They sat quietly in their pew until he came back about fifteen minutes later. When Inga began to ask him where he'd been, he shushed her and quickly led them to the car. Once everyone was safely inside and they were on their way, he told them that his contact had arranged for them to leave next Friday night.

They were all on pins and needles for the rest of the day. When Monday came, they experienced the same routine as last week. By Wednesday, Inga was so frustrated that she actually asked Otto if he was trying to make her fail on purpose or if he was just that stupid. She told them that he refused to talk to her for the rest of the day until her history professor asked him if he was going to tell her what was on the board or just sit there.

Meanwhile, the doctor and Abigail had exactly zero patients all week. In fact, by Wednesday, only Abigail went down to the clinic and that was so she could spend some time with Benjamin. She didn't even close the secret door while she was with him. She told him what had been going on, but she didn't tell him about their plan to leave Friday night. The doctor told her he would tell him when the time came. She didn't understand, but she didn't say anything.

Friday was the longest day in recorded history for everyone. Abigail found herself looking at her watch every few seconds until she finally forced herself to read the doctor's newspaper. After they picked Inga up at school, they all were quiet and antsy. The doctor had told them to pack a small bag with only the essentials, maybe one or two changes of clothes, and to be ready to leave by nine o'clock that night. They were all packed and ready before dinner.

They spent the evening in the living room listening to the radio and counting the minutes until the code was tapped on the door. Since they weren't looking out the window, they were unaware of what was happening just outside.

The security agent was walking back and forth, trying to keep warm on that cold late October night. He had just turned to walk back the other way when there was a thump and the man collapsed to the ground. Simultaneously, the two men in the alley met the same fate. When the dark sedan came around the corner the driver began looking for the agent that was supposed to be walking the beat in front of the house. When he didn't see him, he stopped the car. He opened the door and had just stepped out when he saw the body lying in a heap on the sidewalk. He began moving toward it when there was another thump and he fell in a heap next to the other man.

Out of the darkness, three men came and quietly placed the dead men in the back of the police car and drove around to the alley. There, the other two agents' bodies were placed in the car and all were driven a few blocks away.

The news had just begun when they all jumped at the sound of someone tapping on the door. The doctor got up and hurried to the door. Just as the code was tapped a second time, he tapped the response. The next few seconds seemed to last an eternity until the correct acknowledgment code was tapped back.

Abigail had just come around the corner when her heart stopped. She watched as the doctor reached behind his back and drew a Luger semi-automatic handgun from his belt while he opened the door. The man outside whispered something and the doctor stood aside to let him in. After closing the door, Abigail saw the doctor put the gun back into the small of his back. The two men embraced and then he led him into the living room.

"Everybody," he began, "this is Edgar Devereux, my underground contact. Edgar, this is my family. This is Mrs. van der Walle, our housekeeper, Inga van de Clerk, my granddaughter, and her companion, Abigail Henderson. Corporal Benjamin Nicholson is down in the clinic. When we're ready to leave, I'll go get him."

No sooner had the doctor finished when Edgar said, "No Doctor, we believe Corporal Nicholson is actually an operative for the secret police. We believe that's why they continued to try and break you. They thought that if they could crack you or your family you would lead them to us and our associates."

Abigail was dumbfounded when she heard that. She covered her mouth with her hand and practically fell back into the chair. When everybody looked at her reaction she mumbled, "I let him kiss me and I even kissed him back. Oh my God, I think I'm going to be sick."

Inga sat beside her and took her hand in hers, trying to comfort her. The doctor looked shocked as he addressed Edgar. "Well, what are we going to do with him? We can't leave him here."

Edgar said, "Not to worry. We have a plan that we think will actually turn him to our side. In any case, that's for another time and place. In the meantime, we need to get going." He looked around and added, "Are you all packed and ready to go?"

They all nodded and Edgar said, "All right, here's the plan. In a few minutes, a delivery van will pull into the alley and stop just behind the house. The four of you and your guest downstairs will be blindfolded and led to the van. Once you're safely inside, you will be taken to a safe house on a farm outside of town. You'll lie low there for a few days and then we'll begin the trip to Deep Water Bay and then on to Anglosia and freedom."

"How long do you think the trip will take," the doctor asked.

"Well, depending on troop movements, bombing raids, and the like, we should be at Deep Water Bay in about two weeks. Then, provided we can find a boat, Anglosia a day or two later."

Edgar moved to the back door and looked out. While he was looking for the delivery van, the doctor instructed everyone to go get their bags and stand by. Once they were all in the kitchen, the doctor and Abigail went downstairs and brought Benjamin up to join them.

They had just come back up when there was a knock on the back door. Edgar opened it and three men dressed all in black came in. Edgar looked at the doctor and said, "These men will be blindfolding you and leading you to the van. Once in the van, it would be best if everyone sat quietly until we reach the safe house." He and the other three men began blindfolding them. When they got to Inga, she giggled and said, "You're wasting your time blindfolding me. I'm completely blind already."

None of the men said anything as they finished blindfolding them, including Inga. Then, one by one, they were led out to the waiting van. Each was led to the back door and crawled as far forward as they could. Eventually, everybody was sitting in the now cramped van and the doors were closed. As they began driving away, Abigail couldn't help but think of the last time she was in the back of a truck being taken to an unknown location. It sent shivers down her spine.

They sat in the back of the van for what seemed like hours. Everyone was so frightened, no one said a word as they made their way to the safe house. Suddenly, they heard Edgar say, "Everyone stay quiet. We're coming up on a roadblock." Even in the darkened van, he could see the fear on their faces so he explained, "There's a roadblock on every road out of the city. The authorities like to keep tabs on people coming and going from the capital, especially since the resistance has been so successful with their sabotage missions."

The van began slowing down and eventually came to a stop. Abigail could barely breathe as she heard the soldier come to the driver's window and ask for their travel papers. The driver tried some small talk, but the soldier was all business. Although they didn't know it, another soldier with a German Shepherd circled the van. Abigail was certain they were about to be arrested when the soldier returned. Instead of ordering them all out of the van, he handed the documents back to the driver and told him he could go.

They all began breathing again when the van pulled away from the checkpoint. After about another half an hour, Abigail felt the vehicle begin to slow down again. They turned off the road and onto the long gravel driveway of the secluded farm that was to be their home for the foreseeable future.

CHAPTER FIFTEEN

The van came to a stop and the driver got out. Edgar called through the little door into the back, telling them to remain patient, he would be back in a moment. Abigail was beginning to think they would never come back for them when the back doors of the van were suddenly thrown open. One by one, they were taken out of the van. Eventually, it was Abigail's turn. She felt a rough and calloused man's hand take hers and help her out of the van. Once she was out, she expected the hand to release hers, but it didn't. Instead, she was led a few yards away from the van and a deep voice said, "We'll be going down twenty steps, be careful."

She almost stumbled as she stepped off the first step, but her guide caught her and they continued down the steps into a cold and damp room. Finally, when everyone was together again, they all were allowed to remove their blindfolds. Abigail looked around and found Inga. She moved over and took her hand in hers and gave it a reassuring squeeze.

She looked around the space and saw they were in some kind of underground bunker, or maybe a bomb shelter. She shivered at the memory of the first bomb shelter she had been in. As she looked around, she saw doors leading off the main room. She hoped they led to bedrooms and hopefully a bathroom. There were also rooms without doors and she could see they led to a kitchen and a dining room. Then she looked closer and saw that the room they were in resembled the living room of their old home. There were two or three chairs and two couches, all grouped around a wood stove and a console radio.

She was just describing their new surroundings to Inga when Edgar came down the stairs and smiled at them. "Welcome to your new home. Hopefully, you will only need to be here for two or three days." He held his arm out toward a woman in her thirties and she moved forward. "This is Mrs. Krista Haagensen." The woman nodded to them as Edgar continued, "She will give you a tour of the cellar, and then you can get some rest."

Mrs. Haagensen smiled and said, "If you will follow me, I'll show you where you'll be sleeping."

She led them through a door and said, "This is the men's bedroom."

Abigail looked around and saw two sets of bunk beds, two chests of drawers, and a small closet. There was a rug on the floor, and Mrs. Haagensen explained there was a bathroom behind the door on the other side of the room. Just before they left, the doctor and Corporal Nicholson put their bags on the two bottom bunks. Benjamin, looking exhausted, made his excuses and all but collapsed onto his bunk. As they were leaving, Abigail saw Edgar and another man come in and begin talking to Benjamin.

The next room was for Mrs. van der Walle. This room had the same furniture as the men's room, but the decorations were a bit more feminine. It was a nice room and Mrs. van der Walle looked pleased, especially when she found out she would have the room to herself.

Then they moved to the next bedroom. This one, Mrs. Haagensen explained, was for the girls. Like the other two bedrooms, the furniture was exactly the same, but the room was decorated as if for younger children. It irked Abigail a little to be put in a child's room, but then, she rationalized, she and Inga would at least be together.

The next two rooms were an office and a small infirmary. When they were back in the living room, Mrs. Haagensen asked if anyone was hungry. Inga said she'd love a sandwich or something small like that and Abigail agreed. Mrs. Haagensen smiled and said she'd be glad to make them a little something, and as she went into the kitchen, the girls made themselves comfortable in the living room.

Abigail had just tuned the radio to a music program when Mrs. Haagensen brought them both a chicken sandwich and a glass of milk. While they were eating, Mrs. Haagensen made a fire in the woodstove. It wasn't long before the rest of their party came in and sat down. They all listened to the music show in silence as Abigail took their dirty dishes into the kitchen.

The news was just coming on when she came in and sat next to Inga. The reporter began with news from the battlefront. According to the report, the Army of Truth and Light had nearly completed the conquest of Norminia, a small country on the southern coast of the continent. The reporter went on to tell of the 'nuisance' bombing raids of the enemy and how ineffective they were.

Edgar came in at that moment and said, "Why are you listening to that rubbish? You should be listening to Radio Free Anglosia or Colonial News Radio."

They all gave him a blank stare and he moved over to the radio. After fiddling with the dial for a moment, they heard a man's voice speaking Anglosian. Abigail didn't know much Anglosian but she knew Benjamin did. She got up and said she was going to get him to translate but Edgar told her he would translate for them because Benjamin was busy. She was curious about what he was doing, but after remembering what Edgar had said about him betraying them, decided not to ask.

Edgar told them that the man was saying that the Combined Army of Freedom, which was the name of the armies fighting against the Empire of Truth and Light, was making progress in Norminia. He went on to explain that the massive bombing raids were beginning to affect the war effort by reducing the flow of weapons and ammunition that the empire needed to continue fighting. The announcer then commended the freedom fighters, those brave men and women who were fighting the evil regime from within its borders. Finally, they listened to a speech by the Prime Minister of Anglosia in which he encouraged all free people to do their part in the effort to defeat the evil and demonic Empire of Truth and Light.

When the news was over Mrs. van der Walle asked, "Mr. Devereux, is there a radio station we can listen to with local news?"

Edgar nodded and tuned the radio to a local station that was just starting their news broadcast. Abigail was surprised at how different the two broadcasts were when it came to coverage of the war. She was still contemplating this when the announcer said, "We have just received a report that four agents from the State Security Service have been found murdered in a neighborhood in western Brighton. Preliminary reports are that they were assigned to monitor a suspected enemy collaborator, or collaborators, about three blocks from where they were found. All four men were reportedly shot in the head and driven from the scene. We will have more on this story as the information becomes available."

Everyone looked at Edgar, but he didn't say a word. Finally, Mrs. Haagensen said, "Well, I'm sure you are all tired after such a long and exciting day." She stood and motioned for Edgar to follow her as she said, "Why don't we leave so you can all get some rest. If you need anything, just pick up the phone in the office, it's a direct line to the phone up in the house and someone will come and assist you."

She nodded to Edgar and they both left the cellar. The doctor yawned and said, "I think she's right. We should all go to bed. No telling what tomorrow will bring."

They all shuffled off to their rooms. Just as she was getting Inga settled, Abigail told her she wanted to say goodnight to Benjamin and hurried out of the room.

She knocked on the door of the men's bedroom and the doctor called out for her to come in. When she entered, he said, "Something wrong, Abigail?"

She looked around, but he wasn't there. "Isn't Benjamin back yet," she asked.

The doctor scowled as he replied, "Edgar and his associate took him away to question him about his possible connection to the secret police. If he's innocent, as I expect he is, he should be back with us by tomorrow, if not sooner."

Abigail nodded and wished the doctor goodnight and was just closing the door when Benjamin came limping into the living room. She saw the pain on his face as he slowly made his way toward her. She quickly crossed the room and, placing her arm around his waist, helped him into the bedroom and onto his bunk. The doctor came over and asked him what happened.

Through his gritted teeth he said, "Your friends thought I might be a spy for the secret police. They asked me a bunch of questions and even threatened to kill me if I didn't answer. At first, I thought they were going to kill me, but then they let me go."

Abigail rushed into the bathroom and brought back a wet washcloth and wiped his face as he lay back on the bed. The doctor looked over his old wounds and did a cursory physical exam. Once he was sure there were no new injuries, he excused himself and went to the infirmary for some medication to help Benjamin sleep.

While he was gone, Benjamin took Abigail's face in his hands and made her look at him. "You don't believe I'm working for the secret police, do you?"

She blushed but didn't answer. Instead, she looked away as she asked, "Are you hungry? Can I get you something?"

He nodded and she ran to the kitchen and fixed him a plate of cold chicken and a tall glass of milk. He thanked her and devoured the food almost instantly. When he was done, she asked what Edgar and his friends had done to him and what they asked him.

"They took me to the house and put me in a dark room in the basement for about an hour by myself. It was cold and damp and they left me in the dark. Then, two of them came in and began asking me about my unit and the men in my plane. I explained that this was my first mission and I really didn't know many of the guys in the unit, but that I did know Sergeant Smithers. I explained that he and I were the only survivors when our plane was shot down, but I didn't know what happened to him. They asked me a few more questions, trying to trip me up, you know, but I must have told them what they wanted to hear because after a while they brought me back here."

They sat quietly for a few moments until Benjamin said, "I can't believe anyone could suspect me of something like that. After all you guys have done for me? And exactly how was I supposed to contact the secret police from that hidden room in the basement? I didn't see a telephone and I don't have a radio, as you know. I can't think of any other way I could have been in contact with them, can you?"

Just then the doctor came in and gave Benjamin a pill and a glass of water. He explained that the pill was for pain and would relax him so he could sleep. Benjamin took it and then looked at both the doctor and Abigail and said, "I can't thank both of you enough for all you've done for me. If we ever make it back to the UC, maybe I could show you around."

He leaned forward and gave Abigail a small kiss before the drug claimed him and he fell back on his pillow, asleep. The doctor leaned over and whispered, "Edgar told me that his story checked out. He is who he claims to be, so he's not the one giving the secret police information about us." He smiled and said, "So, the next time he kisses you, you can kiss him back."

Abigail blushed and the doctor laughed. He gave her a quick hug and told her to get out as he wanted to get undressed and go to bed. She wished him sweet dreams and went back to her room and Inga. When she got there, she brought Inga up to speed with what the doctor and Benjamin had told her, and Inga said she was glad it hadn't been him after all.

The next day started off with a nice breakfast and then nothing. It didn't take long before they all became bored and irritable. Around noon, Mrs. Haagensen was in the kitchen with Mrs. van der Walle preparing lunch. All the time, Mrs. van der Walle was hinting that she'd love to go up and see Mrs. Haagensen's home and maybe help bring down the ingredients for that night's dinner. Eventually, Mrs. Haagensen agreed and took her up to her house after lunch.

While Mrs. van der Walle went with Mrs. Haagensen, Abigail and Inga sat in the living room reading and listening to music. Unbeknownst to them, Benjamin had come in, sat down, and was listening, too. When Abigail stopped to get them both a drink, he offered to take over reading for a while. After getting over the shock of finding him there, Abigail and Inga agreed. Ten minutes later each had a steaming cup of tea and Benjamin was reading aloud in broken, but much better Dutch.

About an hour before dinner, the doctor came in and sat down with the girls and Benjamin. They had stopped reading and were talking about the UC. The doctor listened as Benjamin described his home in New Brunswick. "My father is a haberdasher," he explained. "He has a little shop on 33rd Street. There are my parents, my sister, my little brother, and me all living in a three-bedroom apartment above the shop. We aren't rich, but we're not too bad off either. Anyway, when Dutchland became the Empire of Truth and Light and began the war, my father began worrying about his relatives in Agustis. I was fourteen when it was conquered, and from that day on, my father told me it was my duty to both my country and my ancestral home to help defeat General Joshua and return the world to freedom and prosperity. So, when I turned seventeen, my father gave his permission for me to enlist, and after training as a tail gunner, here I am."

Just then, Mrs. van der Walle called them for dinner and they all headed for the dining room. After dinner, it was back to the living room for an evening of their favorite radio programs, then the news, and off to bed. As they were all heading for their rooms, Abigail gave Benjamin a quick kiss and a hug.

The next day, the girls were once again in the living room reading when Mrs. Haagensen came rushing down the stairs. Abigail looked up and saw the panic in her eyes as she burst into the room. "You all need to be very quiet. Don't make a sound! There are three army trucks coming up the drive as we speak. They couldn't possibly know about you or this shelter, but all the same, you need to be as quiet as you can."

Without waiting for a response, she turned and hustled back up the stairs. Abigail jumped up and turned off the radio and then sat back down beside Inga. Soon they were joined by everyone except Mrs. van der Walle. When Abigail asked about her, the doctor just shrugged his shoulders.

Inspector Hoffmann and two army trucks filled with home guardsmen drove into the yard just as Mrs. Haagensen came out of the back door of the house. The inspector stepped out of the car and approached her. When she asked if there was something she could help them with he replied, "Yes, you can show us where Dr. van Heflin and his group of traitors are hiding."

"I'm sorry. I don't know what you're talking about," she replied.

The inspector smiled and said, "Well, perhaps we'll just have a look around and see if we can figure it out by ourselves."

"Help yourselves," she replied.

They were all sitting as still as statues, each straining their ears to hear what was happening above them. Abigail was deep in thought when she saw Mrs. van der Walle coming out of the office area and make her way towards the stairs. Abigail was just about to say something when the doctor looked up and saw her. Quickly and quietly, he jumped up and pulled her from the foot of the stairs. Mrs. van der Walle began struggling against him and screamed before the doctor could place his hand over her mouth.

CHAPTER SIXTEEN

Inspector Hoffmann suddenly stood stock-still. He looked at Mrs. Haagensen and said, "What was that?"

She looked befuddled and said, "What was what?"

The inspector sighed and pulled his pistol out of its holster and pointed it at her. "I grow weary of these games. Now I'll ask you one more time. Where are Dr. van Heflin and his group of traitors? I know they're here. I have an informant in his group and that informant told me they were hiding on this farm but couldn't tell me exactly where. This is your last chance. Where are they?"

Mrs. Haagensen began backing away from him as she raised her hands defensively. "I swear I don't know what you're talking about. There's only me and two hired helpers in the barn. I don't know anyone named van Heflin and I don't know anything about any traitors. Please, we're just poor farmers trying to make a living. We don't want any trouble."

The pistol exploded and Mrs. Haagensen screamed as she fell. Blood blossomed from her leg. The inspector moved over her and said, "I don't like being lied to." He pointed the Luger at her head and said, "Where are they?"

She cried, "Please, there's nobody here but me, Hans, and Edgar, my farmhands! Please, we don't know any doctors! Please don't kill me!"

The doctor was struggling with Mrs. van der Walle as Abigail jumped up and ran into the infirmary. She looked around until she found the drug cabinet, and after scanning the contents, found a sedative. Quickly, she loaded a syringe and ran back into the living room. Without saying anything, she rushed over and plunged the needle into Mrs. van der Walle's neck. As the drug entered her bloodstream, her eyes rolled into the back of her head and she collapsed in the doctor's arms.

While all this was happening, Benjamin hobbled over to help the doctor, arriving just after Abigail had injected her. As she collapsed, he helped carry her into her bedroom and onto one of the bunks. Gasping for breath, the doctor looked at Abigail and said, "See if you can find something to tie her to the bed."

As she rushed out of the room to begin her quest, the doctor helped Benjamin back into the living room and onto one of the sofas. He, too, was gasping for breath because of pain. The doctor hurried into the infirmary and soon returned with something for Benjamin's pain. It wasn't long before all was quiet again in the underground bunker.

While the inspector was dealing with Mrs. Haagensen, the soldiers had jumped out of the trucks and searched the farm. Just as the inspector was threatening to shoot Mrs. Haagensen a second time, a sergeant came up and stood in front of him. He glanced up and the sergeant said, "We've searched the house, the barn, and all the outbuildings. There's no one here but two men who claim to work here."

The sergeant looked over at two men his soldiers were holding at gunpoint. Mrs. Haagensen looked over at them too. "That's Hans and Edgar, my farmhands. Do you believe me now?"

The inspector lowered his gun and said to the sergeant, "Have you questioned them?"

"No, sir. We thought we'd leave that to you."

He nodded and said, "Bring them and the woman into the house. We might as well be comfortable while we have a little chat."

It was nightfall when the staff car and two army trucks pulled out of the driveway.

It seemed to Abigail that the afternoon had lasted for a month when the trap door opened and Edgar came running down the stairs. He slid to a stop and looked around, his eyes filled with panic and blood dripping from his nose and lower lip. Finally, his eyes fell on the doctor and he gasped, "Doctor, come quick! Those bastards shot Krista!"

The doctor jumped up and said, "Wait here while I get my bag."

He ran into his room and was soon back carrying a black doctor's bag in his hand. As they moved towards the stairs, he looked back at Abigail and said, "I'll probably need your help."

She got up and followed the men up the stairs. As they reached the top she said, "Grandpapa, shouldn't we tell Edgar about Mrs. van der Walle?"

And so, as they hurried to the house and Mrs. Haagensen, the doctor told Edgar about Mrs. van der Walle's duplicity. As they entered the house, Edgar sent Hans to guard her until they could question her. He nodded and limped out of the house.

They continued into the living room where Mrs. Haagensen was lying unconscious on the sofa. The doctor looked at Edgar and he explained about Inspector Hoffmann's visit and the wounding of Mrs. Haagensen. In conclusion, he told him about the questioning and finished by saying, "I'm not sure if it's because of the gunshot or the questioning that she's unconscious."

The doctor knelt next to her and began his examination. Thirty minutes later, the bullet had been removed and the wound bandaged. Mrs. Haagensen had been carried to her bedroom, and with Abigail's help, dressed in a nightgown and put to bed. She was sleeping peacefully when Abigail gently closed the bedroom door and headed downstairs with the others.

When they walked into Mrs. van der Walle's bedroom, she was awake. She looked at the doctor and burst into tears. "I'm so sorry, Kurt. They made me," she pleaded. "They took Dierdrick! They threatened to kill him if I didn't give them information on you and the resistance! I thought he was safe in that monastery! I never thought they'd ever threaten a priest! Please, Doctor, you've got to believe me. It was for him that I did it."

"Do you have any idea what you've done," he quietly demanded in reply. "The damage you've caused? Because of you, this farm can no longer be used as a safe house. Because of you, Krista, Hans, and Edgar were forced to endure hours of interrogation by our friend, Inspector Hoffmann. He even went so far as to shoot Krista in the leg and threatened to blow her brains out. Lotte, what are we supposed to do now?"

Abigail and Inga were standing in the doorway as the doctor spoke. Abigail interjected, "Mrs. van der Walle, what did you tell them?"

She looked at Abigail and said, "I told them that Dr. van Heflin was helping the resistance by treating injured fighters. I told them what he told Inga about why he was doing it, and I told them that you and I were helping. Then, Inspector Hoffmann began questioning me about foreign fighters and I mentioned that every now and then, we helped downed pilots and airmen and he began demanding names of these foreigners and I told him."

There was silence as they all digested this news. At last, the doctor asked, "And how did they find us here?"

Mrs. van der Walle sobbed as she replied, "Yesterday, when Mrs. Haagensen invited me up to see her home, she left me alone for a few minutes and I called the inspector and told him where we were. He promised he would return Dierdrick to me if I helped him capture the resistance group you were working for." She sobbed again and looked pleadingly at Dr. van Heflin, "What was I to do? He's my only child."

"I say we kill her," Edgar growled. "She's a traitor! She'd see us all dead if she had her way."

Abigail didn't even realize she did it, but she suddenly rushed forward and stood in front of Mrs. van der Walle, crying, "No! You can't kill her! She was only protecting her family like any of us would have done. Put yourself in her place. Wouldn't you do the same for Inga? And you, Mr. Devereux, don't you have someone you'd do anything to protect? Please don't kill her!"

Inga moved over and joined Abigail. She said, "Grandpapa, you can't let them hurt Mrs. van der Walle. She's a part of our family! Please don't let them kill her!"

"Doctor," Edgar said, "this woman has betrayed you and your whole family. Given the opportunity, she'd betray us again. We cannot take that chance. There are too many lives at stake."

The doctor looked from him to the girls protecting Mrs. van der Walle and back again. At last, he said, "All of you have valid points that need to be considered and I think I'll need some time to consider them. Perhaps we can all get some rest and make our decision in the morning. In the meantime, I think we can loosen the bonds a bit so Mrs. van der Walle can at least sit up."

Although he wasn't pleased with the doctor's decision, Edgar nodded, said, "I'd better go see to Krista," and left.

After they heard the trap door slam, the doctor said, "Abigail, since Mrs. Haagensen is injured and Mrs. van der Walle isn't able, could you make us all something to eat? I would, but I need to speak to Lotte."

Abigail nodded and taking Inga by the arm, left for the kitchen. Half an hour later, they were all in the dining room eating what Abigail euphemistically called a casserole. Even though it was a mess to look at, it didn't taste too bad. Once everyone was full, they all moved into the living room while Abigail took a plate to Mrs. van der Walle and cleaned up the kitchen. Finally, once she had joined them, the doctor turned the radio on and tuned it to the local news.

They were all in shock when the announcer said, "The State Security Service has issued an empire-wide lookout for a group suspected in the recent deaths of four of its agents. The group is led by Doctor Kurt van Heflin formerly of 419 Wilhelm Gade in Brighton. He is in his fifties and described as six feet tall, weighing 225 pounds, with gray hair and a beard. He was last seen accompanied by his fifteen-year-old granddaughter, Inga van de Clerk, a sixteen-year-old slave named Abigail Henderson, and their housekeeper. Both van de Clerk and the slave have recently had their heads shaved and there is no description available for the housekeeper. They should be considered armed and extremely dangerous, so if you see them do not attempt to apprehend them yourselves. Instead, contact the nearest police, State Security Service office, or any military post in your area."

"In other news…" the reporter continued, but Inga spoke over him, saying, "Grandpapa, what are we going to do now?"

The doctor was sitting in stunned silence as she spoke. He seemed to come out of a trance when he said, "I don't know."

"We'll just have to change the way we look," said Abigail.

"How?"

"Makeup and wigs. Grandpapa can dye his hair or maybe shave it off. We can wear boys' clothes or maybe platform shoes. I don't know. We'll just have to think of something."

"Well, whatever we decide to do, we'll have to lie low here or someplace else for a while," the doctor said.

While this conversation was going on, Benjamin hobbled over to the radio and tuned it to Radio Free Anglosia. When the announcer began reporting on the status of the war, they all became quiet. Benjamin translated the news into Agustian and Abigail translated it into Dutch.

The announcer reported that, due to bad weather, all bombing raids over Dutchland had been postponed. Additionally, the fighting in the south was not going well for the Combined Armies of Freedom. The Army of Truth and Light was conducting a counteroffensive on the Norminian coast, and additional men and equipment were finding it difficult landing on the beaches. The news closed with the announcement that the government of Anglosia had closed all its eastern ports because of increased enemy naval patrols.

Doctor van Heflin walked over and turned the radio off. "I think that's enough bad news for one day, don't you? Perhaps we should all just turn in and decide what to do tomorrow."

Abigail got up and was just about to lead Inga into the girl's bedroom when Benjamin said, "Abigail, could I speak to you…privately?"

She nodded and told him she'd be back after she took Inga to the bedroom. Inga interjected that she could find it just fine and that she'd see her later. Once Inga's and the doctor's bedroom doors were closed, she looked expectantly at Benjamin. He patted the sofa cushion next to him and she sat, still looking at him. Looking uncomfortable, he said, "Abigail, I know Edgar and his friends told you all that I was the traitor." When she didn't deny it, he continued, "Did you believe him?"

"Benjamin, we had this conversation the other day. Don't you remember?"

"Yes, I remember. But I also remember that you didn't really answer me."

She hesitated and Benjamin took that as her answer. "I see," he said and looked down at his lap.

"Benjamin, I may have had doubts when Edgar first suggested it might have been you, but deep in my heart I knew it couldn't be true."

He looked at her and said, "I would have thought that after all the time we spent together that you'd have known it wasn't me."

She couldn't think of a response and looked down at her lap. When she looked up, she saw Benjamin stand up. She looked up at the same time as he looked down at her. She could see the hurt in his eyes as he turned and hobbled towards the bedroom. "Benjamin, please don't leave," she begged, but he ignored her.

She walked slowly to her room and quietly crawled into her bed, tears gently falling down her cheeks.

"Abigail," Inga whispered.

She didn't respond.

"Abigail, is that you? Are you all right?"

Inga slipped out of her bed and made her way over to Abigail's. She sat on the edge of the bed and placed her hand on Abigail's back, slowly rubbing her hand in circles. Slowly, Abigail regained control and, through her sobs, told Inga about her conversation with Benjamin.

When she was done, Inga tried to cheer her up by saying, "I'm sure this will blow over and everything will be back to normal in a few days. You'll see." She said it, but she didn't really believe it. Neither of them did.

CHAPTER SEVENTEEN

The next three days were all the same. They would get up and have breakfast and Abigail would bring a plate to Mrs. van der Walle. Then, the two girls would read until lunch. After lunch, they would listen to the radio and discuss how the war was going. After dinner, everyone would gather in the living room, listen to a radio drama, and then finally, the news.

All through this time, Abigail and Benjamin didn't speak unless they had to. He would sit in as they read. He would listen to the radio with them and listen to their discussion of the latest news and the war but would only venture an opinion if asked. Abigail wished she could think of a way to make things better, but try as she might, nothing came to mind.

They were just settling down for yet another afternoon when Edgar burst into the shelter and announced that there were two tanks coming up the drive. "No matter what you hear, don't come up until someone comes and gives you the all clear."

Without waiting for an acknowledgment, he ran back up the stairs and closed the trap door just as the tanks came to a stop about a hundred yards from the house. The staff car that was ahead of them continued into the yard and came to a stop in front of the house and Inspector Hoffmann got out. He was almost at the front door when Edgar called out, "Can I help you, Inspector?"

Hoffmann turned and waited for Edgar to make his way to the front porch before he answered. "Devereux, isn't it?"

Edgar nodded and the inspector continued, "Where's Haagensen? Still recuperating?"

He gave an evil grin when Edgar nodded. "Well, no matter, I can deal with you. As you know, I'm looking for Doctor van Heflin and his cohorts. You also know that I have reason to believe they're hiding somewhere on this miserable excuse for a farm."

Edgar opened his mouth to speak, but the inspector waved his unspoken protest away as if it were a mosquito. "Please don't begin your lame excuses. I'm not interested. Now, I've been patient and I've given you people plenty of time to come to your senses, so now I'll ask you again. Where are Dr. van Heflin and his friends?"

The tanks assigned to the home guard were not the latest models by any means, but that's not to say they weren't well cared for and very capable of causing death and destruction. As they were talking, the two tanks rotated their jet-black turrets toward the barn. When Edgar told the inspector he didn't know anyone by that name the inspector raised his right hand and the two tanks fired their cannons at the barn. When the shells struck the old barn, the explosion was deafening and debris rained down on the rest of the buildings and the house. Edgar had dropped to the ground and covered his head, but the inspector continued to stand, almost oblivious to the debris falling everywhere.

When Edgar stood again the inspector said, "Every time you lie to me, another building will be destroyed." He looked around the farm and smiled. "That means that you can lie to me maybe four more times before we destroy the house. Now, I'll ask again, where is Dr. van Heflin?"

Edgar began to sweat as he repeated his claim of ignorance. The tanks swiveled their turrets and fired at the equipment shed. This time the old tractor and other farm implements, as well as the remains of the building, flew through the air.

This continued until the only building left was the house where Mrs. Haagensen was in her upstairs bedroom. When the inspector repeated his question, he added, "If you refuse to answer me this time your friend will undoubtedly be killed when the house is destroyed. You know that, don't you? You should also know that I won't let you go get her either. So?"

When Edgar didn't answer, the inspector turned, walked off the porch, and over to his car. When Edgar remained standing on the porch, he called out, "I'd run if I were you!"

Edgar watched as the inspector raised his hand again and the tanks turned their turrets toward the house. He continued to watch as flames billowed from the cannons of both tanks. When the shells exploded, destroying the house, Inspector Hoffmann swore he could still see him looking at the tanks.

Abigail clung to the doctor as each building was destroyed. She buried her face in his chest as she heard each explosion. By the fifth explosion, she was almost hysterical, remembering the destruction of her home and the death of her family.

The doctor held her and stroked her short hair, gently reassuring her that everything would be all right.

Abigail wasn't the only one frightened by the explosions. Inga, too, was nearly beside herself with fear as the tanks fired. She didn't know it, but she was sitting near Benjamin when the first shells exploded. When she screamed, he moved next to her and hugged her to his chest as the tanks continued to destroy the farm. Just as the doctor was trying to calm Abigail's fears, Benjamin gently stroked Inga's short hair as he cradled her head next to his heart. While he stroked her, he was softly talking to her, telling her that she was safe and that he wouldn't let anything happen to her.

About an hour later, when no one had heard anything for a while, the doctor looked over at Benjamin and said, "What do you think is happening now?"

Benjamin shrugged and said, "It doesn't sound like anything's happening now." After a moment, he added, "Do you think one of us should go up and take a look?"

The doctor thought about it for a second and then said, "I'll go. You stay here with the girls." As he extracted himself from Abigail's embrace, he said, "Abigail, honey, why don't you check on Mrs. van der Walle while I go up and have a look around?"

She nodded and headed for the bedroom while he climbed the stairs and opened the trap door. Mrs. van der Walle only needed to use the bathroom, but otherwise, she was fine. Abigail released her and re-tied her when she was done. She was just returning to the living room when the doctor came back down the stairs. One look at his face told her that there was bad news.

"The entire farm has been destroyed. Every building has been demolished and is burning," he paused before adding, "Even the house has been destroyed. I saw parts of Edgar's body near what used to be the front of the house."

Abigail felt the tears begin falling down her cheeks as she looked at the others. She saw the doctor had tears in his eyes as he moved to sit in one of the chairs. Then, she looked over at Inga and her heart stopped when she saw her in Benjamin's embrace, her face buried in his chest. Without saying anything to anyone, she walked into the kitchen and began making dinner.

A few minutes after she began working, Mrs. van der Walle came in. Abigail was surprised to see her and it must have shown on her face because Mrs. van der Walle explained, "Doctor van Heflin released me. He said that he understood why

I did what I did, but considering the mess we're all in, he didn't see what further damage I could do. Abigail, I'm so sorry. Can you forgive me for what I've done to you…to all of you?"

Abigail moved over and took the older woman into her embrace and they both began crying. It seemed to Abigail that Mrs. van der Walle cried for the longest time, but eventually, the well of her tears dried up and the two of them began making dinner. After about half an hour, they all sat down for a simple dinner of sausage and sauerkraut.

There wasn't much conversation while they ate, but once everyone was done, the doctor said, "Mrs. van der Walle, if you and Abigail could come and sit down once the table's clear, I think we need to talk about what we should do next."

It only took a few minutes for Abigail and Mrs. van der Walle to clear the table and the doctor began. "As I told you all when I came back down here, there's nothing left of the farm. Judging from what I saw during the few minutes I was up there, there's no one left to help us so we're on our own."

He looked around the table and continued, "Before he was killed, Edgar said that, once the coast was clear, he was going to move us to the next safe house which is in Kreeton, about a hundred and fifty miles west of here. He told me the name of his contact in Kreeton and gave me a brief description, but I'm not exactly sure where the safe house is. Nevertheless, I think we should start heading in that direction in the morning. Does anyone have an objection?"

Abigail was about to speak, but Inga beat her to it. "What about Benjamin's leg? He's not going to be able to walk very far with a leg that's still healing."

The doctor nodded and said, "Well, that's true, he's not going to be able to get too far on that leg. Maybe one of the trucks survived today's destruction, but I doubt it. Anyway, we'll just have to look around for some sort of transport once we get out of here. Does anyone else have any concerns?"

When no one said anything, he looked at Abigail and said, "Didn't you mention disguises the other day after our descriptions were broadcast on the radio? Have you given the idea any more thought?"

Abigail shook her head and the doctor looked expectantly at the others. Mrs. van der Walle looked at Abigail and she quickly told her about her idea to change their looks so no one would know it was them. When she had finished, Mrs. van der Walle said, "I don't know where we'll find boys' clothing, but that's a good idea. As for the doctor, I believe we can cut his hair and dye it black without too much trouble. I think Benjamin can become a blond quite easily, too. That leaves only me. Since they didn't give a description of me on the radio, I should be all right."

They all agreed, and Mrs. van der Walle went about gathering the supplies she needed. When she was ready, she cut the doctor's hair very short and dyed it black. Then she instructed him to shave off his gray beard. When he came out of the bathroom, he was almost unrecognizable.

Then she went to work on Benjamin. Since his hair was already short, she used some hydrogen peroxide to bleach his hair and eyebrows blond. Within an hour, he was a different person.

The next morning, they all packed their little traveling bags and were ready to leave the bunker early. The doctor went up first. They all waited at the bottom of the stairs for what seemed like hours for him to come back and give them the all clear. Finally, just when they were about to go look for him, he came back down. They all looked at him as he came into the room and could see there was something wrong.

"There are two soldiers and a Kübelwagen in the yard, just sitting there," he told them. "I'm not sure how we're going to get past them, but I know it won't be during daylight hours. They both have machine guns and there's no way to sneak up on them."

The disappointment was palpable as the news sank in and the little group walked back into the living room. Abigail looked at the others and could see no one had any ideas on how to get past the soldiers. Suddenly, she had an idea. "Grandpapa," she began slowly, "the news reporter gave our descriptions the other night so there probably isn't any way any of us can go out and talk to them, right?"

He nodded and she continued, "But the reporter said that they didn't have a description of Mrs. van der Walle, so she could sneak out at night and distract the soldiers while you and I sneak up behind them and overpower them."

Doctor van Heflin smiled at the thought of little Abigail overpowering anyone. "I think your idea has merit, but, somehow, I don't see you overpowering a full-grown man. That being said, maybe Benjamin and I can do it."

"Grandpapa, Benjamin's leg isn't strong enough for him to overpower anyone either, but I could sneak up behind one of them and inject them with a sedative like I did Mrs. van der Walle the other day. Then the two of you will be able to overcome the other one."

"Or," interjected Mrs. van der Walle, "we could distract them long enough for you to inject both of them. That way, you'll be in less danger."

"Yes, that may work," the doctor said, thoughtfully. "But we'll have to plan it carefully. What do you think, Benjamin?"

Benjamin thought for a moment and said, "Abigail's idea is probably the best we've got, but we'll have to wait until after dark to try it, and even then, it'll be dangerous."

They all agreed to try it just after dark. They sat down and were just about to listen to the radio when the generator sputtered and died, they were suddenly engulfed in total darkness.

CHAPTER EIGHTEEN

They sat in shocked silence for a moment or two before the doctor said, "Does anyone know where the generator is located?"

When no one answered, he said, "Well, I guess we'll have to move tonight then. In the meantime, does anyone know if there are any flashlights, candles, or some other source of light?"

Abigail said, "There are some candles in the kitchen, and I think there's a flashlight in the office. If you want me to, I can go look."

The doctor said, "That's an excellent idea, but let Inga guide you."

Although he couldn't see her face, Abigail gave him a puzzled look. When she didn't say anything, he explained. "Inga is blind, so she's used to navigating in the dark. She'll know where the obstacles are, whereas you normally rely on your eyesight and will bump into things and could hurt yourself."

Abigail saw the sense of this and said, "Well Inga, I guess our roles are reversed!" They all laughed and Abigail added, "Whenever you're ready."

Abigail felt Inga take her hand and she stood up. Inga, still giggling, led her into the kitchen and, after fumbling around for a few minutes, they came back with three lit candles in a candlestick. After placing it on the coffee table, Abigail took another candle and went to the office. She came back with two flashlights.

They sat, talked, and planned until after dinner. Then, about ten o'clock in the evening, the doctor looked at his watch, stood and said, "Abigail, why don't you and I go into the infirmary and load the syringes?"

They came back a few minutes later and he announced it was time to go. Mrs. van der Walle joined them and the three of them walked up the stairs, stopping at the trap door. They held their breath as they listened for any movement. After a few seconds, Dr. van Heflin slowly opened the trap door enough to look around. Once he located the soldiers, he opened the trap door the rest of the way and they crawled out on their hands and knees.

The doctor pointed at the two soldiers and Mrs. van der Walle and Abigail both nodded. Mrs. van der Walle got to her feet and carefully moved around towards the pile of debris that was once the house, while the other two began crawling toward the soldiers.

It was almost eleven and the two soldiers had been on guard duty since six that evening. They were both home guard members well past forty years old. The tallest one was built like the doctor and the other one was short and willowy. The bigger man pulled a pack of cigarettes from his pocket and offered one to the smaller man, who gratefully accepted it. They had just lit them when the big one remarked, "Really Fritz, what are we doing here? There's no one here and no one's going to come here either."

Just then, Mrs. van der Walle called, "Excuse me gentlemen, but have you seen my friend Krista? I'm sure this is where she said her farm was, but I can't find the house."

The two soldiers dropped their cigarettes and pulled their machine guns from their backs. As they pointed their guns at her, Mrs. van de Walle slowed and raised her hands. But she continued to approach. Finally, the big one said, "That's far enough, Mother. Where'd you come from?"

Mrs. van der Walle approached as she said, "I came from over there," and pointed to the other side of the rubble pile that used to be the house.

The smaller of the two men lowered his machine gun and turned to walk toward the house. Noticing this, the doctor rose up behind him, stabbed the syringe into the side of his neck, and pushed the plunger in one fluid motion.

The big one saw this from the corner of his eye. He had just begun turning toward his comrade when Abigail sprang up behind him and plunged her syringe into his neck. Both men registered what was happening, but before they could react, the drug took affect and they fell to the ground in heaps.

Mrs. van der Walle and the doctor pulled the machine guns from the guardsmen's grip and the three of them moved back to the trap door, calling for Inga and Benjamin to come up. As Benjamin came out of the shelter, he took the machine gun from Mrs. van der Walle and began hobbling towards the unconscious soldiers.

Abigail saw this and followed him, saying, "Benjamin, where are you going?"

He didn't stop, but replied, "I'm going to kill these two soldiers before they wake up. That's what they'd do to us if they got the chance."

She ran past him and stopped in front of the two soldiers. "You can't do that. It'd be murder!"

He came up to her and tried to push her aside. "Get out of the way, Abigail. They have to die, or they'll give us away when they wake up."

Every time he tried to push her out of the way, she moved right back to stand in front of the unconscious soldiers. "No! They don't need to be killed. We can just tie them up or something, but please don't kill them!"

Just then, the rest of them came over and sided with Abigail. "Benjamin," the doctor said, "Why don't we just tie them up and place them in the shelter. That way, it will take time for their friends to find them, and we'll be safely far away from here."

It took all of them to persuade him, but finally he agreed. He was just beginning to help move the bigger of the two when he had an idea. He dropped the man's feet and said, "Doctor, isn't this guy about the same size as you?" When the doctor nodded, Benjamin continued, "Well, do you think his uniform would fit you? If it does, then it would help disguise you even more."

The doctor thought about it for a minute and then moved over to the other soldier. He stretched him out and realized he was about the same size as Inga. Looking over at Benjamin, he said, "Are you thinking what I'm thinking?"

Benjamin looked at the smaller soldier and then over at Inga some more, then he smiled. The doctor called Inga over and told her his idea. When he was done, she blushed and said, "But Grandpapa, don't you think my breasts will be obvious enough that the disguise won't work?"

Mrs. van der Walle had been listening and she interjected. "Oh that won't be a problem. We'll just bind them against your chest and then no one will be able to see them. That shirt looks like it will be loose fitting anyway, so that should work. The hard part will be making your face look like a man's."

They agreed to the plan and the doctor and Benjamin quickly stripped the soldiers down to their boxers and Mrs. van der Walle took Inga back into the shelter to change. Fifteen minutes later, Mrs. van der Walle came back up with a young corporal on her arm. Everyone admired Inga's disguise as she told them, "The uniform fits pretty well, but the boots are way too big. We had to stuff the toes with old newspapers before they'd finally stay on my feet. I can walk, but I don't think I'll be able to run in them."

The doctor took the other uniform and went into the shelter. Ten minutes later, he came back looking like a seasoned old sergeant. Once everyone commented on the transformation of both the doctor and Inga, they moved over to examine the Kübelwagen.

To make it harder to see people inside, they decided to put the top up. Once that was done, they checked the storage compartments and found a map of the area. The doctor examined the map and soon discovered that it showed every checkpoint between them and Kreeton. He looked at the others and said, "If we take the main road, we can be in Kreeton by tomorrow night, but we'll have to go through five checkpoints. If we go the back way, it will take us two or three days to get to Kreeton, but we'll only have to go through one checkpoint."

Benjamin smiled and said, "The back roads it is then."

The others agreed. They all climbed into the army vehicle, and they were off. The doctor, of course, drove and Inga sat in the front passenger's seat. Since she couldn't read the map for the doctor, Benjamin did it from the back seat. Abigail found that, being the smallest, she was wedged between Mrs. van der Walle and Benjamin in the back seat as well. It wasn't too bad at nighttime, but she dreaded the warmth of day. As it turned out, she had nothing to worry about as the doctor decided it would be in their best interest to travel at night and hide during the daytime.

The sun was just coming up when a Kübelwagen turned off the main road onto the gravel drive of the one-time farm, which the doctor and the others had previously vacated. When they pulled into the yard, they couldn't see the guardsmen they were there to relieve. They stopped and turned off the engine. All was quiet as they got out and looked around.

When they had put the guardsmen in the shelter, the doctor and the others left the trap door open so they would eventually be found. Therefore, when the guardsmen heard the Kübelwagen pull into the yard, they called for help. Consequently, it was only a few minutes before the shelter was discovered and the guardsmen were rescued. Well, sort of rescued.

When the oncoming sergeant saw them stripped down and tied up lying on the couches in the living area, he decided to leave them there and call Inspector

Hoffmann. The two bound guardsmen were very unhappy about this decision because the cords were beginning to cut off the circulation in their hands and feet.

After about an hour of them complaining and pleading to be released, the inspector pulled into the farmyard. The sergeant snapped to attention and saluted as he got out of his staff car. He guided him into the shelter and showed him around. All the time the two guardsmen begged and pleaded to be released, or at least allowed to sit up. Neither request was granted.

Finally, the inspector had seen all there was to see and he turned his attention to the two prisoners. Once they were allowed to sit up, the questioning began. The sergeant told him that they really didn't know what had happened. "We saw this woman come toward us from where the house had been and the next thing we knew we woke down here in only our underwear."

The inspector was not impressed. He questioned them for another hour but didn't find out anything else. Finally, he stood and looked down at the two former prisoners and said, "You two are failures." He drew his Luger from its holster and pointed it at the sergeant. He could see the fear in the man's eyes as he said, "And I don't forgive failure."

Shots rang out through the shelter. The inspector holstered his pistol and climbed the stairs, leaving the two men with holes in their foreheads—their eyes still showing their fear. He stopped at the top of the stairs, tossed a grenade into the shelter, and casually strode back to his car. Just as he opened the door, the grenade exploded, collapsing the underground shelter and burying the two dead guardsmen.

***

The doctor's group had traveled about thirty miles or so when the sun began coming up. Since daytime travel was dangerous, and due to their lack of sleep, the doctor suggested that they hide the vehicle in the forest and rest until nightfall. They all agreed, and he began looking for a good place to pull off the road. Eventually, they came across an old, unused dirt track that led into a thick pine forest. The doctor turned right, and they bounced down into a ravine. After about fifteen minutes of bumping down the barely discernible trail, they could no longer see the main road. The doctor turned off the engine.

The Kübelwagen was hidden behind some bushes, well off the track, by the time the sun had risen too far above the horizon. After stretching their legs for a few minutes, they all gathered around the little army vehicle for a breakfast of cold sausage, hard cheese, and bread. They washed it down with tepid water from canteens. Finally, they all decided to lie down on the ground around the Kübelwagen. They were just about asleep when the radio that no one had noticed the night before, crackled into life. "Doctor van Heflin," the voice said, "this is Inspector Hoffmann speaking. We found your hidey hole. Very nice accommodations, by the way, I'm sure you were all sorry to have to leave them. Oh, and, just so you know, the two guardsmen you tied up and left behind are now entombed in that hole of yours."

There was silence for a moment as they all looked at each other. Then, the inspector continued. "We're going to catch you, Doctor. We know you're heading for the coast, but you'll never get there. Every police station, security office and military base now has pictures of you, your granddaughter, and that slave girl, so disguising yourselves in home guard uniforms won't do you much good. We know the registration number of the Kübelwagen you stole, and every checkpoint and roadblock will have that information before noon. There's no escape for any of you, so why don't you just turn yourselves in? If you do, I assure you neither you nor your granddaughter will be executed."

They all looked at the doctor, trying to discern if he would take the offered deal. He looked at each of them and then opened the door of the Kübelwagen, took the microphone, and said, "Go to Hell."

The inspector laughed at his response. He keyed the mic and said, "Have it your way, Doctor. But I assure you, I will make sure you are in Hell long before I am."

He reached back into the vehicle and turned off the radio. Then, looking at the others said, "I think it would be best if we all got some rest."

CHAPTER NINETEEN

They all moved back to the blankets they had spread on the ground and began to settle in for the day's rest. Abigail was just getting drowsy when she looked around for Inga. After glancing around, she realized with a jolt that she couldn't see her. She sat up and was about to call out for her when she spotted her lying on the far side of Benjamin. Her heart stopped.

She lay back down and turned her back on the group, not wanting to see Inga and Benjamin anymore. But every time she closed her eyes, there they were: her one-time boyfriend and her erstwhile best friend, arm in arm, looking blissful in their sleep. She lay down, thinking that any time now the pain and tears would come. She just had to wait. And so she waited and waited. All of a sudden, it hit her, there was no pain and there were no tears. Instead, she felt nothing. No anguish. No jealousy. She felt nothing but a mild sense of happiness for Inga and a feeling of relief that she no longer had to feel awkward around Benjamin.

The doctor gently woke her at dusk, before the others. "Abigail, can you come with me, please?"

She scrambled out of her blanket and followed him a few yards away from the others when he stopped and turned toward her with sadness in his eyes. "Abigail, I'm not sure how to tell you this, but…" he hesitated.

"Grandpapa, what's the matter," she asked, concerned.

"Well," he began, and then stopped. He sighed and said, "There really is no way to tell you that will spare your feelings, so I'll just tell you. When I woke up, I saw that Inga and Benjamin are… shall we say…"

Abigail smiled and interjected, "Yes, I saw they were holding each other in their sleep."

She smiled at the confused look on his face and added, "When we first got to the farm, Benjamin and I had a sort of falling out and it's been really awkward ever since. But now that he and Inga seem to be together, maybe we can be friends again." When he continued to look confused, she added, "I'm not bothered by it at all, really. Maybe we'll be more relaxed around each other now that we're not seeing each other anymore."

He looked deep into her eyes, searching for any lies, but apparently couldn't find any. At last, he said, "Well, if you say so. I just hope this doesn't affect your relationship with Inga. I'd hate to see a boy come between you two."

She reassured him and they were soon back with the others. After waking them all, Abigail and Mrs. van der Walle began doling out their evening meal, which was the same as their morning meal. Abigail didn't say anything, but she had a feeling they were all going to get sick of cold sausage and hard cheese real fast.

About twenty minutes later, they were all in the Kübelwagen heading back to the road. They were just about to turn on the main road when the doctor leaned over and turned the radio back on. It was quiet.

As they traveled down the road, Abigail noticed that both Benjamin and Inga avoided looking at her. At first, it amused her, but after a while, it became boring. It was during their first stop that she took Inga aside and told her that she knew about her sleeping in Benjamin's arms. Inga blushed and began stammering excuses, but Abigail cut her off. In the millisecond of silence before Abigail began speaking, Inga braced herself for the tirade that she was sure she was about to hear. She was positive Abigail would call her a traitor and probably something worse.

"Inga, I'm all right with you being with Benjamin. I'm really happy for both of you. Maybe now, he'll speak to me and stop looking at me like I'm the enemy or something."

When they came back to the group the doctor noticed they were both more relaxed and soon the whole group was too. It wasn't to last though.

They had been driving for about an hour when they came upon their first roadblock. They came around a bend in the road and suddenly saw two tanks blocking the road in front of them. They saw a black uniformed army officer standing in front of the tanks and he was motioning them to stop. As he did this, the machine guns on the tanks swiveled and pointed at them.

The Kübelwagen stopped about fifty yards from the tanks and the army officer walked up to the driver's window. Two soldiers with machine guns followed him. When he was beside the Kübelwagen, he shined his flashlight in the doctor's face and said, "Good evening, Sergeant. May I see your orders please?"

Mrs. van der Walle and the others in the back seat leaned back into the shadows as far as they could while the officer was talking to the doctor. As the doctor was patting his pockets for his non-existent orders, Benjamin slowly cocked the machine gun he was holding. Abigail tapped on Inga's shoulder and signaled her to duck just as Benjamin pointed the gun at the officer. Suddenly, there was machine gun fire from across the road and the two soldiers with the officer fell dead. The two gunners on top of the tanks swiveled their machine guns to the left of the Kübelwagen, but just as they were about to fire, there were machine gun bursts from the other side of the road, and both gunners slumped over their weapons.

The officer had drawn his Luger when Benjamin fired a burst into his chest, killing him instantly. Suddenly, the doctor jammed the Kübelwagen into reverse and they shot backwards. The doctor swung the stubby little vehicle off the road and cut the engine. "Everybody out!" he ordered, and they all dove for the ditch next to the road.

As quickly as they could, they began crawling away from the Kübelwagen. They had only gone about fifty feet when one of the tanks fired its cannon and the little Kübelwagen exploded and flew about twenty feet in the air. At almost the same time, the ambushers mounted the other tank, pulled the hatch open, dropped a grenade, and slammed the hatch shut. No sooner had the man jumped down than the grenade exploded and the tank belched smoke from every opening.

The other tank started moving, but the ambushers stopped it by throwing a grenade into one of the tracks, destroying it and disabling the tank. Then another grenade exploded, destroying the other track. Finally, one of the ambushers climbed on the tank and dropped a smoke grenade into the top hatch. A few minutes later, four soldiers surrendered with their hands in the air.

Abigail and the others were watching the drama when they were suddenly surrounded by almost a dozen men with machine guns. Without saying a word, they all raised their hands and surrendered. The men were surprised to find Abigail and Mrs. van der Walle and were even more surprised when they discovered one of the soldiers was actually a fifteen-year-old girl. Instead of killing them, as they expected, the men took away the two machine guns they had and led them over to the mission leader.

They were walking with their hands behind their heads, approaching the rest of the ambushers, when, to their horror, they were forced to watch the tank crew being lined up beside their disabled tank and brutally gunned down. When they reached the tank, Abigail was positive they were about to meet the same fate when a short, fat man walked over to them.

He looked carefully at each of their faces, and when he came to the doctor, he said, "Dr. van Heflin, I presume?"

When the doctor nodded, the man said, "We were hoping to find you before the authorities did. My name is Gerhart Weitz, and these men are from my underground unit. We were ordered out to look for your group as soon as we heard about Krista and Edgar."

As the man was talking, everyone lowered their arms. When he finished, there was an awkward silence, but the man didn't seem to notice as he pulled a cigar out of his pocket, put it in his mouth, and lit it. Through a cloud of smoke, he looked up and said, "Let's see if we can find you something other than that sergeant's uniform to wear."

They were all chuckling when the man wrapped his arm around Inga and said, "If I had known the empire had such pretty corporals, I'd have enlisted years ago!"

Inga blushed profusely as they moved with the group towards a large army truck. When the doctor gave the man a questioning look, he said, "What better way to go around unnoticed than to use one of their own trucks. There must be hundreds of these things in this area."

They all climbed in the back of the army truck and within minutes had left the death and destruction behind. The group had been traveling for about a quarter hour when Mrs. van der Walle asked, "Excuse me, but where are we going?"

The leader blew out another puff of cigar smoke and said, "Our safe house is on the other side of Waldrand. We should be there in another half hour or so. In the meantime," he reached under the bench and pulled out bottles and bottles of beer. He handed them to the others and said, "Let's celebrate another successful mission without losing a single man!"

Abigail had never drunk beer before and she wasn't entirely sure she was allowed to, so she looked at the doctor for guidance. When he just nodded, she opened the beer, saluted the toast, and took a sip. The men laughed when she pulled a face at the bitter taste. She glared at them and then took a second sip. It wasn't as bad as the first, but she still made a face.

Before long, they entered the city and Abigail got a chance to look around. She was shocked at the destruction, especially in what obviously had been the industrial section. One of the underground fighters leaned over and said, "This area was bombed out of existence almost two years ago. Most of the factories have been rebuilt underneath the rubble. The idea is that the allies won't know they're there. But we know. We tell the allies, and they bomb the rubble until they finally reach the aircraft and armored vehicle factories beneath."

She continued looking out the back of the truck as they continued past the industrial section and came into the slum areas. These too, she saw, had been bombed into almost nonexistence. When she looked at the fighter next to her, he explained, "When the war started, the people living here thought they would be getting good paying jobs. But, when the factories started bringing in outside workers, they rioted. The army came in and destroyed the neighborhood and killed almost five hundred men, women, and children. Instead of accepting responsibility, they tried to blame it on the rioters and the underground. It didn't work though. Everyone knew it had been the army who killed all those people. That's when most of us joined the resistance."

The last area of the city they entered was filled with massive old mansions and what could only be described as estates. Abigail looked at the man and he said, "When we started looking for a place to use for our operations base, we realized that we needed a place big enough for dozens of people to work and some to live too. One of our founders was the original owner of an airplane manufacturing company before the war and when General Joshua took over, he confiscated the business. He promised the government would pay him for the business, but surprise, surprise, they never did. So, to get his revenge, he started this underground resistance group. He was killed during a raid on his factory and now, we use his old house as our headquarters."

***

Inspector Hoffmann stepped out of his staff car and walked over to the army major standing near the remains of the Kübelwagen. The major turned and saluted. The inspector returned the gesture and said, "What happened?"

The major replied. "We received a radio transmission from the lead tank, advising a Kübelwagen matching your lookout was approaching the roadblock. That's the last we heard until we arrived." He motioned for the inspector to look around and continued, "And you see what we found. One tank destroyed and the other disabled and its crew murdered. We found the lieutenant in charge over there, shot in the chest, and the remains of the Kübelwagen is over here. It looks like one of the tanks shot it."

"Anyone in it," the inspector asked.

"No, we didn't find anyone but the tank crew, the lieutenant, and his men over there. Whoever was in the Kübelwagen must have left with the underground fighters."

The inspector nodded and asked, "Any idea where they went?"

"There are tire tracks from a truck over there," the major said as he pointed to a nearby field. "They either came from, or are heading in, the direction of Waldrand. That's the nearest town of any size nearby."

The inspector nodded and returned to his staff car. Moments later, the car drove off towards Waldrand.

CHAPTER TWENTY

The truck pulled into a barn-like building behind the manor house and everyone jumped out. Abigail started moving toward Inga, but stopped when she saw Benjamin was guiding her toward the house with the rest of the group. She moved over next to the doctor instead. When he gave her a curious look she just motioned toward Inga and Benjamin and said, "She doesn't need me to guide her. She's got him."

The doctor laughed and said, "When I saw those two together last night, I was worried you'd be jealous of Inga. Now I see you're jealous of Benjamin. How ironic is that?"

She smiled as he pulled her into a one-arm hug. Together, they walked into the mansion and began looking around. Although the outside of the building was that of a palatial residence, the inside was more like an office building. Aside from the kitchen, all the rest of the main floor rooms were being used for offices and the dining room was the operations center of what appeared to be a large, coordinated resistance movement. As they looked, around they saw at least a dozen men and women all working around a large map laying on the table. When they came nearer, they saw it was a map of the continent and it showed the location of both allied and imperial forces. It also showed the location of all the resistance units operating within the empire.

Then, Gerhart Weitz came over and put his arm around the doctor's shoulder. He said, "Quite impressive, isn't it? Every military unit on the continent is represented on that map. If the empire knew the resistance's coordinating center was only one hundred and fifty miles from their capital, they'd have a fit." He laughed as he began guiding them away from the map. "Why don't we find you something else to wear and then get you something to eat? No doubt you're hungry and tired."

He led them up the stairs to where there used to be bedrooms, but instead there were room upon room of clothing of every imaginable type. There were rooms with civilian clothes for men, women, and children; rooms with military uniforms from both sides; shoes and boots and another with foul-weather gear of every type imaginable. There were rooms filled with camping gear and helmets and all kinds of foul-weather gear, including cross-country skis. Mr. Weitz led the doctor to the room with civilian men's clothes and it wasn't long before he had two new outfits. Abigail noticed that Inga and Benjamin were in the women's clothing room picking out an outfit or two for her to wear instead of the corporal's uniform she had.

There was a woman in each of the rooms they entered and soon they all were given clean clothes and were then sent to other rooms where they were given soap, shampoo, and a clean towel. Then, the men went to one shower and the women went to another. After about an hour, they were together once again.

They were then taken to the underground dormitories. The men were in one dormitory and the women another. When she entered her dorm, Abigail was greeted by a wizened old woman who assigned her to a bunk and told her where to find a pillow as well as the sheets and blankets. She discovered she had been assigned to a top bunk not far from the bathroom, and while she was making up the bed, it struck her; this was exactly like the slave processing center. The thought sent a chill down her spine.

Once she was done with her bed, she moved over and helped Inga with hers. Finishing that task, she escorted Inga to the bathroom and helped her find her way around. Eventually, Inga said she would be all right and they all went to the cafeteria for a much-needed meal. When they walked into the dining room, Abigail was once again reminded of the slave processing center.

She guided Inga through the food line and, finally, over to one of the long tables. As soon as she took her first bite of the food Abigail was again reminded of the slave processing center. After choking down about half of her meal, she decided she couldn't eat anymore of the swill. She looked over at Inga, but she was busy talking and flirting with Benjamin. She turned to the doctor and told him she was going to bed.

***

The staff car parked in front of the State Security Service office in the heart of Waldrand and Inspector Hoffmann stepped out. When he opened the door, he saw an agent with his feet on a desk, listening to music on the radio, and reading a paperback book. He saw that the agent's uniform looked like he'd slept in it for a week. He slammed the door, and the man glanced his way. The inspector saw the man's expression change from bored irritation to terror in less than a second.

The agent jumped to attention and attempted to button his collar and fix his tie as the inspector moved past the little swinging gate that separated the office area from the reception area. He stopped in front of the man and looked him up and down, disgust written all over his face. "Who's in charge?"

"Commander Heitl is the senior agent, sir," the man replied.

The inspector looked at him for a moment or two and then said, "Where is he?"

"In his office, I think, sir."

After a moment, the inspector said, "I'm getting old here, mister. Get him…now!"

The agent saluted and rushed to a door near the back of the office. Seconds later, a middle-aged man rushed out and greeted the inspector with a salute, a smile, and a proffered handshake. It was not accepted.

"You are?"

"Commander Jozef Heitl, sir."

The inspector nodded. He glanced at the desk agent and said to the commander, "Dock that man a week's pay for his slovenly appearance and for reading with his feet on the desk. Now, is there somewhere we can go to talk¬– privately?"

The commander nodded and said, "Right this way, Inspector. We can speak freely in my office."

Once they were in the commander's office with the door closed, the inspector opened his attaché case, pulled out a green file folder and tossed it on the desk. The commander looked at him and he nodded towards the file. Commander Heitl sat behind the desk, picked it up, and examined it. On the left side were pictures of Dr. van Heflin, Inga, and Abigail. On the right side were pages and pages of information. The commander leafed through the documents and finally looked up with a perplexed look on his face.

"I'm looking for those people and I have reason to believe they're in your district."

He reached into his attaché case again and pulled out a red file folder. He handed it to the commander. After he perused the contents, he looked up and the inspector said, "It is believed that he was a gunner on a bomber that was shot down near Brighton about two months ago and the underground took him to van Heflin for treatment. We believe he's still traveling with him."

Slowly, the commander began to comprehend the gravity of the situation, "If we were to capture him…"

"The UC could be forced out of the war, and we would be able to secure the continent and end the war within a year. That's why I need to find him. Now, what can you tell me about the local underground?"

***

Abigail lay in her bunk for hours. As tired as her body was, her mind refused to shut down and allow her to sleep. Consequently, she was still tossing and turning when Inga came in three hours later. She lay perfectly still as Inga whispered her name once, twice, three times. Finally, believing Abigail was asleep, Inga changed and crawled into her bunk, too. Abigail was really dozing off when the air raid siren sounded. Both girls jumped out of bed and threw their clothes on over their nightgowns. Abigail grabbed Inga's arm and they moved toward the door. There wasn't anyone there to guide them, so Abigail looked up and down the corridor until she saw a couple of people moving toward an open door that looked like it led to a set of stairs leading down.

They moved quickly and caught up with the workers just as they were beginning their descent. Abigail asked, and they told her that this was the way to the air-raid shelter. They all hurried down the stairs. When they got to the bottom, they soon found the doctor, Mrs. van der Walle, and Benjamin. As they approached, Benjamin came over, blushed slightly, and took Inga from her.

She moved over to stand by the doctor. She was just about to ask him about the air raid when Mr. Weitz walked over and addressed the doctor. "The allies are scheduled to bomb the underground factories tonight, so we thought it'd be best if we evacuated to the shelter."

No sooner had he finished talking then they began hearing far off explosions. Without waiting for permission, Abigail moved over and told the others what was happening. As she talked, she could see the tension flow from their faces. Then the lights went out. Abigail nearly fainted.

***

"Commander, I want every agent and police officer you have in the district to check every house and building in the area for these people. Leave no stone unturned. I want you to start tonight. Start with your informants. See what they can find out. Do I make myself clear? This is the highest priority and approval has come from the Supreme Commander himself. He wants this boy caught and caught now."

He watched as the commander blanched at the mention of General Joshua and added, "I needn't tell you that I wouldn't want to be the one who tells him we failed. And," he added grimly, "I wouldn't want to be the commander of the district where he eluded capture. That's probably not a pleasant experience."

**

The lights came back on about fifteen minutes later, but to Abigail it felt like an eternity. She looked around and saw Inga was safely in Benjamin's arms and Mr. Weitz was moving toward them from the doorway. Apparently, he had rushed off to see what had happened to the lights and was just coming back to let everyone know. He smiled as he came nearer to them and called out, "No need to be concerned. One of the bombs took out a power station. No worries, though. Our generator just kicked in, so we're fine. The raid is over, and you can all go back to whatever you were doing before."

"Abigail," Inga asked as they walked back to the dorm, "are you sure you don't mind Ben and me spending time together?"

Abigail's mind had been shaken by the air raid and how much this place reminded her of the slave processing center, so she wasn't ready for the question. She jerked back to reality and realized she hadn't been listening. "What?"

Inga said, "Ever since Ben and I started spending time together, you've been kind of quiet and a little distant, and I was wondering if really bothers you that we're, you know, sort of together."

Abigail chuckled and said, "Inga, of all the things that are on my mind, that's quite possibly the least bothersome. Really, the only thing that troubles me about you and Benjamin is that you don't seem to need me as much as you used to."

Inga relaxed a little, but, suddenly, what Abigail had said finally hit her. "Well, if it's not Ben and me, then what is bothering you?"

Abigail explained about the familiarity of the place and how it reminded her of the processing center. When she was done, Inga admitted that that would have bothered anyone. As they both got back into their bunks, Inga said, "Well, hopefully we won't be here very long."

Abigail didn't say anything, but she hoped so too.

***

Two days later, the inspector stepped up to a rostrum in front of a room filled with police, state security agents, military, and home guard officers and began the briefing. The lights dimmed and a projection screen displayed a collage of pictures of Dr. van Heflin, Inga, Abigail, and Benjamin. "These people are somewhere in this district, and I want them found."

***

Mr. Weitz came to the doctor two days later and told him of the impending raids throughout the city. "It would be best for you and your party if we got you out of town as soon as possible. Our informants tell us that the raids will start tomorrow night, so we need to get you folks on your way to Kreeton before they start."

The doctor agreed. Mr. Weitz guided them all to a small conference room where there was a young man waiting for them. He looked like he was about Benjamin's age, but otherwise he was just the opposite of him. Where Benjamin was tall, this boy was only a little taller than Inga. Benjamin's eyes were blue. This boy's eyes were hazel, almost golden. The new boy's hair was bright red, where Benjamin's was normally light brown.

Once everyone was in the room, Mr. Weitz closed the door and began. "Everybody, this is Werner de Groote. Werner, this is Dr. van Heflin, his granddaughter, Inga van de Clerk, their slave, Abigail Henderson, their housekeeper, Lotte van der Walle, and Corporal Benjamin Nicholson from the United Colonies."

As they all shook hands, Mr. Weitz continued, "Doctor, Werner is going to be your guide on your way to Kreeton. His cousin is the leader of the underground there."

The doctor nodded and said, "So, how are we traveling and when do we leave?"

TWENTY-ONE

"We'll leave in the morning, sir. We'll be going by horseback through the forests," he responded.

"Horseback? You do know Inga's blind, don't you? How is she going to ride a horse?"

"That could be a problem," Werner replied thoughtfully.

Benjamin chimed in, "Don't worry about Inga; I'll take care of her. Back home, I would spend the summers at my uncle's farm, and we rode horses all the time. I can tell her how and even take her reins if I need to. It won't be a problem, really."

The woman came and woke Abigail, Inga, and Mrs. van der Walle at five o'clock. They all grumbled a little as they dressed and went to breakfast. When they had finished, Werner came in and escorted them out to the back of the manor house where there were six horses.

Abigail, a city girl, born and bred, had never seen a real horse up close before. She was a little intimidated because her grandparents hadn't kept horses. She tried to hide it from the others, but it wasn't long before Mrs. van der Walle noticed and moved nearer to her. "Don't feel bad, dear. I've never ridden one either. In fact, none of us have ever been near a horse before except maybe the doctor when he was a young boy."

Werner was an excellent teacher. It wasn't long before he had taught them how to mount and dismount their horses. Soon, they were all sitting tall in the saddle. He smiled and told them to go get their things and then they'd be off. Ten minutes later, each member of the party had saddle bags filled with clothes and food and a bed roll tied to the back of their saddle. They headed out just after noon.

Three hours later, the little group had covered about nine miles. They were well out of the city and deep in the forest. Abigail was directly behind Werner and the doctor was behind her. Mrs. van der Walle was next, and Inga and Benjamin were bringing up the rear. Abigail was beginning to get sore, and by looking at the others, she could tell they were too. She called out, "Excuse me, Mr. de Groote.

How much farther are you planning to go today? I think I speak for everyone when I say I'm beginning to get a little sore."

He laughed and said, "Please, call me Werner. I thought we'd ride until sundown and then stop for the night. That's about another hour or two. But, if you all are getting too sore to go on, we can walk for a while. I kind of forgot you aren't used to riding." He chuckled again and added under his breath, "Wait till tomorrow."

They made the next hour and a half and finally stopped for the night. Abigail didn't know how, but she managed to get off the horse and stand, even though her legs didn't feel like they worked anymore. The rest of them climbed down with lots of moans and groans. Soon, they were all grouped around a clearing, watching Werner gather wood and light their evening campfire. He kept it small, so its light didn't attract attention.

Once the fire was going, Abigail and Mrs. van der Walle, slowly and with many groans, started fixing their dinner. Half an hour later, everyone was devouring bowls of beef stew and buttered bread.

***

The staff car containing the inspector and the commander was in front of a line of half-tracks and light armored vehicles rumbling through the streets towards a suspected underground stronghold. Just before midnight, the soldiers were in position and the light cannons opened up on what turned out to be an empty mansion three blocks from the real underground headquarters. After wasting all that time and ammunition, the inspector was not happy. "Impressive Commander, you and your men just signaled to everyone within hearing radius that we're coming. Now what do you intend to do? Bomb the local Catholic church?"

The commander didn't say anything. The inspector got out of the car and called the leaders together. Once everyone was standing near the front of the staff car, the inspector said, "Here's what we're going to do for the rest of the night." He looked over at the police captain and said, "You and your men will go into the neighborhood and begin knocking on doors. If someone answers, you search the house—no matter what the inhabitants say. If no one opens the door, notify the home guard lieutenant and he and his men will enter and search the residence. If either group finds anything, notify a State Security Service agent and we'll interview the occupants before they're arrested. We will also finish searching the building. We have more experience finding hidden rooms and passages than the average policeman." He paused and looked around the group. When no one said anything, he pulled out the photographs and handed them around. As the group was looking at them, he explained, "If anyone finds any of these people or any evidence that they have been somewhere, stop what you are doing and call me immediately." He looked around and said, "Does anyone have any questions? Is everyone clear on their instructions or would you like me to repeat anything?"

Most of the men just shook their heads. The inspector moved over to the hood of the staff car and placed a map on it. "Does anyone have a flashlight?"

One of the policemen handed him one and he shone it on the map. "This is the neighborhood we're in," he said, pointing at a spot on the map. "Now, it's almost one o'clock and I'd like to finish this six-block area before sunrise. Captain," he said to the police official, "do you think there'll be any problem doing that?"

The captain pretended to study the map for a second or two and then, looking up at the inspector, said, "No sir, we can finish that area in about three hours. Perhaps we can do some additional blocks when we're done, if you'd like us to."

The inspector smiled and said, "No, let's just concentrate on these six blocks for tonight. We can do some more tomorrow night if we need to."

The captain nodded and the meeting broke up. Minutes later, the inspector was watching as teams of police knocked on doors and home guardsmen stood in the street, machine guns glistening in the moonlight. "That, Commander, is how you coordinate a large, multijurisdictional raid. Remember that if you ever get to be a commander again."

**

Dinner was over, and the group was sitting around the fire. No one said much. As it got later and later, the temperature continued to fall. One by one, they began to bundle up in their bed rolls near the fire. Abigail had been mesmerized by the fire and sat staring into the depths of the flames when Inga touched her shoulder. She came back to reality with a start and looked up at her friend as she patted her hand.

"Abigail, most of us are going to bed now. Ben says you haven't moved for the last hour. Are you all right?"

As Inga was speaking, Abigail realized she was shivering from the cold. She nodded at Inga and said, "Yes, I'm fine. I guess I was just lost in thought."

Standing up, Abigail walked over to the saddle she had just taken off her horse. She placed it with the others' things and grabbed her bed roll. When she came back to the fire, she saw that Inga and Benjamin were bedded down next to each other and the doctor was next to them with Mrs. van der Walle next to him. That meant that the only place near the fire was between Mrs. van der Walle and Werner.

After she had spread out her blankets and laid down, Werner leaned over and asked her if she was tired. That's when she realized she wasn't. "No," she said. He moved a little closer and said he wasn't either and asked if she would like to talk for a little while. She agreed and they moved even closer so they could talk quietly and not disturb the others.

Werner asked her about herself. She explained about being a slave and everything that had happened since that fateful day when the soldiers had killed her family. When she'd finished, Werner was shocked. "You must be very brave to have survived," he finally said.

Was she? She didn't think so. "Not really," she replied. "The only reason I'm not dead is because of the doctor. If not for him, I probably would have been forced to…" She didn't finish the statement because the thought was just too evil.

"What about you," she asked, changing the subject. "Working with the resistance is dangerous, too. Why do you do it?"

"When the war started, the army came marching into Kreeton and took over the factories for the war effort. Well, one night a bunch of soldiers must have gone drinking and decided to have a little fun. I don't know why they chose our house, maybe because it was on the end of the street or something, but they decided to break in and take whatever they wanted." He was quiet for a few seconds. Abigail was about to ask what happened when he continued. "It turned out what they wanted was my mother and my sister. They killed Papa and then spent the rest of the night raping, and eventually killing, my mother and sister. The only reason they didn't kill me was because I hid in my closet behind some toys. Thankfully, I didn't have to watch, but listening to them attacking and killing my family was bad enough.

"Like a fool, I went to the police station the next morning and they came to 'investigate,' as they called it. But, in the end, no one was arrested, and I was sent to live with my uncle and his family in Waldrand." He paused, and then added, "You met him. He's Gerhart Weitz."

By the end of his story, Abigail was in shock. Even though her story was just as horrific, she was still shocked and filled with pity for the young man next to her. She reached out and took his hand and said, "That's terrible."

He looked at her and smiled. "Yes, it is," he agreed. "But that was six years ago. Now, I help my uncle and his resistance fighters as often as I can."

"But aren't you a member of the underground," she asked.

He laughed and said, "Oh no, my uncle won't let me join till I'm eighteen."

Now, Abigail was really confused and it showed on her face. "But I thought you were Benjamin's age," she blurted.

He laughed again and replied, "Well, I don't know how old he is, but I'm sixteen."

"That's how old I am," she said, without meaning to.

"Well," he said as he moved a little closer, "we have something in common, don't we?"

Before she could answer, he leaned closer and kissed her gently on the lips. She was stunned.

***

The policeman knocked on the manor house's door for the second time. He knew someone was there because he could hear movement inside. He decided to try one more time. Bang! Bang! Bang! went the door knocker. At last, he saw the door handle turn. It was the last thing he ever saw as a hand holding a Luger came out of the crack, pointed at his forehead, and fired. He fell like a sack of potatoes.

The home guardsmen took a second to realize what had just happened and then another second to react. As their leader called out to the other units for help, a dozen armed men came pouring out the door of the manor, their machine guns blazing. Thirty seconds later, there were no living guardsmen.

The inspector heard the gunshots and began running back to his staff car when the resistance fighters mowed down the guardsmen. He screamed at his driver, and they shot towards the manor house as fast as the V-12 engine could go. He was too late.

The army colonel in charge of the armored vehicles and half-tracks ordered his men to attack the manor. As the vehicles came into position, two light tanks, stolen from the local army depot, came around the house and opened fire. The first two armored vehicles exploded and flew into the air, lighting up the night. Before the last two could react, the tanks fired again and they, too, became fireballs. The half-track drivers quickly reversed from the area but found themselves under attack from resistance fighters with grenades. Within seconds, the half-tracks were on fire and all the soldiers were dead. By the time the inspector reached the scene, the people from the resistance were gone.

He screamed at the former commander to gather his people and whoever else he could find and storm the house. Ten minutes later, there were fifty heavily armed men approaching the house. As the one-time commander pulled open the door, the entire house was engulfed in an explosion that killed everyone within a hundred feet. Inspector Hoffmann picked himself off the road and looked out from behind the ruined hulk of his staff car as the rest of his forces, as well as the underground headquarters, went up in smoke.

***

It had begun snowing sometime in the night. When Abigail woke, she found she was wrapped in two blankets and two strong arms. That realization shocked her into complete consciousness. She quickly looked around and found no one else was awake yet. As her heart began to slow to something near normal, she remembered how she had ended up in this predicament. After talking until well after midnight, both she and Werner realized they were freezing! Werner got up and hurriedly put more wood on the fire and then said, "You know, if you would be willing, we could... we could... it's not like..."

She began to get suspicious as she could clearly see him blushing. "We could do what?" she asked.

He knew he was stammering, but he couldn't help himself. He continued, "It's not like I would try anything, you understand...it'd just be for warmth."

"Werner, what are you trying to say? What would be just for warmth?"

"We could lie down together and cover up with both our blankets. That way, we would have double the blankets and we could share our body heat." He could see the suspicious look on her face and he quickly added, "I promise I won't try anything, you know. We'd both still be fully dressed…well, except for our boots that is. But we could even sleep back to back if you wanted to."

She started laughing as she watched him try to explain what he meant. "Werner," she finally said, "I'm freezing, and if you promise not to try anything, I think we can share body heat." He looked relieved, but then she added, "But if you do try anything, I promise you'll regret it by the time I'm through with you. Not to mention what the doctor will do to you."

In the end, he promised and they even started out lying back to back. But, sometime during the night, Werner must have turned over and draped his arm over her, and, somehow, she couldn't begin to figure out how, he had gotten his other arm under her, and she had woken up snuggled next to him, blissfully warm and secure inside his embrace. She smiled to herself when she realized she liked it.

CHAPTER TWENTY-TWO

She quickly looked around and saw that no one else was awake. She rolled over so she was facing Werner and said, "I thought you said you wouldn't try anything. Now look at us."

He woke with a start, his eyes opening to the size of melons and his heart sinking to his toes. What had he done in his sleep? he wondered. Then he saw she was smiling and quietly laughing at him. Without thinking, he pulled her closer and kissed her. She wrapped her arms around him and kissed him back. After a few minutes, she said, "We'd better get up before we get caught and have to explain why we're doing whatever it is we're doing."

He kissed her again and crawled out from under the blankets. He shook the snow out of his hair and put on his boots. While he was doing this, Abigail wrapped herself in both blankets and said, "Let me know when you've got breakfast ready."

Werner stooped, grabbed a handful of snow, and tossed it at her, barely missing her. They both laughed and Abigail got up to begin making breakfast. Once Werner had the fire blazing, the others slowly began waking up too. By the time everyone was awake, breakfast was ready.

***

Snow was falling on what was left of the manor house as Inspector Hoffmann, now covered with bandages, inspected the ruins. Others were collecting the bodies and still others were keeping the curious people away from the carnage and the wreckage. Even from the other side of the street though, there was plenty to see.

The regional military commander arrived just after daybreak and he was not pleased. "Tell me again Inspector, exactly how these men were massacred and on whose orders were the raids conducted?"

He looked at the general as he explained the mission and its importance to the empire and the Supreme Commander. Without saying anything, the general walked over to the destroyed vehicles and the dead soldiers. He watched as some soldiers removed the dead and others moved equipment into place to remove the mangled remains of the four armored vehicles and the two half-tracks.

Without looking at the inspector, the general walked over and inspected the two destroyed light tanks. He turned and looked at a major, the dead colonel's executive officer, and screamed, "How did they steal two tanks without you knowing?!"

The major replied he had no idea, and the general retorted, "I hope you keep better control of your tanks when you arrive on the southern front, Captain!" The major blanched.

The general walked back to the inspector and said, "Since there are no living members of the State Security Service left in this district, thanks to your incompetence, you will be assigned here until the Service sends someone to replace you."

"But sir," the inspector complained, "what about my mission?"

"Inspector, I don't give a damn about your mission. But if you think your mission is so bloody important, I suggest you plead with your headquarters to send someone as quick as they can. Then, you can go chasing across the country for an old man, two little girls, and some boy from the UC. In the meantime, I will expect your detailed mission report on my desk by 0700 hours tomorrow morning." Without waiting for a reply, the general walked over to his half-track and drove away, while Inspector Hoffmann gaped after him.

***

Once the fire was out and everybody saddled their horses, Werner checked each cinch to ensure security, and they were off. At first, Abigail's backside told her how unhappy it was to be back in a saddle, but after a while she began to get used to it. Even though her backside was sore, it was the cold that really bothered her. She felt that the sun must be on vacation somewhere down south as she glanced up to the grey, cloud-strewn sky. *At least it stopped snowing*, she thought.

Finally, around noon, the clouds began to break up and the feeble winter sun began shining down on them as they continued to travel through the forested countryside. Once the sun decided to make an appearance, it began to feel almost bearably cold instead of bitterly cold. They stopped for a light lunch in a clearing sometime around one o'clock. While they were eating, they all looked up as dozens of what looked like bomber aircraft flew overhead. After finishing their meal, they were all happy to get back underway because it was warmer when they were traveling compared to sitting still.

As they traveled, Abigail and Werner talked. Dr. van Heflin saw the change in Abigail, as did Mrs. van der Walle, and they were both happy to see she was no longer moping around. In fact, they were discussing that very topic when the fighter plane trailing smoke and flames, came screaming overhead, narrowly missing the treetops. When it did, it not only startled the humans, but it frightened the horses. Abigail's horse suddenly reared, throwing her to the ground with a bone crushing thud, and bolted from sight. It took the others a moment or two to gain control of their horses and another moment to realize what had happened. Immediately, Werner jumped from his saddle and rushed to help Abigail but he had no sooner reached her side than the doctor was there, examining her. While he checked her for broken bones he said, "Werner, she seems all right, just a few bruises and the wind was knocked out of her. Since she's in no danger, don't you think you should try to catch her horse?"

He nodded, jumped back on his horse and began following Abigail's. Just as he rode out of sight, they heard the explosion that could only mean the fighter plane had crashed not too far from there. The explosion frightened the horses again. It was all they could do to keep them from bolting like Abigail's had done.

Abigail lay on the ground, trying to breathe. Every time she tried to inhale, she felt a sharp pain in her right side. Soon, she began coughing and was shocked by the pain. The doctor forced her to sit up and began prodding her right side. Suddenly, she screamed as he found the broken ribs. "Lotte," he said as he continued prodding, "she has at least two broken ribs. Can you get my bag and help me bandage them?"

Mrs. van der Walle dismounted her horse, as did the others. She handed the reins of her horse as well as the doctor's horse to Benjamin, who was standing a few feet away. She took the doctor's bag down from behind his saddle and moved over to help him. As she walked, she said, "Benjamin, turn around and face away. We'll have to take off her blouse and you don't need to watch." He did as he was told.

Once the doctor was sure there were only the two ribs broken and nothing else, he helped her take off her coat and blouse. Her body was covered with goosebumps, and she was shivering as Mrs. van der Walle and the doctor began wrapping her injured rib cage. She was told to hold her arms above her head and to exhale and hold it. They wrapped her ribcage as fast and as tight as they could. When the doctor told her she could breathe again, she didn't think the bandages would let her.

She had just put her blouse and coat back on when Werner came back leading her horse. After being told about her ribs, he agreed to go slowly for the rest of the day. The doctor offered to help her get back into the saddle and she soon found herself in the last place she wanted to be—on a horse walking through the woods. Every jarring step sent bolts of pain through her ribs, and she was never happier than when Werner decided to stop for the night. They never did check on the downed fighter.

***

It took three days before the inspector's temporary replacement arrived. During that time, he had filed his report with both the general and his superiors back in Brighton. Neither was pleased, but both agreed that he had followed standard procedures and was not to blame.

Now, he finally had a new staff car and a new driver, so he could resume his pursuit of Dr. van Heflin and the UC boy he was helping. During the three days he had been stuck in Waldrand, he had been contacting other State Security Service offices between him and the coast. He told each office about the doctor and the colonist he was helping. He gave each office a detailed description of the doctor, the two girls, and Benjamin. Each promised to begin searching their areas as soon as their other duties allowed. The inspector had bellowed, screamed, and threatened each of the commanders, but after the debacle in Waldrand, no one was afraid of him anymore.

The inspector and his driver arrived in Kreeton in the middle of the night. Their first stop was the State Security office, but it was closed. *No surprise there*, thought the inspector. They went to the nearest inn, took two rooms, and ordered dinner. When the hotel staff balked, the inspector threatened to have the place closed down and the entire staff arrested for giving aid to the enemy. Dinner was ready and sitting on their table by the time they reached the dining room.

The office opened at eight o'clock in the morning and the inspector was waiting out front before the first person arrived. By 8:15, he was sitting in the commander's office berating him for not starting the search. By 9:30 the process had begun.

***

Abigail's ribs were killing her as the fourth day of riding those awful animals came to an end. It was after dark when they reached the edge of Kreeton. It was almost ten o'clock when they finally arrived at the safe house on the far side of the town. She was so tired and sore that she could barely climb off her horse. When she did, she almost collapsed, but Werner caught her before she hit the ground. Almost instantly, the doctor was there, and he gently took her from Werner and took her inside the house while Werner took care of the horses.

The owner of the safe house was a woman named Margot Dumont. She was very tall and quite friendly. She took one look at Abigail and helped the doctor carry her into one of the bedrooms. Within a few minutes, Abigail was in a clean nightgown snuggled deep in the warm embrace of the soft bed, feeling the pain medicine taking effect. Shortly after that, she was sound asleep.

The rest of the party enjoyed the first home-cooked meal they had had in almost a week. As they ate, Mrs. Dumont told them all about the ill-fated raid on the Waldrand headquarters. Werner asked about his uncle, and she told him that no one had been caught and very few had been hurt. "They just moved their operation to another location and were back in business within hours."

Mrs. Dumont then told them the news about the war. The empire had begun a counteroffensive in the south and had almost driven the allies off the continent. While the empire was exerting most of its strength in the south, she told them, the allies made a landing on the coast of Francovia, driving almost fifty miles inland before they met any real resistance. Although that was good news overall, it complicated their escape plans.

"How far from Deep Water Bay is the fighting," the doctor asked.

"Deep Water is now in the hands of the allies. The last I heard, the front is about twenty miles east of Deep Water, near the town of Lutton."

"How are we supposed to get through to Deep Water now?"

"You're not. There's no way you can get there without getting caught or killed. Instead, we decided to send you to Spreitenstadt in the north. It's farther away, but it's still under the empire's control, so it will be easier to get to." Before the doctor could say anything, Margot added, "As soon as the girl can travel, we'll have you taken there. They're in a hurry to get your colonial friend back home where he belongs."

The doctor nodded and didn't say anything. Inga did though. "What's the hurry? Who would want Ben so badly?"

Margot didn't answer. Benjamin said, "Inga, my name isn't really Benjamin Nicholson."

She looked confused as she turned in his direction. "What is it, then?"

Everyone at the table was looking at him and he cleared his throat. Just as he was about to answer, Margot said, "No. You're not allowed to tell them. Suffice it to say that if the empire was to capture him, the war would be over in less than a year and we'd all be saluting the Supreme Commander for the rest of our lives. No, it's best if you continue to know him as Benjamin Nicholson."

Abigail slept for almost 24 hours before she finally woke up. When she did, she was starving and really had to go to the bathroom. While she was eating, the doctor brought her up to date on their new plans and introduced her to Margot. Everyone had come in and joined her as she ate, but, when she looked around, she realized that Werner was gone. She turned to Margot and said, "Mrs. Dumont, do you know where Werner is?"

"He went back to Waldrand, the day after you arrived." She saw the disappointment in Abigail's face and added, "But, he left you a letter."

She got up and went into another room and returned shortly with an envelope. She handed it to Abigail, who quickly opened it and read:

Dearest Abigail,

Thank you for a truly enjoyable journey and all the wonderful memories. You are a marvelous girl and I wish we had more time to get to know each other better. The nights we spent talking and bundling up together will always be some of my favorite memories.

Please remember me, and after the war, if you're ever in the area, feel free to look me up. I'd love to see you again.

All my best,

Werner

PS: In another place and time, we might have had something together.

When she finished reading, there were tears in her eyes. The doctor leaned over and placed his arm around her. "Abigail, honey, are you all right?"

Without speaking, she smiled and nodded.

***

As he did in Waldrand, the inspector gathered police, military, and home guard leaders for a briefing. He gave the same speech and passed around the same pictures. When he opened the floor for questions, there must have been at least a dozen questions about the botched operation in Waldrand. He answered the first few of these questions but soon began trying to ignore them. Someone would ask and he would tell them that he wasn't going to talk about that right now. He was only willing to talk about operations here, not in Waldrand. That tactic didn't work too well though, the questions kept coming. Finally, he lost his temper. "The next person to ask about Waldrand will be thrown out of this meeting and will not be allowed to participate! Now, can we get back to this operation?"

The regional army commander, a colonel, stood and said, "If you expect me to commit assets to your wild goose chase while the allies are less than five hundred miles away, you have to give me some assurance that your operation won't be a suicide mission like it was in Waldrand."

Before he could respond, the police commissioner stood and said, "All my best men have been conscripted into the army. What I have left are old men and cripples. I don't think we can help you." When he finished, he turned and walked out, taking the rest of the police officials with him.

The rest just sat there. He looked at them and said, "Anyone else want to leave?"

No one did.

***

Three days after arriving in Kreeton, Abigail was feeling almost back to normal. Her ribs still hurt, but at least she could walk, talk, and breathe without too much pain. When she told the doctor this, he and Margot decided they would leave that night.

CHAPTER TWENTY-THREE

The group was dressed, packed, and ready to go by eight o'clock. They sat together in the living room and waited for Margot to come and get them. The clock struck nine and she hadn't come yet. The clock struck ten and she still hadn't come. Abigail and Inga fell asleep just after ten. The clock struck eleven and Margot came striding into the room with a huge middle-aged man. Abigail and Inga woke up as soon as she began speaking.

"Dr. van Heflin, this is Horst Kristoffersen. He'll be taking you to Spreitenstadt in his truck. If you're ready, I'll help you load up and you can be off."

The doctor nodded and everyone stood up. They all followed Margot and Horst out the back door and into the barn behind the house. Parked in the middle of the barn was a tractor-trailer rig that looked as if it wouldn't make it across the street, let alone go three hundred miles with cargo in the trailer. Horst could see their incredulous looks and laughed. When he stopped, he said, "She doesn't look like much, but there's more to her than you can see."

He took them over and showed them the bright, shiny new engine hiding under the rusted hood. Then, he took them back to the trailer and showed them the secret compartment under the floor. "There's enough room in there for a dozen full-grown men and all their gear. I'm sure you five will have more than enough room. And look," he continued, "there's ventilation and a light so you won't suffocate or get claustrophobic."

Abigail could see that they all had misgivings, including Inga, but she could also see they really didn't have a choice. Then, Margot told them the rest of the plan. "You will all hide in the secret compartment. Horst will pick up a load of cargo and haul it to Spreitenstadt where it will be loaded onto a freighter bound for Cape Friesland. Once the truck is empty, he'll stop near a fishing boat that will smuggle you out of the country and on to Anglosia. If all goes well, you should be safely in St. Thomasville within a week, ten days at the most."

The doctor thanked Margot for all her help and he and his compatriots climbed into the secret compartment in the belly of the trailer. Immediately, Abigail was reminded of the boxcars she and the other slaves were forced into. When the hatch was closed, it took her breath away. As she did in the boxcar, she moved until she was near an opening and could see out. Slowly, she could feel her heart rate return to near normal as she gazed out the ventilation hole.

It didn't take long for Horst to climb into the cab and start the truck. Soon they were on the way to the freight yard near the railhead in the industrial section of town. Abigail felt the truck come to a stop and begin backing into a loading dock. They all listened as men and machines loaded crates and pallets of freight into the trailer, eventually covering the escape hatch and trapping them in the compartment.

***

The informants had reported and the search teams were ready. The inspector and the commander, together with the home guard captain, police chief, and reluctant army colonel, were at the head of the convoy as they headed for their first raid of the night. A small shipping company near the factories was first on their list. As they neared the company's loading docks, the inspector noticed a beat-up, old semi-truck pulling out of the lot. *No matter*, he thought.

Abigail looked out of the ventilation hole as the truck finally began moving. When they pulled out of the lot, she was surprised to see a caravan of civilian and military-type vehicles pulling into the loading docks they'd just left. Ten minutes later, they all heard the explosions.

The convoy had just come to a stop and the soldiers and guardsmen were getting out of the trucks when it seemed the whole world began shooting at them. The inspector cursed as one of the trucks' fuel tanks exploded and it flew in a high arc, landing just a few feet from his car. He jumped out and drew his Luger as his driver gave a whimper and fell face-first over the steering wheel. He fired the entire magazine into the loading dock while the horn on the staff car blared.

The two half-tracks were equipped with mounted machine guns. Within seconds of the first shots ringing out, the gunners pointed their weapons at the docks and opened fire. It was over within minutes. When the machine gunners stopped firing, the remaining soldiers and guardsmen stormed the freight offices, guns at the ready. They searched each room, but only found the dead and injured people and lots of perforated freight.

Abigail was near panic as she listened to the machine guns firing. She was sure the soldiers would soon be chasing them down the highway until they were captured or killed. She kept taking deep breaths as she waited for the chase to begin. Slowly, she came to the realization that no one was following them, and they were relatively safe.

She felt an arm pull her into a hug and looked around to find Inga next to her, trying to reassure her. She smiled, even though Inga couldn't see it, and hugged her back. "Thanks, I needed a friend," she whispered.

Inga gave her shoulders a squeeze and said, "Don't worry. We'll be fine."

The truck continued traveling at a steady pace and Abigail began to calm down. Suddenly, she realized she was freezing! She began feeling around until she found her bag and pulled out her blanket and her other coat and covered herself as best she could. It didn't help much, and as the hours and the miles passed, she felt it was only getting colder. Just before daybreak, she began to wonder if they wouldn't all freeze to death before they ever reached Spreitenstadt.

***

The medical corpsmen were tending to the wounded, while the inspector and the other commanders walked around the ruined freight yard and inspected the carnage. Thirty soldiers, guardsmen, policemen, and State Security agents were dead, twenty-five more were injured, and two vehicles were destroyed. On the plus side, the freight yard owner was taken alive and was talking. They'd have the local resistance unit dismantled and its members dead or in jail by this time tomorrow. But, even with all that, he still hadn't caught van Heflin and his group! Then, he remembered that truck.

***

The sun was just coming up over the horizon when the truck began slowing down. Abigail hadn't been able to sleep in the cold, so she was the first to sense the change in vibration, but it wasn't long before they were all awake. Eventually, the truck came to a stop and Horst shut off the engine. Abigail was straining to hear anything when she suddenly heard men's voices.

Horst had gone almost seventy miles before he came to the first checkpoint. Something wasn't right. He could feel it as soon as the soldiers motioned for every semi to pull over for inspection. He pulled into the parking area and shut off the engine, waiting for his turn. He didn't have to wait long.

Three soldiers walked over to the truck and the one with the sergeant's insignia motioned for Horst to climb down from the cab. As he opened the door, the sergeant called out, "Bring your log and manifest!"

He grabbed his logbook and the manifest and climbed down. When he was on the ground, he handed both documents to the sergeant. He examined the manifest. He handed it back to Horst and opened the logbook. Suddenly, he looked up and said, "When did you leave Kreeton?"

"Last night," Horst replied.

"What time?"

"Around one or two o'clock this morning. Why?"

The sergeant didn't reply. Instead, he handed the logbook back to him and said, "Open the back."

As they were walking towards the trailer doors, the sergeant motioned to an officer who hurried over to them. While Horst was opening the doors, the sergeant and the officer conferred. Within minutes, there were a dozen soldiers and a portable loading platform working to unload the trailer.

Abigail and the others could hear the soldiers emptying the trailer. As time slowly crept by, they could hear the heavy boots moving deeper and deeper into the belly of the trailer. They all held their breaths as the soldiers removed the last of the crates. Then the soldiers began banging on the walls and floor and ceiling of the trailer while others opened each crate and pallet.

Time seemed to have stopped as Abigail struggled to keep calm. It was a losing battle as she began to feel the sweat trickle down into her eyes even though it was barely above freezing. Finally, she heard the soldiers leave the trailer and all was quiet. She began to breathe easier.

When the soldiers began removing the freight from the trailer, Horst marched up to the lieutenant and began complaining bitterly. "What do you think you're doing," he demanded. "You're going to make me miss the ship and then what am I going to do with all this stuff!?"

The lieutenant remained calm and replied, "Your logbook said you came from the Therkelsen Freight Company in Kreeton and we were told to look out for trucks smuggling contraband from that company. If we don't find anything I'll make sure the men reload your freight and you'll be on your way. Now, go stand over there, out of the way."

When everything had been removed and searched, he walked over to the lieutenant and said, "I told you I wasn't smuggling anything. Now, can you load me back up so I can get going? If I hurry, I just might make it to Spreitenstadt before the ship sails off without this stuff."

The lieutenant nodded, and an hour later, they were back on the road headed for Spreitenstadt. Once they pulled away from the checkpoint, Abigail began breathing again.

***

The interrogation of the freight company owner lasted for over ten hours, and it had taken almost half that time before he admitted he had helped smuggle Dr. van Heflin and his group out of Kreeton. It then took almost another two hours before he told them what truck they had hidden in and where they were going. With that bit of information, the inspector ordered that every checkpoint and security officer between the two cities be notified and told to stop that truck. Then, he secured another staff car and driver and sped off towards Spreitenstadt as fast as they could go.

***

The truck began to slow down again, and Abigail began to get nervous. She peeked out the hole and found they were entering a large city. *This must be Spreitenstadt*, she thought, as they made their way through early afternoon traffic toward the harbor. At last, the truck pulled up to the security post just outside the docks and Horst handed over his documents. Once the home guardsman had examined the papers, he told him where the ship was docked and allowed him to proceed.

***

The staff car screeched to a stop outside the State Security office in the heart of Spreitenstadt. The inspector jumped out and actually ran into the office. The duty agent was startled out of his usual afternoon stupor when he burst into the office. He slowed down only long enough to find out where the commander's office was.

Seconds later, he burst in on the commander's afternoon 'meeting' with his secretary.

***

The longshoremen had just finished unloading the truck when the State Security commander finished his meeting and left his office, accompanied by a thoroughly irritated inspector. Hoffmann was fit to be tied when the commander ordered him out of his office and even had two agents escort him to the waiting area. Finally, an hour later, the commander came out and listened as Hoffmann briefed him. Ten incredibly long minutes later, they were both in the commander's staff car. He had flat-out refused to ride in the inspector's car as they headed for the docks.

The doctor and the others had all thanked Horst and climbed the gangplank onto the Sankt Andreas, a fishing boat that would take them to Anglosia. They were met by the first mate, a man called Ruffie, as they came aboard. It was hard to guess his age, but he was somewhere in his mid-to-late forties. His hair was still brown, as were his eyes and his tanned skin. When he spoke, it was with an accent that Abigail had never heard before and she found it hard to understand him. The doctor, however, didn't seem to have a problem. He told them that Ruffie was going to show them to their cabins and then they'd shove off.

***

The truck had made it back to the checkpoint when the State Security staff car was stopped at the gate. Inspector Hoffmann began yelling at the home guardsman to stop that truck and jumped out just as the exit gate was going up. Hoffmann ran around the staff car and into the path of the semi. Horst had just begun moving forward when he slammed on the brakes, coming to a stop inches from plowing into the inspector.

He drew his Luger, pointed it at the windshield, and motioned for Horst to exit the cab. After turning off the engine, Horst climbed laboriously from the cab and raised his hands. Hoffmann ordered him to the back of the truck and then to open the trailer, which he did. Hoffmann and two home guardsmen climbed in and inspected the empty truck, but they didn't find the hidden compartment.

He jumped down from the trailer and walked over to Horst, his Luger still in his hand. "Where are they," he demanded.

Horst didn't even blink as he replied, "Who?"

Hoffmann pointed the gun at Horst's left leg and said, "Van Heflin and his little band of traitors. Where did you drop them off?"

"I don't know what you're talking about."

The bullet tore into Horst's left knee, and he screamed in agony as he fell. The commander pulled the gun from Hoffmann's hand and threw him to the ground. One of the guardsmen came rushing over and helped the commander subdue Hoffmann as another guardsman attended to Horst. The third guardsman was on the phone to their superiors, and within minutes, Horst was on the way to the hospital and Hoffmann was in handcuffs in the back seat of the staff car on the way back to the State Security office, screaming all the way.

CHAPTER TWENTY-FOUR

They were just getting settled as the captain radioed the harbormaster for permission to depart. It was granted, and before long, the 120-foot fishing boat was happily chugging along, heading for international waters three miles off the coast. At first, the ocean was a bit choppy and the boat was tossed and thrown about, but it wasn't long before they were in deeper, smoother waters. Abigail and Inga were sharing a cabin, trying their best not to get seasick as the boat was tossed about. Once they had reached smoother waters, the doctor came and told them the captain wanted to meet everyone in the mess.

Abigail and Inga got out of their bunks and followed the doctor into the little mess. When they entered, they saw Ruffie and a man they didn't know sitting at the head of a table. Once they were all seated the man began. "Folks, I'm Igor Norgaard and I'm the captain of the Sankt Andreas. And this is my first mate, Rudolf Robinovich, whom you've met."

Everyone introduced themselves and the captain continued. "If we have decent weather and the seas are fairly calm, we should make it to Anglosia in about four or five days. While we're at sea and it's not too choppy, feel free to move about as you wish. I only ask that you stay out of the way of the fishing operations. I wouldn't want anyone to get hurt or accidentally pushed overboard."

He paused for a moment, hoping for a chuckle or two, but continued when he didn't get one. "Now, there are warships and patrol boats in these waters and it's not unheard of for a fishing boat to be boarded and searched. Ruffie and I will be on the lookout, and if we see a ship coming toward us, we'll let you know, and you'll have to head for the hideaway." He stood and motioned for everyone else to stand, too. "Follow me and I'll show you the hideaway."

He led them to the stern of the ship and into the engine room. Toward the back, on the port, or left, side of the boat, there was a small hatch that led to the propeller shaft. He opened the hatch and yelled over the engine noise, "The hideaway is inside here. Just crawl in and head for the bow. After a few feet, you'll see a crawl space that leads to the keel. Once you're in there you'll find a hatch that covers the crawl space. From the outside, the hatch blends so well that it's almost impossible to see unless you know it's there."

He looked at each of them, making sure they understood. Finally, he said, "All right, I want you to crawl into the hideaway one at a time. Once you're all in there, close the hatch and wait. When the coast is clear, one of us will knock on the hatch to let you know that you may come out."

They all looked at each other to see who would go first. When nobody moved, Abigail took a deep breath and moved toward the hatch. Just as she was about to crawl in, the captain handed her a flashlight and bellowed, "When you get in there, look to the right of the hatch and you should see a little light switch. Just flip the switch and a light bulb should come on, so that you can see."

Abigail nodded and proceeded to crawl into the narrow space. After a minute or two, she entered what was actually the bilge. She flipped on the light and was surprised to see about two inches of brackish water sloshing around near the bottom of the boat. After a few minutes, the rest of the group had joined her, and Benjamin closed the hatch.

It was a little crowded, but not as claustrophobic as the hidden compartment in the semi-trailer had been. Although the space was larger, there was no ventilation, and it wasn't long before it became stuffy and hot. With the water sloshing around their feet, Abigail fervently hoped they weren't boarded before they reached Anglosia.

***

It took three calls to headquarters and six hours before the inspector was released from custody. He was still fuming when he made his way to the hospital and Horst's room. When he walked in, Horst was asleep—his leg bandaged and resting outside the covers. He slapped the bandaged leg and Horst woke with a scream of pain. "Where did you drop them off," he demanded.

"I dropped my cargo off at pier 47 and it was loaded onto a ship headed for Cape Friesland. I don't carry passengers, only freight."

Hoffmann slapped the injured leg again and Horst screamed in agony. A nurse came running in but scurried away when she saw the State Security uniform. Hoffmann walked over and locked the door. "Now, let's start again, shall we?"

***

The torpedo boat was designated as T-37. She had been launched just two years into the war and had, so far, sunk over 375,000 tons of enemy shipping. Her captain was Commander Elkhart Finzel. He and his patrol boat had just come off a three-week patrol of the Nordic Sea and he was still in his cabin finishing his log and other paperwork when there was a knock at the door.

"Enter," he called, and the radio operator came in and saluted. He handed him a dispatch and left, closing the door behind him. He sighed as he adjusted his glasses and read the dispatch.

TO: COMMANDER IMPERIAL TORPEDO BOAT T-37

FROM: COMMANDER NORDIC SEA FLEET OPERATIONS

COMMANDER FINZEL:

STATE SECURITY SERVICE HAS REQUESTED THAT ALL PATROL BOATS IN THE NORDIC SEA IMMEDIATELY BEGIN SEARCHING FOR ANY AND ALL VESSELS THAT MAY HAVE LEFT THE HARBOR IN SPREITENSTADT WITHIN THE LAST 48 HOURS. ALL VESSELS ARE TO BE BOARDED AND SEARCHED FOR DR. KURT VAN HEFLIN, INGA VAN DE CLERK, ABIGAIL HENDERSON, AND AN UNKNOWN ADULT FEMALE. THEY WILL BE ACCOMPANIED BY A UNITED COLONIES AIRMAN POSSIBLY NAMED BENJAMIN VAN NICHOLSEN, OR A SIMILAR NAME. IF THEY ARE LOCATED, THESE PEOPLE ARE TO BE TAKEN INTO CUSTODY, TRANSPORTED TO THE NEAREST NAVAL FACILITY, AND HELD FOR STATE SECURITY.

YOU ARE TO DEPART AS SOON AS POSSIBLE.

VICE-ADMIRAL SIGMUND WIRTH

IMPERIAL NAVY

NORDIC SEA COMMAND

He got up and walked into the radio room. When the radioman looked up, he said, "Otto, contact base operations and tell them we will be departing as soon as we have completed refueling and resupplying. Also, contact the crew and have them report by 0600 hours tomorrow." The radioman nodded and began making the notifications as the skipper left the room. His next stop was the XO's cabin. By 0700 hours, the next day, T-37 was casting off.

***

It began to rain the second day out from Spreitenstadt. By noon, the sky was as black as midnight. All fishing operations were suspended, and the little boat turned its bow toward the coast. Hour after hour, the boat bobbed in twenty-foot seas, and hour after hour, Abigail tried to keep from getting seasick.

The two girls sat in their cabin trying to keep their minds off the storm by reading. Abigail had read one book and was just starting on the second when the rest of their party came in. "We heard you reading and thought we'd like to listen too," Mrs. van der Walle explained as they all came in and sat down.

So she read, and read, and read until her voice was hoarse. Then it was the doctor's turn to read. He had just finished his second chapter when there was a knock on the door. Benjamin opened it and saw the old cook standing there. "It's too rough to make a full meal tonight folks, but there're sandwich fixin's in the galley if you're interested."

Benjamin thanked him and they all made their way to the galley. Abigail made herself and Inga half of a ham sandwich and a small glass of milk while the others ate a more robust meal. When everyone was finished, they all decided they didn't want to read anymore, and since there was nothing else to do, they figured they might as well go to bed and try to sleep. Maybe the storm would be over when they woke.

***

T-37 was being tossed about almost as badly as the Sankt Andreas, but the skipper kept a steady helm. Hour after hour, the lookouts scanned the sea for any other vessel. The boat would be almost airborne when it crested a wave only to be partially submerged as it reached the trough. They'd been at it for almost twenty-four hours when Commander Finzel decided to head toward the coast.

Ruffie was at the helm when the bow lookout pointed out the torpedo boat off the starboard bow about five miles away. He watched as the imperial craft turned directly towards them. Without a second thought, he called the captain.

The forward lookout spotted the fishing vessel and called out to the conn. The first officer had called Finzel and he was on the bridge watching as they turned toward the other boat. He had no idea how he was going to board the boat in these seas, but he'd worry about that when they caught them.

Captain Norgaard woke them by pounding on their cabin doors. He quickly told them of the approaching torpedo boat and told them to head for the hideaway. Abigail and Inga threw on their clothes, grabbed their bags, and dashed for the engine room. Everyone else followed and it wasn't long before they crawled into the stuffy little space in the keel of the boat and waited for the all clear.

T-37 was about a mile off when the radioman made contact with the Sankt Andreas. Commander Finzel ordered the boat to stand down and prepare to be boarded. "We'll be glad to try, Commander," Captain Norgaard replied, "But, I'm not sure you'll be able to board us in this weather. Instead, is there something you're looking for that we might be able to help you with?"

"Negative Captain, just prepare to be boarded when we get there."

It took them almost an hour to come alongside the fishing boat. Once they were close enough, both ships deployed all their fenders and ropes were cast over to the Sankt Andreas. Slowly, and with great care so as not to damage either vessel, the two crews pulled the ships together, finally securing them. Commander Finzel and six heavily armed sailors boarded the Sankt Andreas and were met by Captain Norgaard and Ruffie.

"Captain, I'm Commander Elkhart Finzel of the Imperial Navy of the Empire of Truth and Light, and I've been ordered to board and search every vessel that set out from Spreitenstadt within the last two or three days. Where are you coming from and where are you going?"

"We did indeed set out from Spreitenstadt, but it's been more than two or three days since we set out. In fact, it's been more like a week. We're a fishing boat, as you can see, and we set out to fish for northern cod. They should be running within the next few days."

"How many crewmen do you have on board?"

"There are fourteen men and Ruffie and me... that makes sixteen. Oh, and the cook, too. I forgot him."

"Very well, have the crew assemble in the mess while we search the ship." He looked over at two of the sailors and told them to go with the captain and ensure everyone was accounted for before they began the search.

Norgaard and the rest of the crew were all in the mess, guarded by two of the sailors, as Commander Finzel and the other four searched the boat. The search took almost three hours to complete. Finzel and two of the sailors searched the living quarters, while the other two sailors inspected the mechanical areas of the ship. Finally, the fish hold was inspected, and they all came back to the mess.

Norgaard put his coffee cup down on the table as the navy commander strode into the cramped room. He looked around, making sure to look at each person. Finally, he turned to Norgaard and said, "Is this your whole crew? There's no one missing?"

Norgaard nodded and the commander looked around again. Then he reached into his pocket and pulled out Inga's nightgown and held it up over his head. He slowly turned in both directions as he called out loudly, "Then who is the pervert that sleeps in a woman's nightgown?"

The crew members all laughed as the commander continued to display the nightgown. Unseen by the commander, Ruffie nudged a young man near the back of the room and he raised his hand. The commander looked at him and said, "This is yours?"

The man blushed and nodded. As he came forward, he explained, "I just got married before we sailed and that's my new wife's. She gave it to me to remember her by."

The commander and the others were laughing even harder as he tossed it to him. The young sailor caught the nightgown and returned to his place. The commander waited for the laughter to end before he brought out his next surprise. "Well, let's see what other interesting items your crewmen left lying around."

The room was dead silent as they waited for the next bombshell. The commander smiled as he placed his hand in his pocket and slowly pulled out a pair of Mrs. van der Walle's bloomers. "Does anyone want to claim these beauties?"

This time, it was Norgaard who nudged one of the crewmen. At nearly sixty, the engineer was the oldest member of the crew, and when he raised his hand most of the crew remained quiet. "Those are mine," he called out. "They're a souvenir from my last visit to—a certain house in Spreitenstadt where there's a woman who likes to spend time with me. She and I like to get together and talk about the first thing that comes up."

The room burst into tumultuous laughter as he grabbed the garment from the commander. As the laughter died down Norgaard said, "Well Commander, did you find any other mementos that we can all enjoy, or is the entertainment over?"

The commander smiled and said, "No, Captain, the rest of your crew are either better at hiding their souvenirs or are too boring to have any." He nodded at the six sailors and said, "I think we're ready for the big reveal."

Two of the sailors walked out of the room and returned a moment later with the doctor's Luger pistol and Benjamin's machine gun. The commander looked at the stunned look on Norgaard's face and said, "Somehow, I don't think these are treasured keepsakes from wives and lovers, Captain."

Igor was thinking fast, but it was Ruffie who said, "Every ship needs a couple of guns, Commander, to ward off pirates and such and to scare off birds and sharks and whatnot."

No one was laughing as the commander moved towards Ruffie. He cocked the Luger and said, "Is this another attempt to explain incriminating evidence with lies and humor? Somehow, I don't hear anyone laughing."

He pointed the gun straight down and fired off all nine rounds. When the echoes had died, he handed the gun to Ruffie and said loudly enough for all of them to hear, "I have no doubt that you're a bunch of liars and probably traitors too, and if I had one speck of evidence, I'd haul all of you back to base and put you in front of a firing squad. But I don't have any evidence, so you're free to continue your fishing." He turned and walked to the door. Just before he walked out of the mess, he turned and said, "Oh, and Captain, the next time you're boarded and claim to be fishing, you might want to have some fish in your hold."

***

When the commander fired off the Luger, Abigail had to shove her knuckles in her mouth to keep from screaming. In fact, she bit so hard on her hand that she drew blood. When the ninth round had been fired and silence had returned, she noticed two things: first was the doctor scrambling over to Mrs. van der Walle's body, which had slumped over. Abigail's brain seemed to be working in slow motion as her eyes took in the blood, but her brain didn't register what it meant. The second thing she noticed was the water in the bottom of the keel was rising—fast.

She shook herself and slowly came back to reality. She scrambled over to Mrs. van der Walle's side and began helping the doctor treat the numerous gunshots to her legs and abdomen. She whispered to Benjamin to hand them the doctor's little black bag, and once he had, she began rummaging in it for gauze, bandages, and forceps. She took out a bottle of antiseptic and poured it over the six gunshot wounds, while the doctor tore the clothing away from the area. Then she poured some on his hands and gave him the forceps.

The doctor was working feverishly, trying to probe the wounds for the bullets and stem the blood flow before she bled to death. His hands were a blur as he worked, but all the time, Mrs. van der Walle's breathing was getting shallower and more ragged. Abigail wiped away the blood as fast as she could to allow the doctor to see what he was doing, but the more blood she wiped away, the more blood there was. Soon, the doctor told her to stop wiping and to put pressure on as many of the bullet wounds as she could.

Benjamin reached over and began helping to put pressure on the wounds, too, and Inga reached out and took Mrs. van der Walle's hand as the doctor and Abigail struggled to save her life. He had just removed the fourth bullet when Mrs. van der Walle's heart stopped beating. He tried again and again to get it to restart, but it never did.

CHAPTER TWENTY-FIVE

The commander nodded to the six sailors and they left the mess and headed for the deck. A few minutes later, T-37 had cast off from the Sankt Andreas and began pulling away at speed, looking for its next victim.

As soon as the commander had left the mess, the chief engineer and three others darted for the engine room to look for damage from the nine bullets fired into the hull. They surveyed the engine room, finding no damage. The engineer had just opened the hatch to the propeller shaft when Norgaard ran in. He gave the engineer a questioning look and he said, "There's no damage to the engines, Captain, I was just goin' to check the shafts and the keel when you came in."

Igor watched as the engineer sent one of the younger, smaller men into the cramped space. Moments later, he called out that one of their passengers was dead and they were taking on water. "There must be holes in the keel 'cause we're takin' on water, Skipper—lots of water."

The engineer shuffled over and started the bilge pumps to begin pumping the water out while the captain and the engineer's mate helped Dr. van Heflin and the others pull Mrs. van der Walle's body out of the hideaway. Eventually, the engineer's mate and Benjamin were told to take her back to her cabin and Abigail and Inga followed, both silently shaking with sobs.

Once the area was free of people, the captain crawled into the bilge to inspect the damage. They were indeed taking on water. He took his flashlight and shone it into the bloody water. He really couldn't see much, so he began feeling for any holes. There they were—six holes about the size of a pencil and one larger hole where more than one bullet had crashed through the hull. And the water was just pouring in! He crawled out and described the damage to the engineer. "We can plug 'em Skip. Wait a sec 'n I'll get some corks and a mallet."

A few seconds later, he came back and handed the captain a dozen corks of all different sizes, and a rubber mallet. "Try these," he said as he tipped the corks into his hand, "and pound 'em in with this."

The captain nodded and returned to the leaking keel. He began feeling around and finally found the holes. He plugged three of the smaller holes and the larger one with no difficulty, but the last three small holes proved more problematic. Eventually, he plugged them too. He breathed a sigh of relief and crawled out of the narrow space to find he had bigger problems.

***

Commander Finzel finished his after-action report and the radioman had sent it within an hour of leaving the Sankt Andreas. He was just preparing to pour himself and the first officer a glass of brandy when the radioman tapped on the door. When he answered, the man snapped to attention and said, "This just came in from Fleet, sir," and handed him the dispatch.

He nodded, took the sheet of onion paper and closed the door. He had just sat down again when he read:

TO: COMMANDER IMPERIAL TORPEDO BOAT T-37

FROM: COMMANDER NORDIC SEA FLEET OPERATIONS

COMMANDER FINZEL:

YOU ARE TO LOCATE THE SANKT ANDREAS AND SINK HER. YOU ARE TO ENSURE ALL ABOARD ARE DEAD AND REPORT BACK TO ME IMMEDIATELY. STATE SECURITY SERVICE REPORTS INFORMANT HAS CONFIRMED ESCAPEES WERE ON THE BOAT WHEN SHE LEFT SPREITENSTADT.

ACKNOWLEDGEMENT OF YOUR ORDERS REQUIRED.

VICE-ADMIRAL SIGMUND WIRTH

IMPERIAL NAVY

NORDIC SEA COMMAND

He handed the dispatch to his second-in-command and walked out of the cabin, heading for the bridge. The first officer finished reading, got up, and headed for the radio room.

"Captain on the bridge!" called the duty officer as the commander walked through the hatch.

He acknowledged the duty officer and said, "Ensign, I have the conn."

"Aye aye, sir, you have the conn," replied the ensign, exiting the captain's chair.

"Helm," he commanded, "turn the ship about and find that fishing boat. Command wants us to sink it."

***

"Captain!" called the radio operator. "That torpedo boat has just been ordered to come about, find us, and sink us. Seems the State Security Service knows about our passengers and wants them dead!"

Norgaard was visibly shaken as he listened to the radioman's report, but he suddenly came back to himself. He nodded and hurried from the engine room, heading for the bridge. When he came rushing in, Ruffie turned and stared at him. "Ruffie, that torpedo boat is about to try to sink us. See if you can hide from her long enough to get into Anglosian waters."

Ruffie nodded and pushed the twin throttles full against their stops. The diesel engines roared, and the boat shot back out to sea. In next to no time, they were hurling towards the Anglosian Islands and safety. Only time would tell if they would make it.

***

Abigail shooed everyone out of Mrs. van der Walle's cabin. "Get out," she commanded. "I don't need an audience while I clean her up."

When Inga asked if she could help, Abigail agreed, and the two friends began the daunting task of preparing the body for burial. Constantly wiping tears from their eyes, it took longer than they had expected. When they were finished, they allowed the doctor and Benjamin to come back in. Both were moved at the transformation of Mrs. van der Walle. When they had brought her in, she had been literally covered in blood (hers), sweat (everyone's), and tears (everyone but hers). Now, she was lying on her bunk looking as if she were just sleeping; her hair was clean and brushed and her face was made up as if she were ready to go to church. And she was wearing her best clothes.

The doctor gave Abigail and Inga both hugs, telling them that they had done a beautiful job. "Lotte looks as if she's ready to go to the finest restaurant in town."

Then, they felt the boat speed up and looked at each other, fear clearly showing on their faces. Benjamin hobbled as quickly as he could out of the cabin and towards the bridge with the doctor right on his tail. They reached the bridge just as Ruffie turned hard to starboard, or right, and the ship slewed away from the coast and out to sea. They all had to grab on to something to keep from falling as they raced back out to sea.

Norgaard turned and bellowed above the roar of the engines and the sea, "Go back down below, Doctor. There's nothing you can do up here except get in the way!"

The doctor bellowed back, "What's happened? Why are we going so fast?"

"That torpedo boat that boarded us earlier is on its way back to sink us. The State Security Service told the navy they had proof you were on board, and they ordered them to sink us! We're gonna run for Anglosian waters as fast as we can. Hopefully, we can get there before our friends find us! Now, please go back to your cabins and stay there. I'll keep you informed if anything changes!"

The doctor nodded and he and Benjamin headed back down below to tell the girls. They found them sitting in the mess. They said they didn't feel like being alone in their cabin. The doctor nodded and told them what was going on and what the captain's plan was. Although they both looked frightened, neither began crying. They just nodded.

***

They'd been searching the open waters for over three hours and there was no sign of the Sankt Andreas. They had returned to the coordinates where they'd left the fishing vessel, but it wasn't there. He hadn't thought it would be. He and the First Officer had checked the charts and tried to figure out just how far the boat could have gone and then guess in which direction they went.

"If the State Security is right and that colonist is on that boat, then I would guess they're heading for Anglosia," the first officer said. "And if that's the case, then they'll have probably headed out to sea a bit and are making a mad dash to Anglosian waters, here." He pointed to a spot on the chart.

Finzel nodded and the first officer continued, "I would recommend we head in that direction, too. Only, we stay closer to the coast. You know, to try and force them further out to sea. Then, if we see them, they'll be in international waters and we'll have 'em."

Finzel nodded and said, "Make it so." He stood up and said, "You have the conn. Call me if you see them. I'll be in my cabin."

***

He looked at Ruffie and said, "How much farther?"

Ruffie studied the chart for a minute or two and said, "If we can keep up this speed, and if that torpedo boat don't find us, I figure we should be in Anglosian waters in about four or five hours."

***

"Abigail," the doctor said, "Would you please go to your cabin and get the book we were reading?"

She nodded and retrieved the book. She handed it to him and sat back down. He began reading as they continued racing towards freedom.

***

"Captain to the bridge! Captain to the bridge! We have a sighting! Captain to the bridge!" was heard over the intercom system.

"Captain on the bridge!" called out the first officer as he walked through the hatch.

He acknowledged and said, "I have the conn."

"Aye aye, Captain, you have the conn."

He sat down in the captain's chair and said, "Report."

The first officer replied, "The forward lookout spotted a ship similar in shape and size to the Sankt Andreas ahead and to starboard. Estimated range is seven miles. We should catch up to her in about an hour, give or take."

The commander nodded.

***

"Captain, I think we've got company," Ruffie called out over the roar of the engines.

Norgaard looked up and Ruffie continued, "The stern lookout said he sees a ship coming up fast behind us. Said it looks like it could be that torpedo boat."

"How far to Anglosian waters?"

"About an hour or so."

"Turn towards port and see if we can get another knot or two out of those old engines."

Ruffie called the engine room and then relayed Norgaard's orders to the helmsmen.

***

"How long until we're in firing range?" the commander asked.

The first officer consulted the weapons officer and said, "Between twenty and thirty minutes, sir."

"And how far are they from Anglosian waters?"

"Thirty to forty-five minutes, sir."

***

Abigail tried to listen to the doctor as he read page after page of the book. He was a good reader, and the book was one of those thrillers that, under normal circumstances, would have kept her on the edge of her seat. But it was hard to listen to a fictional thriller when you were deep in the middle of a real-life thriller that was better than any book could ever be. She looked around at the others and saw they didn't seem to be having any trouble listening.

She couldn't take it anymore and got up. Immediately, the doctor stopped reading and asked, "Where are you going?"

She began walking toward the hatch as she replied, "I can't take it anymore, I've got to see what's happening!"

She didn't listen as he tried to call her back. She stepped onto the bridge just as Ruffie called out, "Incoming torpedo, starboard side!"

The captain yelled, "Hard to port!"

CHAPTER TWENTY-SIX

"Skipper, we have a firing solution," the first officer called out.

The commander nodded, "Tubes ready?"

The weapon's mate called out, "Tubes one and two are ready, sir. Tubes three and four are being loaded as we speak."

"Fire tube one!"

"Fire one," echoed the weapons officer into the intercom.

The torpedo sped from the tube and hit the water already at speed. The commander sat as the reports began coming in. "Fish is away," the weapon's mate announced. "Running hot and true. Distance to target, six thousand meters." There was silence on the bridge as he continued his report.

"Distance to target is now two thousand meters. Target is changing course, veering to port at speed. Fish is not changing course. Fish has passed the target. Shot is a miss. I say again, the shot is a miss."

***

"Torpedo coming up fast on the starboard side, 'bout two hundred yards back," Ruffie called out.

"Hard to port," the captain bellowed, and the ship began moving to the left.

Abigail grabbed hold of the back of the captain's chair as the turn deepened. Ruffie called out, "Torpedo now fifty yards astern. Stand by for impact!"

They all tensed, expecting to hear and feel the explosion, but it never came. "Torpedo has passed five yards astern, Captain. All clear!"

He took a deep breath and called out, "Return to original course and maintain present speed. How far to Anglosian waters now?"

The question was never answered.

***

"Range to target?"

"Five thousand meters, sir."

"Do we have a firing solution?"

"Stand by," the first officer replied. Seconds later, he called out, "We have a firing solution!"

"Tubes two, three, and four ready, sir," called out the weapons officer.

"Fire tubes two and three. Stand by tube four and reload tube one. We might get another shot before they're in Anglosian waters."

"Tubes two and three are off! Both fish are in the water, running hot and true. Distance to target, four thousand meters." Seconds later, the weapon's mate called out, "Target has turned to starboard. Distance to target is now three thousand meters. Fish two is a miss, fish three still on target."

***

"Two torpedoes incoming," yelled the lookout.

The helmsmen pulled harder on the helm, willing the boat to move further to the right. "Radio a distress call. Maybe the Anglosians are close enough to help," Norgaard called out.

"Mayday! Mayday! This is the Sankt Andreas. We're a fishing boat out of Belekota. We're being pursued by an imperial torpedo boat, and they're firing on us! Mayday! Mayday!"

***

"Captain, we're receiving a distress call from a fishing boat nearby. They say they're being pursued by an imperial torpedo boat."

"What's their location?"

"About seven miles east northeast of our present location, sir."

The captain leaned forward and said, "Tell them we're on our way and then tell Fleet." Then to the helmsmen, he said, "Set an intercept course. Flank speed."

"Sankt Andreas, this is the HMS Fortitude. We are approximately seven miles from your present location. What is your status?"

"Fortitude, this is the Sankt Andreas. The imperial torpedo boat is approximately one to two miles astern and closing fast. They've fired on us twice, both misses. Please hurry."

***

"Skipper, we have a firing solution for tubes one and four!" the weapons officer called out.

"Are you sure this time, Ensign? We've fired three fish and haven't hit yet. Make sure we don't miss this time."

The weapons officer blushed and double-checked the figures. "Range is 2500 meters. Speed is 16 knots. At present course and speed, both torpedoes should impact two minutes after they're fired, sir."

The commander nodded and said, "Fire both tubes and man the deck gun."

"Fire!"

"Two more incoming," Ruffie called out.

"Hard to starboard," bellowed Norgaard.

"Both fish away; both are running hot and true," the weapons mate called out.

"Fortitude, this is the Sankt Andreas. They've fired on us again!"

"Target turning starboard. Fish one is a miss; fish four still on target. Five hundred meters. Impact in twenty seconds—ten seconds. Impact is imminent."

***

The crew watched as the wakes of both torpedoes came speeding towards the Sankt Andreas. They all were praying to whatever god they believed in when one torpedo sped past them to the left. Unfortunately, the other one didn't miss.

The torpedo struck the fishing boat on the starboard side of the stern. The men in the engine room felt the collision and expected to die immediately. They didn't. Instead of exploding, the torpedo simply tore through the hull, severing the starboard propeller shaft and slammed into the starboard engine. Seconds later, the engineer and his two mates were out of the quickly flooding engine room and trying valiantly to close the hatch as the freezing ocean water came pouring in.

Once the hatch was secure, they hurried to the bridge. As the engineer came rushing in, he yelled, "Skipper, that last torpedo punched through the hull and the starboard propeller shaft. It didn't explode, but the engine room is filling up fast. Recommend we abandon ship as soon as we can 'cause we won't stay floatin' much longer!"

***

The helmsmen called out, "Speed's down to 10 knots, Capt'n and still goin' down!"

Norgaard nodded and said, "Radio the Anglosians and prepare to abandon ship. Helm, keep us headed for Anglosian waters as fast and as long as you can. Everybody move, now!"

"Fortitude, this is the Sankt Andreas. We've been hit in the stern. The torpedo didn't explode, but it did breach our hull. We're taking on water and are about to abandon ship. Are you close enough to help?"

"Affirmative, Sankt Andreas. We see you now. We're about a mile away and should be there within minutes. Proceed with your evacuation. How many crewmembers are on board?"

"Seventeen crewmembers and four passengers for a total of twenty-one. We're beginning evac now, Fortitude. Hope to see you soon. Sankt Andreas out."

"Sir, the Sankt Andreas is slowing down and appears to be taking on water. We must have hit her with at least one fish, but it must not have exploded," the weapon's mate called out.

"Sir," the radioman cut in, "the Sankt Andreas put out a distress call and an Anglosian cruiser, the HMS Fortitude, is responding. Last transmission placed them approximately a mile out. The crew of the Sankt Andreas is abandoning ship, sir. They claim to have four passengers on board."

"Get as close as possible and strafe the survivors before that Anglosian ship gets here."

***

Abigail ran back towards the mess only to find the doctor and the others rushing up the stairs. She glanced beyond them and could see the water seeping steadily up the deck toward the staircase. "Come on everyone! The captain has ordered us to abandon the ship. We've got to go!"

Just as she finished speaking, Ruffie came rushing up to them and yelled, "Follow me! Got to get you all in life jackets 'afore we hit the drink!"

No one spoke. They just hurried behind him to the closest life jacket station. Ruffie pulled out the life preservers and began handing them out. The doctor and Benjamin were easy to fit, but try as he might, Ruffie couldn't find ones small enough for Inga and Abigail. Eventually, he took some rope and tied the too-big life jackets on both of them and led them back to the bridge where everyone else had gathered to wait for the order to jump.

***

"Imperial torpedo boat, this is the HMS Fortitude. You are interfering with a rescue mission. Leave the area or you will be fired upon. Acknowledge."

There was no response, and after informing the bridge, the radioman repeated the admonishment.

"No response, sir!"

The captain rubbed his hands together and said, "Very well, we gave them warning. Lower the ship's boat and pick up the survivors of the Sankt Andreas. Helm, all stop. Weapons, have the forward guns prepare to fire upon that torpedo boat," the captain ordered.

***

"Everyone, here's how we're going overboard. Each of you choose a partner and stand by the starboard rails. Doctor, your group will go second and third. Drew, you and Rieckhoff go in first and help the others as they come. Everyone, once you're in the water start swimming away from the boat, when she goes down, she'll create a small vortex that could pull you down with her." He looked around and said, "Does everyone understand? Anyone have any questions?"

When no one answered, he said, "Good. Ruffie, you and I will rig the helm to continue straight and keep the throttles at full. We'll be the last off, so swim fast." To the others he said, "All right, start evacuating now."

***

"Sir, the Anglosian ship has ordered us from the area. They say they'll sink us if we don't leave," the radioman reported.

The commander nodded and said, "Ensign, do you have a firing solution on that cruiser?"

"No sir, I…"

The commander cut him off. "I want a firing solution firing all forward tubes followed by a 180 degree turn and then firing all aft tubes and I want it now!"

Two minutes later, the first officer called, "Firing solution for four forward tubes complete, sir. Aft tubes solution will be ready before we've turned around."

"Fire!"

CHAPTER TWENTY-SEVEN

"Captain, four incoming torpedoes!"

"Full astern and hard starboard, helm! Sound General Quarters! Advise forward gunner he may fire at will!"

The light cruiser's propellers began churning the water, hoping to gain purchase and reverse the ship's forward momentum. At first, the ship slowed and began turning to the right, but after what seemed like ages, it began going backwards and left. Meanwhile the forward gun turret swiveled and pointed its three cannons in the direction of the Imperial torpedo boat and began firing.

"Forward four fish are away, running hot and true," the weapons mate called out.

"Helm, full about and full speed for home," Commander Finzel ordered.

"Rear tubes one and two are ready. Firing solution acquired, sir."

"Fire!"

"Incoming torpedoes one thousand meters and closing. Time to impact is two minutes."

"Brace for impact!"

***

Drew and Rieckhoff climbed over the rail and jumped as far away from the crippled boat as they could. The doctor tapped Benjamin on the shoulder and said, "You and Inga go first. Abigail and I will follow."

Benjamin nodded and took Inga's arm. He told her, "When I tell you, jump as far out as you can and hold your breath until you come back up. I should be beside you within a few seconds. If not, just lean back and your life jacket will keep you afloat. Ready?"

She nodded and he helped her over the railing, but just as he was climbing up himself, she jumped into the freezing water. Abigail could hear him curse as he dove out and back towards where Inga had gone in. No sooner had they cleared the rail than she and the doctor climbed up and immediately jumped.

The water felt like hot knives even as the cold forced every ounce of air out of her lungs. Within seconds, she surfaced and began looking around for the doctor and the others. Soon, they were together and struggling to swim towards Drew and Rieckhoff. It seemed to take forever, but eventually they made it. All of them were huffing and puffing and Abigail could feel her hands and feet going numb from the cold.

***

"Skipper, incoming shells," bellowed the first officer.

"Verdomme!" cursed the commander as three six-inch shells struck the stern. The shells tore through the decking and two of them exploded in the engine room, killing everyone instantly. The other shell entered the torpedo boat just forward of the engines and exploded in the ship's magazine. Almost instantly, the boat was virtually vaporized.

***

The HMS Fortitude's propellers dug deep into the icy Nordic Sea, trying desperately to reverse itself and live to fight another day. Slowly at first, but eventually faster and faster, the light cruiser came to a stop and began reversing. But would it be enough? The entire bridge crew held their breath as the sonar man reported, "Four torpedoes off the starboard bow. Speed: 40 knots. Time to impact: one minute."

Sweat was beginning to trickle down the captain's forehead as the seconds ticked past. "Report," he said.

"Four torpedoes still inbound at the same speed. Time to impact: twenty seconds."

"Sir," called out the communications man, "the forward lookouts report the torpedoes are just off the bow."

Twenty seconds later, the sonar man called out, "Torpedoes have missed the bow and are continuing out to sea." They had just begun cheering when the sonar man yelled, "Two more torpedoes inbound!"

***

Abigail couldn't feel her arms or her legs anymore, and looking around, she was sure the others felt that way too. Suddenly, she was horrified as she saw the doctor's eyes closing. She reached out and punched him in the shoulder, but he didn't react. She moved as close as she could and took her numb hand and slapped him across the cheek, saying, "Stay with me now, Grandpapa! Don't leave me!"

"Time to impact?"

"Ten seconds," replied the sonar man.

"Any chance they'll…"

The bow of the Fortitude exploded as the two torpedoes struck the very tip. Water and shrapnel filled the air as the bow disappeared. Inside the ship, alarm bells and sirens were sounding as damage control parties tried to shore up the bow and make it as watertight as possible. Corpsmen rushed forward to see to the wounded and to save as many as they could.

The ship's boat had been launched before the torpedo attack had forced the Fortitude to reverse course in an effort to evade the incoming torpedoes, so it wasn't long before they arrived to recover the survivors of the Sankt Andreas. The sailors were just beginning to pull the crewmembers onto the boat when the bow of the light cruiser was blown off. The sound was horrific, but the waves were worse. The little boat was tossed about as if it was a toy and the remainder of the survivors were washed away from it in every direction.

Abigail watched in horror as she and the doctor were forced farther and farther from the rescue boat. She tried to grab the doctor's life jacket and pull him back to the boat, but either he was too heavy or she was too tired. Whatever the reason, no matter how hard she swam toward the boat, it didn't seem to be getting any closer. The water was so choppy that it seemed like every other breath was nothing but salt water. She coughed and sputtered as she continued to drag the doctor toward the boat.

They weren't going to make it, she realized, as she tried once again to clear the salt water from her lungs. There were stars at the edges of her vision, and she knew that she was going to pass out any second now. Still, she pulled the doctor along as she struggled toward the boat. Then, she gave one last ditch effort and her body went limp.

Benjamin had gotten Inga into the boat and had followed her. They were sitting in the middle of the boat watching the sailors struggling to recover all the others when he saw Abigail and the doctor flailing about fifty yards from the rescue boat. He called to one of the sailors, but he didn't, or couldn't, hear him. His heart stopped when he saw Abigail go limp. Without thinking, without saying anything to anyone, he dove back into the freezing water and struck out for Abigail and the doctor.

Seconds passed before anyone was aware of them, and in that time, Benjamin reached the two stricken swimmers. He checked and found that both were still alive, but just barely. He grabbed the rope on Abigail's life jacket and pulled her to the rescue boat. While the sailors were pulling her onboard, he swam back and grabbed the doctor.

Abigail woke as the boat neared the crippled cruiser. They pulled up to the gangway and were met by over a dozen sailors. She watched as some of the sailors helped the ambulatory survivors up the stairs and the others were loaded onto stretchers and carried to the ship's sickbay. Abigail protested but was forced onto a stretcher. She watched helplessly as the doctor, still unconscious, was also loaded onto a stretcher.

There were eight survivors who suffered hypothermia from their time in the water. Each was treated and most released within hours. Those who remained were the doctor and Captain Norgaard, the chief engineer, and one of the deckhands. Abigail was taken to one of the officer's cabins where she found Inga wrapped in someone's oversized tee shirt. She giggled when she saw her until the steward handed her one and told her to strip. "We have clothing for the men, but we don't have any women's clothing, so we'll clean and repair yours as best we can, and you can wear this till we're done." She was blushing profusely when she held her wet clothes out the cabin door and the steward took them.

Two hours later, the steward returned with the clean and repaired clothing and told the girls that once they had changed, they would be escorted back to the sickbay to see the doctor who was asking for them. They left the cabin five minutes later.

The doctor was sitting up in his bed when they were allowed to enter. They both ran to his side and gave him monstrous, rib-cracking hugs. "Easy girls," Benjamin said with a chuckle, "you might break him!"

They all laughed and had a good reunion until the ship's doctor came in and shooed them away. "He'll be good as new tomorrow, but right now he needs his rest. Come back tomorrow afternoon and you can take him with you."

They kissed him good night and headed out the door. When they entered the corridor, they realized they had no idea where they were or where they were going. As they were contemplating this, a young man came up to them and saluted. "Begging your pardon, sir, ma'ams, but the captain would like to see you in his cabin. If you'll follow me, please?"

Abigail took Inga's arm and the three of them fell into line after the sailor. They turned this way and that way and finally ended up at a cabin not far from the one Abigail and Inga were sharing. The sailor knocked and was told to enter. He opened the door and said, "The two ladies and the colonist to see you, as you requested, sir."

He stepped aside and motioned for them to enter. When they did, they were greeted by the captain with a smile and a handshake. He was a nondescript man, neither tall nor short, neither thin nor fat. He probably was about forty or so, but you really couldn't tell by his face. He reached out and shook Benjamin's hand and then Inga's. He warmly greeted both of them, and when Benjamin said his name, the captain winked at him.

Finally, it was Abigail's turn. She took the captain's hand and shook it as she told him her name. He glanced down, saw the brand on her hand and gasped. Without letting her hand go, he turned her arm so he could see her tattoo. His smile became a frown as he asked, "When and where were you taken?"

Abigail blushed as he let her hand go, but she told him an abbreviated version of her story. When she was finished, he said, "I had a cousin who lived in Agustis. She and her two sons were killed when the city fell."

The rest of the evening went well. The captain had them as guests for dinner and they got to meet the remainder of the ship's officers. The next day, they were taken on an extensive tour of the ship, not including the damaged areas. Finally, they met the doctor and they all went to dinner in the officer's mess.

It took the crippled ship almost two weeks to limp back into port. When they arrived, there were three men in overcoats and fedoras waiting for them at the bottom of the gangplank. Abigail felt her pulse quicken at the sight of them, but when they made it to the bottom of the gangplank, the leader smiled, shook everyone's hands, and introduced himself.

It turned out he was from the UC Embassy and was there to escort them to the ambassador's residence. Then he introduced the two men with him. Just as he was finishing the introductions, a large limousine, followed by a second sedan, pulled up in front of them. The driver popped out and opened the rear door and the man motioned for them to get in for the ride to the embassy.

Thirty minutes later, the limo pulled into the courtyard and up to the entrance. As they got out, they were greeted by the ambassador himself and an army general. Abigail stole a glance over at Benjamin and saw he'd gone pale as a ghost.

CHAPTER TWENTY-EIGHT

When the doctor exited the limousine and straightened up, Abigail saw the ambassador smile. He hurried down the steps and took the doctor's hand, shaking it vigorously. In Dutch, he declared, "Doctor van Heflin! How good it is to finally meet you, sir. The whole country owes you a debt of gratitude for what you've done!"

Abigail was baffled as the ambassador turned to Benjamin and pulled him into a great bear hug and exclaimed in Anglosian, "Nicholas, my boy, thank God you're all right! Your mother and father have been worried sick! Not a day goes by that I don't get a cable from your father asking if you'd been found, where you were, and when you'd be back in allied territory! It's been a nightmare, but you're back in Lexington at last. Safe and sound."

Benjamin, or Nicholas, or whatever his name really was, was blushing when he said, "Thanks Uncle David. It's good to be back."

The ambassador next greeted Inga, but he didn't shake her hand. Instead, he wrapped his burly arms around her and gave her a big bear hug. He slipped back into Dutch and exclaimed what a pleasure it was to meet such a beautiful young lady from a beautiful country that was, unfortunately, being ruled and destroyed by a misguided regime bent on conquest and destruction. "It's not the people of Dutchland we're at war with, you know. It's their horrible leader, General Joshua."

Finally, it was Abigail's turn. She blushed as the ambassador took her in his embrace and welcomed her. When he pulled away, he saw her tattoo and a shocked look came across his face. Before he said anything, Nicholas interjected, "Uncle David, it's not what you think. Although Abigail is technically a slave, Dr. van Heflin and Inga have never treated her like one. In fact, she's more like Inga's older sister."

Abigail blushed and nodded. "They're like family to me, Mr. Ambassador. I've never been mistreated by Inga, Grandpapa, or Mrs. van der Walle."

The ambassador looked confused, so Nicholas explained, "Mrs. van der Walle was their housekeeper. She was killed when an Imperial torpedo boat boarded and searched the fishing boat we were on. One of them fired a pistol through the hull and some of the bullets struck and killed her. But, before that, she was a wonderful, caring person—even if she did betray us."

"Well, I can see there's quite a story here and I can't wait to hear it, but now I think we all need to go in and get settled. There will be a reception tonight in your honor, so I expect everyone will need to rest and get some appropriate clothes. Come, let me show you to your rooms." As they started up the steps, the ambassador added, "Nicholas, I believe General Ashley would like a few minutes with you. He has some questions he'd like you to answer."

Nicholas nodded and stopped in front of the general, coming to attention and saluting, even though he was in civilian clothes. As Abigail and the rest were led into the residence, she saw Nicholas being led back down the stairs towards a military sedan.

The ambassador handed them off to the domestic staff, begging their pardon and explaining he had to send a cable to Nicholas' parents and attend to some last-minute details for the reception that evening. They all said their goodbyes and were soon taken to their rooms. When the butler opened the door for her, Abigail's heart stopped. She had never seen such a huge bedroom, or bed, either! There were two chairs, a chaise lounge, and two couches near a huge fireplace with the most welcoming fire blazing in it that she had ever seen. "Is this all for me?" she asked the butler as he turned to escort the others to their rooms.

"Yes mademoiselle, this suite is just for you. We hope it will be satisfactory."

She nodded and walked into the palatial bedroom. As she looked around, she realized that this one bedroom was bigger than the whole apartment she and her family lived in before the war! She moved over to the bed and tested it. It seemed soft, but not too soft. Next, she moved over to stand near the fire. It was giving off the most wonderful warmth and glow that she instantly felt sleepy. She thought she'd just sit on one of the sofas for a few minutes. She slipped out of her shoes and sat on the couch. Before she knew it, she was stretched out, sound asleep.

She hadn't been asleep for very long when a maid gently woke her. "Me mournfully sleepless us," she said in broken Dutch, "cloth dress form yester eve, hore."

Abigail laughed at her. She couldn't help herself. But almost immediately, she felt ashamed of herself at the look on the girl's face. Blushing she said in Anglosian, "Please forgive me. It's just that what you said was funny and didn't really make any sense. But I speak Anglosian if that's easier for you."

The maid was blushing, too, as she said, "What I was trying to say was that I'm sorry to wake you, but there is a lady here with some dresses for you to choose from for the reception tonight."

Abigail apologized again, and the maid told her not to worry about it. As she left, an older woman came in with two assistants and a mobile clothes rack with dozens of the most beautiful gowns Abigail had ever seen. "Good afternoon, Miss Henderson," the woman said in perfect Agustian. "My name is Madam Couture and I will be assisting you with your gown for this evening's gala."

She turned and pointed to the rack of gowns and said, "I've taken the liberty of bringing a few examples for you to peruse. If you don't see anything you like, I can bring more. The ambassador's instructions were that you and Miss van de Clerk are to be dressed as princesses tonight. Anything your heart desires will be provided."

Abigail was flabbergasted as she looked at the gowns on the rack. Slowly, she began examining each one. There were gowns of every color and every fabric she could imagine. Suddenly, she saw a pale green silk chiffon gown and stopped. Madam Couture smiled and said, "Yes, I thought you'd like that one. I was told you had pale green eyes and I thought it might match them."

Abigail pulled it off the rack and held it in front of her. Without speaking, she went over to the full-length mirror and gazed unbelievingly at her reflection. Madam Couture came and stood behind her, studying her. "Yes, I think that will look lovely on you. Why don't we try it on you and see?"

The gown was way too long and way too big in the bodice, but Madam Couture said that could be fixed. She snapped her fingers and her two assistants attacked Abigail with tape measures and pins. They measured this and pinned that and spun her around, looking at the dress from various angles, until she was quite dizzy. Finally, they were satisfied, and it was time to select her shoes. In the end, they selected a pair of black patent leather pumps and a clutch to match.

At last, Madam Couture was satisfied and was heading for the door when she said, "Thank you, mademoiselle. Your gown will be delivered an hour before the reception. Now, if you will excuse me, I must see to the other young woman."

"Wait," Abigail called, "I'll come with you." When Madam Couture gave her an inquiring look, she explained, "Inga is blind and it's my job to help her with her clothing and such."

Madam Couture nodded and the four of them made their way to Inga's room. They knocked and entered to find Inga sitting next to the fire crying. Abigail rushed over to her and exclaimed, "Inga! What's the matter?"

She looked toward Abigail, and when she sat next to her, she flung herself into her embrace and wailed, "Oh, Abigail, they've taken Grandpapa away and Benjamin is gone and Mrs. van der Walle is dead and nobody would tell me where you were and I was so alone and so afraid! Please don't leave me! I don't know what I'd ever do without you!"

Abigail hugged her as she cried and told her that she would never leave her, no matter what. "But they told me that since we aren't in the empire anymore that you aren't a slave and that you'd probably leave us and I'd be all alone and, oh, what would I do then?"

She patted Inga's back and said, "Even if I'm not your slave anymore that doesn't mean that we're not still friends. I love you like a sister and I have no intention of leaving you and Grandpapa. And even if I did, where would I go? You guys are all the family I have."

It took a few minutes, but Inga finally calmed down and Abigail told her about Madam Couture and her helpers and the need to pick a dress for the reception tonight. Inga agreed and soon she was the center of a whirlwind of activity. Eventually, they selected a dark red strapless gown with a black sash and matching shoes. When the fittings were done and Madam Couture and her helpers had left, Abigail and Inga collapsed on the sofas in front of the fire, thinking they could relax until it was time to get ready for the party. They couldn't have been more wrong.

They had just put their feet up and were stretching out when there came a loud knock on the door. Inga called out, "Come in," and the most flamboyantly dressed man came bustling in with four people trailing him, each pushing a cart or a chair or carrying an oversized case. "There they are," he called to his assistants. "There are the two girls we're supposed to turn into goddesses by six! Oh, good gracious!"

Abigail began to giggle as Inga said, "Who are you and what do you want?"

"Oh, good gracious," he called out. "I, my dear young lady, am Mr. Bonaventure."

Inga gave him a confused look and, when he didn't continue she asked, "And I care because?"

Sounding wounded and exasperated, he replied, "Surely, you've heard of me? I'm the most famous, most sought after hair and makeup artist in Lexington! Why, I do all the movie stars and even the royal family. Everybody's just dying for me to do their hair! Oh, good gracious!"

Inga laughed and said, "Well, I don't know just what you can do with this." She reached up and ruffled her stubby hair.

He put on a look of great consternation and came closer to examine both girls' heads. "Well, yes, I see your point. Nevertheless, I'm sure we'll come up with something and simply everyone will be copying it by tomorrow! Oh, good gracious!"

Abigail was still giggling when one of the assistants grabbed her by the arm and forced her into the portable stylist's chair. Seeing her brands and tattoo, Mr. Bonaventure exclaimed, "Oh, good gracious! So you're the little slave girl that everyone's talking about! Why, you're even prettier than everyone said you were!" Then he turned to Inga and said, "Then that makes you the little blind girl everyone says the president's son is in love with! Oh, good gracious!"

Both girls stopped giggling. "Everyone's talking about us," Inga asked.

"President's son?" Abigail queried.

"Oh, good gracious, didn't you know? Why, the papers are full of the story of how he changed his name and enlisted to fight the fascists and how his bomber was shot down over Brighton. The papers say that you and your grandfather nursed him back to health and protected him from the secret police and then you escaped with him. Oh, the stories about your journey to freedom are riveting. Simply riveting! And when they described how you got away from that Imperial torpedo boat and the time you spent in the freezing water, I thought my heart would just explode! Oh, good gracious!"

Abigail and Inga were in shock as the assistants plopped Inga in the stylist's chair and Mr. Bonaventure began working on their hair. After being wheeled into the bathroom, having her hair washed and being wheeled back into the main room Abigail finally came back to her senses and asked, "How did that end up in the newspapers?"

"Oh, good gracious," Mr. Bonaventure exclaimed as he began clipping here and there. It was surprising how much hair he cut off considering neither girl had much. "I heard that the Colonial Army put out a press release as soon as he was safe on board that Royal Navy ship. That's what the reception tonight is about. It's a celebration of his return to safety and a thank you for you and your grandfather, and your master, too I suppose, except slavery is illegal in the kingdom and in the UC, too, I believe, so I..."

Their hair was done and it was time for their makeup. Both girls were ushered into the bathroom and bathed in the most luxurious bath oils Abigail had ever imagined. Soon, they were back in the stylist's chairs and Mr. Bonaventure was applying eye shadow, rouge, lipstick, and foundation. Finally, when they both felt they couldn't take one more minute of it, he said, "Oh, good gracious, don't you two just look like a pair of angels fresh from heaven!"

He handed Abigail a hand mirror and she gasped when she looked into it. Who was that woman? She wondered. Then she looked at Inga and exclaimed, "Inga, you're beautiful!"

CHAPTER TWENTY-NINE

Mr. Bonaventure had just finished when there was yet another knock on the door. Inga automatically answered, "Come in."

As Mr. Bonaventure and his entourage packed up and left, two people walked in and introduced themselves. "Miss van de Clerk, Miss Henderson," the man began, "my name is Harry Johnston, and this is Mrs. Emma Goldstein. We're here to instruct you on the protocol for the reception this evening. I take it that neither of you have ever been to a diplomatic reception before?"

Both girls shook their heads, and he went on, "Very good. Then we're starting from scratch."

For the next two hours, Mr. Johnston instructed them on what would be expected of them, and Mrs. Goldstein taught them how to walk in high heels. Neither girl had learned to wear high heels before, nor how to curtsy, or walk and talk. By the time they had finished, both of their heads were spinning, and Abigail wondered if she'd be able to remember any of it.

When the clock chimed six, an usher came to escort them to the reception. As they neared the entrance, Abigail was surprised when he led them to a waiting room just outside the ballroom where the reception was being held. As he opened the door, she was happily surprised to see the doctor, wearing a tuxedo, sitting on a sofa waiting patiently.

Both girls let go of the usher and ran to the doctor and he gave them a warm, welcoming hug. The usher cleared his throat and said, "Please, be seated. Mr. Johnston will come get you when it is time for your entrance."

They were just admiring how each other looked when Mr. Johnston tapped on the door, opened it, and said, "Well, shall we go?" They nodded and the evening began.

As they entered the room, a voice said, "Ladies and gentlemen, His Excellency, Ambassador David Southerby and the Embassy of the United Colonies are proud to introduce the guests of honor. Please welcome Doctor Kurt van Heflin, Miss Inga van de Clerk, and Miss Abigail Henderson."

They proceeded into the room to tumultuous applause. Abigail looked around and saw what she thought must have been hundreds of elegant men and women, all smiling and applauding for them. Then she looked in front of her and saw the ambassador, a lady she didn't know, and a young man in a formal army uniform that could only have been Benjamin, or Nicholas, or whatever his name was. *No matter what you call him,* she thought, *he's gorgeous!* He was standing there, next to the ambassador, in a dark blue uniform with three medals and, what was that on his arms, sergeant's stripes? He was a corporal, wasn't he?

When they reached the head table, Mr. Johnston began the formal introductions. "Dr. van Heflin, Miss van de Clerk, Miss Henderson, may I introduce Their Excellencies, Ambassador David and Mrs. Allison Southerby."

The doctor bowed and shook the ambassador's hand and then bowed and kissed his wife's. Inga, facing in the ambassador's general direction, curtsied to him and his wife. The ambassador reached out and gently kissed her on both cheeks. Then it was Abigail's turn. She, too, curtsied to the ambassador and his wife. Then, the ambassador leaned towards his wife and said, "Allison, this is the Agustian slave girl I was telling you about."

Abigail blushed as he was speaking and looked down at the floor. The ambassador's wife reached out and pulled her into the warmest, friendliest hug she had ever had. "Oh, my dear child, you must tell me your story! I can't wait to hear about your ordeal!" She looked at her husband and said, "David, you must tell Andre to change the seating arrangements. I simply must sit beside this charming young lady this evening!!"

Then Abigail found herself standing in front of the boy she thought she had known, but who was now someone else. Mr. Johnston said, "May I introduce United Colonies Army Sergeant Nicholas Southerby."

She curtsied as he blushed. Then he leaned over and gave her a kiss on the cheek. "We'll talk later," he told her as she was shuffled along.

The doctor and the girls joined the receiving line and were introduced to the rest of the guests. Abigail met and was greeted by ambassadors from every allied country, the Prime Minister of Anglosia and his wife, and even the crown prince! Every single person gazed at her branded hands and her tattoo. She had refused to wear long gloves to hide them.

Finally, everyone had been introduced and they moved to the tables and the meal was served. Abigail found herself seated between Mrs. Southerby and General

Ashley, the general who had met them that morning. As the hors d'oeuvres were served, Mrs. Southerby asked her to tell her about how she became a slave and what it was like being one. So, Abigail began her tale. They had just started their dessert when she finally finished. Mrs. Southerby had been a great listener and had even asked a few pertinent questions along the way. "My goodness," she said, "You really have lived an extraordinary life, especially for one so young."

At last, the evening was over, and Abigail finally got to try out that magnificent bed. She was just dozing off when she heard a light tap on the door. "Come in," she called out automatically. She rolled over just as Inga came in the door and asked, "Abigail, are you still awake?"

She sat up as Inga came over to the bed and sat down. She could see the girl had something on her mind but was hesitant to say anything. After a few moments, Abigail said, "Is there something wrong?"

Inga shook her head and said, "No, I just didn't want to be alone, and I thought you might want to talk for a little bit." Before Abigail could say anything she continued, "Did you have fun tonight? I did."

Abigail knew that wasn't what was bothering her, but she went along with the conversation, hoping they'd get to the point sooner or later. She sighed and pulled the covers back, "Come on," she said, "Climb in and let's talk like we used to."

Inga crawled between the covers, and they began discussing the reception. Inga wanted to know all about her conversation with the general and the ambassador's wife. Then, she got to what Abigail believed was the real reason for the late-night visit. "Abigail," she began when there was a lull in the conversation, "Do you think Nick likes me? Really likes me, you know?"

She had to think for a second who Nick was. "Oh, he goes by Nick? I didn't know. Well, yeah, I think he likes you a lot. Why?"

"Well, it turns out he's important and I'm just a little blind nobody and I was wondering if maybe I was just a fling or something. You know, not the kind of girl he could get serious about. I'm kind of scared, you know? I really like him. He's like nobody I've ever known. He's…"

Abigail gave her a little hug and said, "You're silly; of course he likes you. Just look at how much time he's spent with you since we left Brighton. To tell you the truth, I've been kind of jealous. You've spent so much time with him that I was beginning to think you didn't need me anymore."

Inga laughed. "Actually, when we started spending time together, I thought you didn't want to spend time with me. After all, I did steal him from you."

She laughed, "You didn't steal him. I lost him, remember? He thought I wasn't loyal enough when they thought he was the one spying for the empire. You didn't do anything, I did."

They talked for about another hour and then fell asleep in Abigail's big bed.

***

He was sitting outside the deputy's office smoking his fourth cigarette. He knew this meeting wasn't going to go well. He had been given all the resources of the empire and had expended millions of muntens and been responsible for the deaths of countless men in pursuit of that colonist. And he still got away.

He took out his handkerchief and wiped the perspiration from his forehead. Suddenly, the telephone on the secretary's desk rang. He looked up as the woman answered it. When she hung up, she looked at him and said, "The deputy will see you now."

As he walked over, she opened the door for him and he entered the office. He walked up to the front of the desk on legs that barely carried him, snapped to attention, and saluted. The deputy waved the salute away and told him to sit. He did.

The deputy shuffled the papers in a rather thick folder and said, "I've been reading your report, Eric, and I find it difficult reading, difficult indeed." He put the file down on the desk and said, "One boy. One young boy was all you had to capture. I didn't care about that doctor or any of the others. I only wanted that one boy."

He sat back in his desk chair and sighed. "What am I to tell General Joshua? I'm sorry, my leader, but my best man couldn't catch one injured youth. Instead, he kills over a hundred men and destroys millions in equipment, including the most decorated torpedo boat in the entire fleet? Frankly, I'm at a loss what to tell him. Perhaps you should tell him."

Inspector Hoffmann blanched at the thought of standing in front of the Supreme Commander and admitting to failure. "Please sir," he begged, "Isn't there some other way I can make up for my failure? I'll do anything! Anything at all."

The deputy shook his head and said, "No, Inspector. I think the best thing is for you to explain to him what happened. And the sooner, the better."

Without waiting for a response, the deputy picked up his phone and said, "Can you call the leader's office and see if he's available for the final briefing on the Southerby case?"

They sat in silence for a few minutes. He listened as the clock seemed to be ticking down the remainder of his life. He pulled his handkerchief out and mopped his forehead again when the telephone rang. His heart stopped beating as the deputy answered it, listened for a few moments, and then hung it up again.

"He said he would love to hear your excuses, but he doesn't have time. He told me to give you the option of hanging, firing squad, or the southern front as an infantry captain. Oh, then he added that suicide was an option too, if you'd prefer."

He squirmed in his seat and suddenly felt ill. "I'm sorry, sir, but may I be excused? I need to use the restroom."

The deputy nodded and he stood. He left the office and the anteroom and headed directly for the nearest men's room. The deputy was still sitting behind his desk when he heard the sound of a single gunshot. He picked up the phone. When his secretary answered he said, "Call the leader's office and tell them that Inspector Eric Hoffmann has decided on the last option."

***

The limousine pulled onto the tarmac and stopped in front of a Colonial Army Air Corps passenger plane. An army officer opened the door and Abigail, Inga, and the doctor got out. Once they had straightened up, the officer led them to the stairs, and they ascended into the airplane. The stairs were wheeled away, and the door closed. Moments later, the plane began taxiing for takeoff and the seventeen-hour journey to the United Colonies.

Abigail and the others smiled when they entered the cabin of the airplane. They were greeted by four flight attendants, General Ashley and two other high ranking army officers, and standing alone looking a little out of place was Nicholas. She greeted the others warmly and then moved towards Nicholas. When she reached him, she gave him a kiss on the cheek and sat in the row of seats just behind him. Inga, of course, gave him a big kiss and hug and then spent the rest of the trip either holding his hand or resting her head on his shoulder. The doctor sat with Abigail.

As soon as they were airborne, Abigail leaned in between the seats and said, "Okay, let's hear the real story, Nicholas or Benjamin or whoever you are."

He smiled and blushed a little but didn't say anything. "Yes, let's," added Inga. "Why didn't you tell us who you really were?"

"I couldn't. My father agreed to allow me to enlist, but only if I didn't use my real name or let anyone know who I really was. He was afraid that if I was captured and the empire found out who I was, they'd use me to blackmail him into surrendering or at least withdrawing from the war. So, I used my first name as my last name and kept my middle name. I took my grandfather's first name and used that.

"The other condition was that I would be in the air corps and not the infantry and that my bodyguard would be with me wherever I went."

"Bodyguard," Abigail interrupted.

"Yeah, my bodyguard was Sergeant Smithers. I found out that the underground wouldn't let him stay with me and forced him to go home. He should be in Williamston when we get there. Anyway, it seems that the empire had spies and discovered I was in the air corps and exactly which airplane on which I was a gunner. When we flew our mission over Brighton, their fighters concentrated on shooting us down so they could capture me and force the Colonies out of the war. Although they knew where we went down, they didn't think the underground would get to the wreckage before they could.

"Anyway, that's why they were trying so hard to capture us when we were trying to escape. Well, that's the story. You all aren't angry with me, are you? I swear I never wanted to lie to you, and I would have told you sooner, but there really wasn't a good way to do it." He paused and looked into each of their faces before he said, "Can you ever forgive me?"

The others said they forgave him, but Abigail asked, "Back in the shelter at the farm, you told us your father was a haberdasher and you were from New Brunswick. Where did that story come from?"

Nicholas smiled and said, "That was my mother's story. Her father was from Agustis and she was the little sister in the story. In fact, it's his first name I used when I was Benjamin Nicholson."

There was silence for a moment or two and then the doctor said, "So what's going to happen when we get to Williamston?"

"Well, I imagine my parents will throw a big party and lavish their appreciation on you guys, and I'll be grounded for the rest of the war."

They all laughed. Abigail leaned back, thinking about Nick's story. She fell asleep somewhere over the Froth Ocean.

CHAPTER THIRTY

Abigail woke with a start when the steward gently shook her. "I'm sorry to wake you Miss Henderson, but we should be landing in Williamston in an hour and Mr. Johnston thought you might like to freshen up a bit before we get there."

Abigail nodded and began rubbing the sleep out of her eyes. She got up and went to the lavatory and washed her face. When she came out, Mrs. Goldstein was there with a freshly ironed white dress. She smiled, took the dress, and went behind a partition to put it on. When she came back around, Mrs. Goldstein handed her a pair of high heels, smiled and moved on to Inga.

Ten minutes later, Inga was back beside Nick wearing a pretty, flowery blue dress and matching high heels. Mr. Johnston came over and briefed them on the arrival ceremony and how to address the president and his wife. He had just finished when the pilot announced they were coming in for a landing and everyone needed to return to their seats.

It was late afternoon when the plane touched down at the air corps base outside the capital. The airplane taxied to the middle of the arrival area and the pilot shut down the engines. As the portable stairs were rolled into place, the chief steward opened the door. Just as the stairs thumped against the side of the plane, the music started.

The first out of the plane were the important military men. They went single file down the stairs and were met by the president, his wife, and two other generals. Abigail could tell the generals standing beside the president were of higher rank because they had more gold on their uniforms.

The president greeted each of the officers with a smile and a hearty handshake. The president's wife shook their hands and then they moved on. The music ended for a second or two and then began playing the old Dutchland National Anthem. Nick put his hat on and took Inga's arm, guiding her down the stairs with him. Abigail and the doctor followed.

When they reached the bottom of the stairs, Nick leaned over and whispered in Inga's ear. She nodded and stopped while he released her hand, came to attention and saluted the generals and the president. The generals returned the salute, and the president opened his arms. Nick took Inga's hand and moved into his father's embrace. The hug was long and genuine, and when they broke apart, he turned to his mother and received an even longer, tearful embrace. While Nick and his mother were hugging, the president took Inga's hand and said, "So you're the girl we've heard so much about." Before she could do anything but blush, he continued. "You all are all over the newspapers and I hear you've even made the newsreels in the movie theaters. That's quite an accomplishment these days. I don't even make them as often as I'm told that you two have in the last few weeks," he continued, laughing at her as she stammered and blushed.

Nick and his mother had just broken apart when he took Inga's hand and said, "Mother, I'd like you to meet Inga van de Clerk. Inga, this is my mother, Nancy Southerby."

Inga looked in the general direction of Mrs. Southerby and curtsied. In a heavily accented voice she said, "It is a pleasure to meet you, Your Excellency."

Mrs. Southerby reached out and took Inga in a warm embrace saying, "Nonsense, it is I who is honored to meet you. Nicholas' father and I owe you, your family, and friends a debt of gratitude we can never repay."

In the meantime, Abigail and the doctor were being greeted by the president. When she was introduced, she curtsied, but he would have none of the formalities. He took her in his arms and gave her a bear hug such as she had never had, all the time telling her how much he and his wife were indebted to them for the return of their only child.

Soon the welcoming ceremony was over, and they all climbed into the limousine and were whisked off to the presidential mansion. That night's celebration exceeded all the others by far and it was well after two o'clock in the morning before the party ended and they were all allowed to go to bed. Abigail didn't remember how she made it to her room that night. She only remembered waking up warm and comfortable in the most beautiful bedroom she had ever seen.

***

The knock on her door in the morning reminded Abigail that she was in a foreign country, in their president's mansion. She called out for the inquisitor to come in and a maid came in with a freshly laundered dress. She put it on, and the whirlwind day began.

After breakfast, they were taken on a tour of the city. Their guide told them that this was just a familiarity tour and that any sightseeing they wished to do could be arranged on a later date. Soon, it was back to the presidential mansion and a luncheon with the president's wife and a group of very important women.

While she was shaking hands, everyone noticed her brands. Some were coy about it, just glancing quickly, but others were blatant about it, openly staring at her hands. One woman actually pulled her hand up and examined it closely. After satisfying herself that it was indeed real, she exclaimed, "It is true! You really do have brands and a tattoo! One hears so much these days that one doesn't really know what is fact and what is fiction."

Abigail blushed slightly as she showed everyone the brands and the tattoo. Suddenly, that was all anyone wanted to talk about. She spent the rest of the luncheon telling her story. Finally, the luncheon was over and the ladies had gone. Abigail felt drained and Mrs. Southerby apologized at least a dozen times.

The circus continued for about a week and then slowly things returned to normal, or at least whatever normal was in Williamston. Inga was having a worse time of it since she and Nicholas were all anyone wanted to talk about. One night, Inga and Abigail were in Inga's room talking and Inga said, "I can't believe how rude some of these people are. Can you believe that one reporter wrote that the only reason Nick was dating me was because he felt sorry for me because I'm blind? Can you believe it?"

They were both giggling when Inga suddenly stopped and asked, "You don't think that's true, do you? Nick really loves me, doesn't he?"

Abigail looked at her and laughed, "Don't worry," she said amid her giggles. "He's crazy about you!"

The next day at breakfast, Dr. van Heflin told the girls that with the president's help, he had received his license to practice medicine and that they would soon be moving to an area of town where there were many Dutch families. "They call it Little Dutchland. I'm going there this morning to try and find a house and an office for my practice. Do either of you want to come?"

Abigail and Inga declined the offer because they were going sightseeing with Nick. They went to museums and monuments and even received a private tour of the Capitol Building. That night, there was yet another reception at the mansion they were expected to attend.

As with almost every reception or gathering they attended with the Southerby's, Nicholas kept Inga by his side while they mingled. That left the doctor and Abigail to fend for themselves. Well, what actually happened was that Mrs. Southerby displayed Abigail as if she were a champion show dog and the doctor spent his time with the president. This being the third reception and the fourth time she had been put on display, Abigail was getting a little tired of it. Near the end of the reception, she found herself temporally alone. She looked around and found the doctor was sitting alone too. She walked over to his table and sat down. He smiled and said, "I can see that you grow weary of being put on display."

She nodded and replied, "Yes, but I can't think of any way to avoid it without appearing rude."

He nodded and said, "Well, maybe my news will help. I've found us a small house in Little Dutchland and the owner has agreed to let us move in next week. I've also found a little office, not too far from there, for me to start my practice. It won't be long before we all get a chance to start our new lives."

Although Abigail was glad to leave the spotlight, Inga was not. She whined and pouted the entire time they were decorating the new house and office. Finally, the doctor had had it and told her that if it didn't end, he was going to find a boarding school to send her to. That shut her up. As a consolation, he told her that she could invite Nick over anytime she wanted.

Eventually, they were all moved in, and life began to fall into a familiar and comfortable routine. That is until Nick came over one night and told Inga that his leave from the Air Corps was about to end and that he was being deployed back to Anglosia. There were plenty of tears and pleading and begging, but in the end, none of it did any good. He was scheduled to leave the following Tuesday.

Nick came and picked up Inga on the day he was to leave and took her with him to the air base. The doctor and Abigail followed in the doctor's 'new' old luxury car. His departure from Inga was filled with tears, hugs, and promises to write. Abigail stood with Inga at the fence as Nick's airplane taxied and took off. Inga kept her face buried in Abigail's shoulder as she cried the entire ride home.

Inga sulked and moped around the house for the rest of the week until the doctor came home one day and told them that they had both been enrolled in a private high school and they would start the following Monday. By the next month, both girls had tons of friends and life had resumed as if they had never left Brighton.

EPILOGUE

"And that's the story of how we came to be here," she concluded. "Are there any questions?"

The house lights came up and Abigail could see dozens of hands fly up. She smiled and said, "Yes, you, the boy in the green shirt in the fourth row."

The boy stood up and said, "So what happened to Dr. van Heflin and Inga?"

She replied, "Grandpapa lived many years and sent both of us girls to college. He also lived to see both of us married and even to see Inga's first daughter. As for Inga, she and Nick married as soon as she finished college. They have four children and live in Lexington, Anglosia, where he serves as the ambassador."

The boy sat down, and Abigail pointed to a girl near the back. She stood and said, "Your last name is de Groote. Does that mean that Werner de Groote escaped and you two got married?" Before Abigail could answer, the girl added, "How did he get away?"

"Werner helped the underground for three years before State Security identified him and came after him. By then, the allies were only a few miles from Kreeton, and late one night, he snuck through the front lines and turned himself over to them. He had been severely wounded so he spent about a month in a hospital before he was allowed to travel.

"One day, while I was home from college, there was a knock on the door. When I answered it, there he was. At first, I didn't recognize him. He was much thinner and his hair was darker, but after he identified himself, I invited him in. Before long, we renewed our friendship and eventually fell in love. We were married a year after I finished medical school, and we have three beautiful children."

The girl stood up and asked, "Is he still alive?"

"Yes. He would be here, but he's giving a presentation at another school."

The girl sat down, and Abigail pointed to another girl sitting in the front row. She stood and said, "Did you ever find out what happened to your father?"

"Yes. He was killed two days before my mother and brother. He was one of the defenders of Agustis."

She sat and Abigail pointed at a boy on the far-left side. As the others did, he stood and asked, "Did you ever hear about any of your school friends from Brighton?"

Abigail smiled and said, "Yes, we heard from Frida just after the war. She knew where we lived because of the news coverage of Nicholas' rescue. We received a letter that was actually almost a year old, but it began a lifelong correspondence between the three of us. Frida survived the war and eventually married. Unfortunately, the same could not be said of her cousin, Jurren. He joined the army and rose to the rank of major. He was killed in the Battle of Brighton. About half the girls we were friends with at school survived the war. Frida said that most married, had families, and are still alive."

The next question came from one of the teachers. "Have you ever been back to Brighton or Agustis even?"

"I traveled back to Agustis after the war and attended the dedication of the National War Memorial and Museum. I never went back to Brighton, but Inga and Nicholas did. If you're interested, our old house survived and there's a new family living there."

Another boy, near the back raised his hand and she acknowledged him. He stood and asked, "Did you ever find out what happened to the housekeeper's son? The one the secret police used to make her spy on you guys?"

"Once we were settled into our new lives in Williamston, Grandpapa wrote a letter to Dierdrick explaining what had happened to his mother. He gave the letter to our local priest and eventually it found its way to him in Dutchland. Not long after the end of the war, Father Dierdrick visited us. He told us that the secret police held him for almost a year. During that time, he was tortured and beaten mercilessly. In fact, they had beaten him so badly that his right hand was more like a hook than a hand and he could no longer use it. But once the secret police found out that Mrs. van der Walle died on the Sankt Andreas they let him go and he returned to the monastery where he was ordained the next year."

She looked around and saw a very little girl near the front had raised her hand. She smiled and nodded at her, and she stood up. In a very small voice, she said, "Dr. de Groote, if you could go back and change anything, what would you change?"

Abigail thought for a moment and said, "In spite of the pain, in spite of the lost loved ones, and all the suffering we all had to endure, I don't think I'd change a thing." She smiled at the little girl's shocked look and continued, "You see, if I went back and changed anything, then I may not have had all the great friends, my truly wonderful husband or my beautiful children, not to mention my grandchildren. No, I don't think I'd change a thing."

She looked around and saw there were no other hands in the air. She asked, "Are there any other questions?"

When no one raised their hands, the principal walked up and shook Abigail's hand. He moved over to the podium and said, "Thank you, Dr. de Groote, for coming and addressing our school." Then he looked at the students and said, "Let's all thank Dr. de Groote for sharing her fascinating life story with us today."

The whole auditorium stood and gave her a standing ovation. She smiled and slowly walked off the stage. As they were applauding, Freddie Watson leaned over and said, "So, that's your grandmother?"

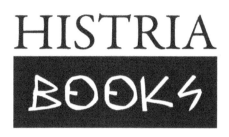

Exceptional Books for Young Adult Readers

For these and many other great books visit
HistriaBooks.com